The Language of Ethics and Community in
Graham Greene's Fiction

The Language of Ethics and Community in Graham Greene's Fiction

Paula Martín Salván

First published 2015 by
PALGRAVE MACMILLAN

Palgrave Macmillan in the UK is an imprint of Macmillan Publishers Limited, registered in England, company number 785998, of Houndmills, Basingstoke, Hampshire RG21 6XS.

Palgrave Macmillan in the US is a division of St Martin's Press LLC, 175 Fifth Avenue, New York, NY 10010.

Palgrave Macmillan is the global academic imprint of the above companies and has companies and representatives throughout the world.

Palgrave® and Macmillan® are registered trademarks in the United States, the United Kingdom, Europe and other countries.

ISBN 978–1–137–54010–2

This book is printed on paper suitable for recycling and made from fully managed and sustained forest sources. Logging, pulping and manufacturing processes are expected to conform to the environmental regulations of the country of origin.

A catalogue record for this book is available from the British Library.

A catalog record for this book is available from the Library of Congress.

Typeset by MPS Limited, Chennai, India.

To Carlos, who always carries my books

Contents

Introduction: Occasions for Unselfing

In a typical Graham Greene novel, a male character – we can tentatively call him the Greenean hero – becomes estranged from his communities of origin, such as family, profession, nation. He becomes a monad, unable to relate to others in a meaningful way, until he leaves and makes a fresh start in a new, often distant location. In this new setting, he will be given a second chance to engage in the life of another, usually marginal, community. The initially reluctant hero becomes thus committed to a cause or to a people, through acts of compassion and sacrifice. Most of Greene's novels, however, end with a twist that upsets the apparent integration of the hero into a community, questioning the nature of his commitment.[1]

This outline emphasizes the persistence of some narrative elements (character types, kernel events, chronotopes) and some lexical items (commitment, compassion, community) in Graham Greene's fiction. In this book, I would like to map out the lexico-conceptual articulation of Greene's narrative dramatization of ethical situations. This main aim issues from three working hypotheses: In the first place, a reduced set of terms such as *peace, despair, pity,* and *commitment* have a striking lexical recurrence in Greene's texts. I consider them as keywords that articulate his discourse at a conceptual level. In the second place, those keywords are invested with narrative potential. I believe they have the capacity to generate narrative situations and developments. And in the third place, they articulate a particular narrative pattern. I contend that such lexico-conceptual articulation is shaped mainly as ethical conflict dramatized in narrative form.

The lexical recurrence of specific terms in Greene's work has been observed in previous criticism, but it has been statistically noted as either a peculiarity of his style, or as an index of thematic prominence assumed uncritically. Lynette Kohn's early monograph *Graham Greene: The Major Novels* (1961) illustrates this critical approach, ascribing a key term to each novel as the unifying thematic element: *Brighton Rock* (1938) is about evil, *The Heart of the Matter* (1948) is about pity, and so on. What this approach does not take into account is the fact that Greene's usage of such terms is idiosyncratic, and often deviates from common usage.

Narrative and thematic patterns, on the other hand, have been explored before, but the general tendency has been to chain those recurrences to the author's biography, or to pre-existing political or religious frameworks.[2] The main problem with this methodology is that it stands on a classification of Greene's texts into religious and political ones.[3] These critical stances tend to perceive only some of Greene's novels – the ones in which the political-secular or the religious-Catholic elements respectively are thematically explicit – as the direct expression of his concerns, while the others are relegated as indirect symptoms of such concerns. That is to say, the religious readings of Greene's work consider the Catholic cycle as their main object of interest, yet claim that the discursive role of Catholicism permeates in a sublimated form the so-called non-Catholic novels through his concern with salvation, compassion, and sacrifice. Similarly, political readings of Greene's texts tend to focus on novels that dramatize imperialist and postcolonial situations, while simultaneously claiming that issues of justice, representation, and political and cultural colonization are indirectly present in the religious texts as well.[4]

My own critical approach benefits from the critical insights of previous explorations of lexico-conceptual and narrative recurrences in Greene's work, while tackling the shortcomings previously sketched. On the one hand, I propose a conceptual archaeology of Greene's keywords, in order to explore the resonance of religious, political, and philosophical discourses in his idiosyncratic uses. On the other hand, I intend to overcome the political/religious bias by proposing that the nature of narrative conflict in Greene's fiction is ultimately ethical. I contend that the religious and the political are two possible answers to the same question posited by Greene's characters, which could be formulated in Kantian fashion: "What should I do?" (*Pure* 677).[5]

The search for pattern

It has become a recurrent nod among Graham Greene's critics to quote his celebrated assertion that "a ruling passion gives [...] to a shelf of novels the unity of a system" (Shuttleworth and Raven 41).[6] Giving the unity of a system to shelves of novels is, after all, what literary critics do. Greene, however, was quite defensive when it came to acknowledging critics' attempts to systematize his fiction. Only a few lines before, in the same interview, he said: "I agree with you, of course, when you say that there is a relationship between, let us say, Anthony Farrant in *England Made Me* and Pinkie, or Scobie, even – but they are not the same sort of person even if they are expressions of *what critics are pleased to call my fixations*" (41; emphasis added). Greene repeatedly mentioned his fear that his work was narrowly interpreted by critics on the basis of recurrent narrative patterns. Both in *Ways of Escape* (1980) (134–35) and in the series of interviews edited by Marie Françoise Allain, he expressed his anxiety over the effects this might have on his work: "In anybody's work there's always a pattern to be found. Well, *I* don't want to see it [...] Otherwise I think my imagination would dry up" (Allain 23). Recent critical work like Stephen K. Land's *The Human Imperative* (2008) is structured precisely around recurrent elements in Greene's work, providing readers with a sort of "morphology" in a formalist sense.[7] Land focuses specifically on Greene's characters and on the transformations in characterization patterns through what he calls the three phases in Greene's career.[8] The idea of pattern seemed to Greene something to escape from. Talking about the possibility of using a first-person narrator for the first time in his career, Greene observed: "Here seemed an escape from the pattern, a method I had not tried" (*Ways* 135). Indeed, as he feared, criticism of his work has endeavored to "unroll before his eyes the unchanging pattern of the carpet" (134).[9]

The kind of work developed by Land lays bare the presence of recurrent elements, precisely in the way Greene did not want to be made aware of. Considering the "all too many repetitions" (Allain 23) that make up what De Vitis calls "the overall pattern of Greene's novels" (*Graham Greene* ii), one may wonder about their nature: what narrative elements tend to constitute the "pattern in the carpet" in Greene's fiction? Characterization, a tendency toward foreign settings which has earned his work the label of "international fiction" (Couto 111), the repetition of some plot elements, a particular style some have identified with the use of cinematic techniques, or with the recreation of the "seediness" he often alluded to in his essays and travel books?[10]

To these, I would add another level of recurrence, constituted by his use of a specific set of terms, a reduced vocabulary, to which he resorts once and again in the attempt to define his narrative universe. Words such as "peace," "despair," "pity," "commitment," or "bargain" are so recurrent in his work that some critics have been led to point out their conceptual importance. Rarely, however, have they gone beyond the mere observation of the lexical recurrence of a word as an index of the thematic importance of a particular topic. An early instance of this critical approach is found in Kohn (1961): "When one surveys the works of Graham Greene, one notices certain themes recurring so frequently that they are clearly central to the author. These themes are related to his primary concern for man as a moral and rational being" (Kohn 1). Twenty-five years later, Grahame Smith, in *The Achievement of Graham Greene* (1986), still discusses the main themes in Greene's fiction, such as "the fear of betrayal" (216) or characters' longing for "peace" (215), without questioning or analyzing what the terms "betrayal" and "peace" imply in Greene's fiction. Even later, still looking for patterns, Robert Hoskins sets out to explore, in his 1999 study, Greene's "obsessional themes" (xi), taking for granted once more that the lexical recurrence of specific terms is just a symptom of thematic prominence.

I consider that the recurrence of a particular set of words in Greene's work deserves deeper critical attention: to begin with, because Greene's use of the terms does not usually coincide with regular, common usage. Thus, his understanding of "pity" as enacted in *Brighton Rock*, *The Confidential Agent*, and, above all, in *The Heart of the Matter*, does not fit the dictionary definition of the word as "sympathetic sorrow for one suffering, distressed or unhappy,"[11] but needs to be assessed in contrast to its twin term, "compassion." As he explains in *Ways of Escape*, pity has for him a negative connotation related to the position of superiority in which the one who pities places him/herself regarding the one pitied. "Compassion," the preferred term to express a positive relation to another's suffering, is posited as the appropriate term indicating a truly ethical behavior. Understanding Greene's use of these terms is fundamental to grasp why characters like D. in *The Confidential Agent* (1939) or Scobie in *The Heart of the Matter* despise themselves for their feelings of pity toward others.

Similarly, in order to avoid misreading characters like Pinkie (*Brighton Rock*), Arthur Rowe (*The Ministry of Fear*, 1943), the Whisky Priest (*The Power and the Glory*, 1940), and Querry (*A Burnt-Out Case*, 1960), it is crucial to understand Greene's peculiar usage of the term "peace." All these characters long for "peace," but they do not wish for "freedom from civil disturbance" or "a state of security or order"; nor do they seek mere "tranquility or quiet." Their desire for peace needs to be understood, within Greene's fictional universe, as opposed to action, intervention, or commitment, thus dramatizing these characters' estrangement from the communities that may exact from them some form of active engagement in their affairs.

The principal aim of this book is to develop a lexico-conceptual exploration of Greene's fiction. The first step, sketched in this introduction, is delimiting and defining the basic vocabulary structuring Greene's fictional universe. I contend, moreover, that the terms which tend to be most prominently recurrent in his work may be analyzed as structuring elements from a narratological point of view. The second step involved in my reading, therefore, is the analysis of the narrative potential of those keywords. In this sense, I broadly share David Lodge's early assessment of Greene's Catholicism as "a system of concepts, a source of situation, and a reservoir of symbols with which he can order and dramatize certain intuitions about the nature of human experience" (*Graham Greene* 6).

Individual, community, and the ethical pattern

The theoretical framework for my study of Greene's fiction emerges from a double critical stance.

First, the nature of narrative conflict in Greene's novels is ethical. Although some critical readings have emphasized the religious or political formulations of conflict in specific novels – the religious dimension being thematically emphasized in *The Power and the Glory,* the political in *The Honorary Consul* (1973), for example – it is my contention that those formulations may be subsumed under the wider scope of the ethical. My understanding of the ethical is informed, on the one hand, by the theoretical work of critics like Derek Attridge and J. Hillis Miller, who have applied Jacques Derrida's speculative engagement with ethics to the analysis of literary works. In this theoretical framework, the oppositional nature of ethical choice regarding organized forms of morality is emphasized, often expressed as a conflict between individual "calling" and communitarian law. The ethical, in the Derridean schema, is necessarily a transgression of the Law, an act of disobedience on the part of an individual, a jump into the moral void of a law that is unwritten. In Greene's novels, a recurrent storyline is created around a character whose conflict with community is expressed as the need to betray the norm that grants him permanence in such community. The double bind in which most of Greene's characters find themselves may be understood in terms of what Derrida calls "the paradox of Abraham" (*Gift* 78), a branching out of moral behavior into separate and conflicting calls for action, the call of the Law, and the excessive and transgressive call to violate the Law, a demand to take responsibility through action, a praxis "that exceeds simple conscience" (25). There is always, in Greene's fictional world, a two-level understanding of morality: a superficial one, expressed in socially regulated behavior, and a deeper, transgressive one that exceeds the first and involves a reversal of official religious and political vocabularies – broadly coincidental with the Derridean distinction between Law and the ethical.

On the other hand, my theoretical approach to ethics partly draws on Alain Badiou's definition of the ethical. Several elements of Badiou's ethics are relevant to my reading of Greene's novels – in the first place, his understanding of ethics in universalist terms (*Ethics* 27). This ethics, in Greene as in Badiou, is defined as a *truth*, and it is understood to be universal – "indifferent to differences [...] the same for all" – eternal – "something we have always known" – and oppositional, in the sense that it opposes and is obscured by official discourses – "even if sophists of every age have always attempted to obscure its certainty" (*Ethics* 27). Behaving "ethically," in this context, means being faithful to the event of a truth, which is made self-evident in a particular situation, making the subject conscious of the existence of something that cannot be reduced to "what there is" (41):

> To be faithful to an event is to move within the situation that this event has supplemented, by *thinking* [...] the situation "according to" the event. And this, of course – since the event was excluded by all the regular laws of the situation – compels the subject to *invent* a new way of being and acting in the situation. (41–42)

At this point, Badiou's formulation touches Derrida's, in that both recognize the inaugural and transgressive nature of ethical action. Moreover, according to Badiou, "every truth erupts as singular" but "its singularity is immediately universalizable" (*Saint Paul* 11). The idea of a "universalizable singularity" (11) finds a sharp formulation in novels like *The Power and the Glory* or *The Heart of the Matter*, where individual characters recognize the necessity of a particular course of action – the need to become faithful to a particular truth, in Badiou's vocabulary – acknowledging the singularity of this recognition, while simultaneously recognizing its universal nature, even in the face of others' ignorance of it. In other words, in Greene's fiction, all human beings are bound to the same ethical impulses, but only his "heroes" answer the call to enact them. The idea is expressed in *The Heart of the Matter*: "This was a responsibility he shared with all human beings, but that was no comfort, for it sometimes seemed to him that he was the only one who recognized his responsibility" (109).

Second, narrative conflict of an ethical nature is articulated as a conflict between individual and community, often dramatized in the establishment of alternative, oppositional communities. Ethical impasse, as it has been sketched above, is something that happens necessarily in connection to others, in a double framework of collectivity. On the one hand, the isolation of the character with his responsibility is opposed to what Derrida would call "universal generality" of moral duty (*Gift* 66), incarnated in the institutional communities to which the character belongs (familial, professional, national). The ethical, in this schema, is dramatized as a conflict between community and individual, or specifically between communitarian morality and individual ethics. On the other hand, Greenean ethics is, as Derrida would say, following a Lévinasian approach, an ethics of the other.[12] There is always a recipient of the main character's ethical decisions and actions, even if sometimes this connection between both remains secret (which is precisely the melodramatic element introduced in *The End of the Affair*). In this sense, Greene's work may be said to explore the potential constitution of forms of community based on ethical action, established as alternative – often opposed – to official or institutional communities.

The analysis of such dialectical interaction between opposing models of community finds an apposite critical tool in Tönnies' sociological distinction between *Gesellschaft* and *Gemeinschaft* (17). The *Gesellschaft*, or society, would stand in Greene's fiction for the institutionalized forms of community in which the main character has been initially entangled: family, profession, official Church, national allegiance. Once uprooted from these, the hero contacts other forms of community, represented as smaller forms of natural interaction among human beings, roughly corresponding with Tönnies' *Gemeinschaft*.[13] These tend to be represented as pastoral communities, depicted through organicist metaphors – home, roots, blood ties – which betray an element of nostalgia for lost wholeness of a romantic kind. Meaningful, permanent integration into these communities is rare for Greene's characters. Yet, it is in the context of the *Gemeinschaft* that a third form of communitarian interaction emerges, through acts of compassion and commitment that were impossible in the context of the *Gesellschaft*. Attention to this third form of community is almost nonexistent in criticism of Greene's novels, which tends to remain focused on representations of the *Gemeinschaft* as the realization of a particular ideological or doctrinal position.

I intend to explore the ways in which ethics interact with communal structures in Greene's novels. The narrative dramatization of ethical conflict finds its most complex expression in the realization that neither *Gesellschaft* nor *Gemeinschaft* provide permanent solutions for the Greenean hero. Regarding the analysis of models of community and the potential conflict between individual and community, my research applies contemporary theories of community developed by Jean-Luc Nancy, Maurice Blanchot, Giorgio Agamben, and Roberto Esposito, among others. All of them have taken as their departure point the alleged collapse of some forms of community in the contemporary world and the search for alternative models. What their theoretical approaches have in common is a reconsideration of what a community is, drawing on Bataille's philosophical explorations of radical communities in *Inner Experience* (1954). The models of community explored in their work are non-identitarian, that is, not based on individual subjectivities sharing what is proper to them (Esposito *Communitas* 6; Blanchot *Unavowable* 65), and they tend to be codified as contingent and often ahistorical, rooted on universalist conceptions. Their articulation entails a reconsideration of notions of ethics, humanity, and human rights. This is the main reason why they seem to be particularly relevant for the analysis of a corpus in which ethical behavior, and its problematic definition regarding standard social normative behavior, seem to be a central concern.

Ethical aporias

Critics have identified his taste for paradox as one of Greene's frequent stylistic devices.[14] Even the Holy Office referred to *The Power and the Glory* as "paradoxical" in its letter condemning the novel (*Ways* 86). Sunita Sinha's Sartrean reading, for instance, emphasizes the paradoxical nature of commitment in *The Comedians* (1966), according to which even non-commitment can be perceived as an act of commitment to nothing (95).[15] Conflict, in his novels, tends to be dramatized in the form of a double bind, a situation in which a character's course of action is directed by contradictory claims of a moral or ethical nature, often resulting in narrative paralysis (Sinha 91). Paradox, in this context, is enacted as a moral problem, and formulated as the doubling or unfolding of the semantic field covered by a specific term into conflicting meanings. Greene's fictional dramatization of ethical conflict enacts Jacques Derrida's claim that all ethical concepts are intrinsically paradoxical: "the concepts of responsibility, of decision or of duty, are condemned a priori to paradox, scandal and aporia. Paradox, scandal and aporia are themselves nothing other than sacrifice, the revelation of conceptual thinking at its limit" (*Gift* 68). Specifically, Derrida's understanding of ethical aporia puts it in connection to responsibility in a sense that seems crucial also for Greene: "a sort of non passive endurance of the aporia was the condition of responsibility and of decision" (*Aporias* 16). Perhaps the character who most directly embodies this articulation of ethical responsibility as inextricably linked to uncertainty is Monsignor Quixote in the 1982 novel of the same title, for whom certainty appears a nightmarish possibility that would deprive him of his faith (*Monsignor* 68–69).

The paradoxical nature of ethical articulation in Greene's novels has been defended by Hayim Gordon in *Fighting Evil: Unsung Heroes in Graham Greene's Fiction* (1997), where he claims that critics' perception of a "cleavage between right and wrong and good and evil" is a sign of critical myopia (90). In order to justify his claims, Gordon repeatedly uses dictionary definitions of the terms whose meaning he is trying to fix in connection to Greene's fiction, and in contradiction to common readings of it (66, 85–86, 122). This evinces the need to pinpoint the exact meaning of ethical terms in any discussion of Greene's fiction.[16]

As has already been pointed out, Greene's work has been interpreted in a theoretical key as a discussion of specific ethical or religious problems. In an early essay on *The End of the Affair*, Ian Gregor focuses his discussion of the text on whether it was appropriate for the novel to engage in theological debate. Gregor notes how many Catholic readers "fail to distinguish between theology and theology-in-fiction, between 'views' and 'the use of views' as artistic material" (110). Beyond Greene's taste for theological matters on a purely speculative ground, however, lies the ultimate problem of the ethical demands made on human beings. His concern is with the difficult, often impossible, passage from thought to action. The answer to the Kantian question, "What should I do?" is never answered easily by Greene's characters. If answering that question is a conflictive matter, and not simply the application of an ethical, moral, or religious code to human behavior on a universal basis, it is precisely because of the discontinuity between moral systems and individual action.

This line of thought leads to the field of moral philosophy, straight to Kant, first, and, closer in time to Greene himself, to Theodor W. Adorno, Jean-Paul Sartre, Simone Weil, and Iris Murdoch. All of them, more or less overtly taking their cue from Kant's discussion on the need to ground morality on universal reason, have discussed the problematic passage from moral codes of general application to individual behavior. From their contributions, an understanding of ethics as opposed to morality in terms of individual versus social behavior has emerged in more recent theorizations. In particular, the work of Jacques Derrida, Derek Attridge, and J. Hillis Miller has traced a redefinition of ethics in terms of an opposition between the normative character of morality as codified in custom and social regulation, on the one hand, and genuine ethics, on the other hand, demanding individual acts of disobedience or rupture with previous codes. This was expressed by Derek Attridge in the following terms:

> We can only continue to use terms with ethical implications like "responsibility" and "obligation" – indeed "ethics" itself – if we are prepared to make some kind of distinction between the most fundamental ethical demands, which always involve unpredictability and risk, and specific obligations governing concrete situations in a given social context, which require the greatest possible control of outcomes. To the latter, the name "morality" is often given. (126–27)

Attridge opposes the idea of risk involved in specific ethical behavior to the controlled scope of the normative and the generalized application of morality. This definition entails a double deviation from earlier articulations of morality. On the one hand, Attridge's conception of the ethical opposes the consideration that human behavior can be regulated through convention and tradition. Codes that may be applied by all individuals in an automatic manner, without posing a challenge to individual consciousness, are not ethical, but social forms of regulation. On the other hand, it draws on an emotivist approach to ethics, as opposed to the Kantian conception of morality as grounded on universal reason. Attridge partakes of the conception, shared by Derrida among others, that the ethical cannot be abstracted into universal rational principles, but must remain on the level of particular, contingent moments of unprecedented decision born out of compassion for another's suffering. In the ethical model one can intuitively deduce from Attridge's words, an active decision is made, one that cannot be contained within the normative framework of social behavior nor grounded on universal rationality, and it involves the deliberate adoption of a course of action (often conflicting with morality, as Derrida's celebrated argument on Abraham's sacrifice in *The Gift of Death* illustrates).

The ultimate source of narrative development in Greene's novel tends to lie within the scope of the asymmetry between what different codes demand from the individual regarding his relationship with others, and the individual's reluctance to comply with a specific course of action. From the friction between individual and community – expressed through its different ethical, moral, religious normative codes – emerges, in some cases, a course of action one feels tempted to call – at least tentatively – individual ethical action. One crucial aspect of this pattern in Greene's fiction that, in my opinion, has not been sufficiently analyzed in a consistent manner is the identification of the source from which this call to ethical action comes for the heroes in Greene's novels. In the so-called Catholic cycle, this source is usually God. The rationale for ethical behavior would be then described as a divine summons to act in a particular way in a given situation. This issue has received plenty of critical attention. Nevertheless, no continuity has been traced between this group of novels – texts like *The Power and the Glory*, *The Heart of the Matter*, *The End of the Affair*, or *A Burnt-Out Case* would be easily placed in this category, although some may be reluctant to include texts like *Brighton Rock* or *The Honorary Consul* as "Catholic novels" – and the rest of Greene's "serious novels" or his "entertainments." Let me formulate this as an interrogation on Greene's work: What is the ethical rationale justifying an individual's decisions and actions in novels like *The Quiet American* or *The Comedians*, where religion is not an issue? Both novels posit the hero's passage from disengagement to action on the grounds of an implicit commitment to a politically oppressed community (the Vietnamese, the Haitian resistance against Papa Doc's dictatorship). Yet, the nature of their impulse to behave ethically remains unchanged regarding the openly religious texts.

Similar situations may be found in several of Greene's "entertainments." In *The Confidential Agent*, *The Ministry of Fear*, or *Our Man in Havana*, the heroes come to be engaged in resistance and struggle processes for the sake of specific communities (Spanish Republicans during the Civil War in the first case; British Intelligence Services, in defense of British interests, in the other two cases). In these novels, a factor stressing the manner in which individuals alien to the struggle are brought into it is the fact that all of them had unrelated occupations and are slowly drawn into active engagement: D., in *The Confidential Agent*, is a history professor; Arthur Rowe, in *The Ministry of Fear*, is a retired journalist; and Wormold, the protagonist of *Our Man in Havana*, is a vacuum cleaner retailer.

My argument is that the same rationale is found, in one version or another, in most of Greene's novels, including the "Catholic" ones. In *The Power and the Glory*, the Priest's religious affiliation is clearly marked as opposed to official politics, and his activity has a very strong subversive connotation regarding the community of those oppressed by the Mexican local authorities under General Calles and Governor

Garrido Canabal's regime. In *The Heart of the Matter*, Greene complicates things by having two opposing codes collide within one character, as Scobie represents both legal authority – meant to protect the social community – and is subject to a religious summons which, in his distorted view of the matter, clashes against his professional duty.

In *The Heart of the Matter* and *The End of the Affair*, Catholicism does not have the explicit subversive potential it has in novels like *The Power and the Glory*. Still, it is not the "official" or institutional code regulating morality. Catholicism summons the characters affected by it to a community from which those closest to them are excluded (Helen Rolt, Bendrix). Hence, it creates a split in the characters' communitarian life, as other characters will not understand their motivations and actions, guided by Catholic principles. In these two texts, being a Catholic constitutes a deviation from regular social standards. Being Catholic is, for Scobie and Sarah, being marked as different from the rest of the members of the communities to which they belong (professional, social, personal).

Perhaps the text in which the religious and political elements are brought into a single stance with greatest clarity is *The Honorary Consul*. Here, Father Leon Rivas embodies the conflation of Catholicism as a subversive, non-official code, and the process of political resistance to its institutionalized version, at the service of political interest. As in *A Burnt-Out Case*, *The Power and the Glory*, or *Monsignor Quixote*, two versions of Catholicism are opposed. On the one hand, there is the institutional Church, often in close contact with a governing social or political community: the Bishop and Father Herrera representing the curia intent on repressing the deviant Father Quixote; the Catholic community at Luc, led by the Pharisaic Rycker, in *A Burnt-Out Case*; the prelates of the Church, aligned with power, escaping from persecution and abandoning the people to their luck in the other two novels. On the other hand, there is the ecumenical practice of Catholicism on the part of the less favored social groups: the lepers, the Mexican peasants, the Paraguayan poor. Their unadorned understanding of religion is recurrently described as primitive and closer to original Christianity, and it is on this side of the dichotomy that Greene's heroes, Father Quixote, the Whisky Priest, Querry, Parr, and Rivas, are aligned. In structural terms, it could be claimed that both Catholic and non-Catholic novels dramatize the same narrative function, and that the religious element itself is not a determinant feature of the function per se. Rather, the central element of this narrative function is the oppositional nature of a marginal community, presented by Greene's narrators as preferred to the official or institutional one. Rendering this in communitarian terms, this narrative invariant may be explained as the hero's preference for a subversive *Gemeinschaft* and its codes – religious or political – over the official *Gesellschaft*.

The narrative pattern explored in this book, then, takes its point of departure in personal detachment and frequently extreme individualism, transformed by means of a summons to engage in an oppositional communitarian logic (which may be or not religious, but has always an ideological direction). This commitment leads to a specific course of action, sometimes resulting in the betrayal of other allegiances, which ends up demanding that the individual sacrifices for the sake of his fidelity to his commitment. The key moment in most of Greene's novels happens when a character is shaken from his lack of involvement and comes in contact with a reality/an individual/a community forcing his commitment to a cause or an idea. As a consequence, he abandons his passive role and adopts an active, heroic one, in which decisions are made and actions undertaken. The question that helps to articulate the narrative pattern to be analyzed in each of the novels could be: What makes the character turn from passive spectator to actively involved hero?

An overview of some of Greene's major novels from this perspective may illustrate the persistence of the narrative pattern just sketched, and the recurrence of a shift from detachment to commitment as a central narrative device. In *The Power and the Glory*, political persecution forces the hero into marginality, which in turn awakens him to the suffering of the poor: the shift toward commitment has already taken place when the novel begins, but the picture of the Priest hanging on the wall of the police station reminds us that, in the past, he used to lead a very different kind of life, surrounded by the powerful and richer social strata and enjoying the privilege of being protected and pampered by them. In *The Heart of the Matter*, it is unclear when this shift actually happens. In this sense George Orwell may have been right when he wrote that if Scobie had it in him to create such a fuss around him, he would probably have done it much earlier (Orwell 108). However, it may be said that the scene with the dying child constitutes a turning point in the narrative. It is in attending to the petition made to God regarding the dying child that the course of events which will lead to Scobie's destruction is symbolically set in motion (although from the Orwellian perspective one may also argue that things had started to go wrong with Scobie helping the Portuguese Captain and borrowing money from Yusef). *The End of the Affair* picks up on the idea already explored in *The Heart of the Matter*: What if God hears your prayer and concedes the miracle you ask for? It will inevitably tie you forever to whatever promise you have made, or to whatever course of action you have committed to. Here, the turning point comes in the moment of Sarah's prayer for Bendrix's life, which creates an obligation she cannot escape. Sarah's commitment is to God and the promise made in prayer, but also to Bendrix in an indirect sense. In *A Burnt-Out Case*, the symbolic scene of the anointing of the sick is staged in Querry's search for Deo Gratias in the bush. This passage splits the narration in two regarding Querry's "healing" process: after it, he apparently regains an interest in life, perceived by the priests in the *léproserie* as a more authentic life path, closer to primitive Christianity. In *The Quiet American* the shift in Fowler's attitude can be said to derive from a double motive: the threat of losing his current life (not only represented in Pyle's courtship of Phuong, but also in the news that he is to return to England) and the direct witnessing of terror and death, as suffered by the Vietnamese people. The problem remains as to which of the two impulses comes first: is it first personal and then collective/ideological/moral? Or is it the other way around? In both *The Comedians* and *The Honorary Consul*, the main character's detachment from the unstable political situation around them is highlighted, only to favor the greater contrast with the course of action adopted by other characters who are shown to believe in a political cause (the Smiths or Doctor Magiot in *The Comedians*, Leon Rivas and his fellows in *The Honorary Consul*). The instant when commitment is adopted is obscured in both novels, as it is in *The Quiet American*. Commitment is, for Brown and Plarr, a double process of attaining ideological conscience and membership in a native community. As Brown explains in *The Comedians*, finding "home" and "roots" implies finding something to die for.

The typical departure point in Greene's fiction is the disengaged liberal subject,[17] for whom no categorical imperative of a Kantian kind operates as internal self-directing principle of moral obligation, and for whom tradition and convention offer no moral solace. This state of disengagement exists at the outset of most of Greene's novels, when the hero expresses his skepticism and distance regarding moral codes that he perceives as arbitrarily imposed. Alasdair MacIntyre's working hypothesis in *After Virtue* may illuminate this view. McIntyre argues that the contemporary world is characterized precisely by the lack of an accurate moral vocabulary. We live, MacIntyre claims, on the fragments of a conceptual scheme which is no longer operative, but we continue to use many of its key expressions in the absence of their original context (2):

all those various concepts which inform our moral discourse were originally at home in larger totalities of theory and practice in which they enjoyed a role and a function supplied by contexts of which they have now been deprived. Moreover the concepts we employ have in at least some cases changed their character in the past three hundred years; the evaluative expressions we use have changed their meaning. In the transition from the variety of contexts in which they were originally at home to our own contemporary culture "virtue" and "justice" and "piety" and "duty" and even "ought" have become other than they once were. (10)

In noticing the peculiarities of Greene's usage of particular terms belonging to the fields of morality and ethics, characters' lack of an intrinsic moral vocabulary shared with their communities of origin is brought to the foreground as the primary dramatic expression of this fundamental issue. The moment of engagement or commitment in Greene's fiction is usually codified as the acknowledgment of an ethical imperative through which one of those terms – like "pity" or "commitment" – is reinvested with a meaning recognized as already existing, but somehow forgotten. Quite frequently, this is expressed as a return to a native community (*Gemeinschaft*), as happens in *The Power and the Glory*, *A Burnt-Out Case*, or *The Honorary Consul*.

A relevant aspect of such acts of commitment is that they happen in spite of the hero's reluctance or skepticism about himself, and against all chances of success. The most prominent of Greene's "reluctant hero" type are the main characters in *The Quiet American*, *A Burnt-Out Case*, and *The Comedians*. In these novels a man who claims that his motives are selfish and unalloyed by an ethical impulse ends up becoming a hero in the defense of an ideal or a people. This is particularly the case with Jones in *The Comedians*, a soldier of fortune turned into a guerrilla leader fighting against the Tontons Macoute, who ends enacting the part he had been mischievously playing before. Indro Montanelli's *Il Generale Della Rovere* (1959) comes to mind as a possible precedent for Greene's Mr. Jones. Nevertheless, the idea of becoming a hero in the attempt of living up to the myth that has been created around the character is a classical theme in Joseph Conrad's fiction, explored with special intensity in *Lord Jim* (1900) and *Nostromo* (1904). In all these cases, what is demanded from the hero of Greene's novels is that he becomes, like Conrad's Nostromo, "of the people." This implies, as Conrad illustrates in the aforementioned two novels, a sacrifice of individuality for the sake of a community, formulated in terms close to what Iris Murdoch called "an occasion for unselfing" (*Sovereignty* 82): "we cease to be in order to attend to the existence of something else, a natural object, a person in need" (*Existentialists* 58).

The immediate narrative consequence of such acts of commitment in favor of oppressed communities is the rejection and often persecution of the hero by the representatives of the institutional communities (*Gesellschaft*). The dissociation between the hero's ethics and the social norm, or simply the misunderstanding of the hero's motives and actions becomes a narrative trigger. For different reasons, the Priest (*The Power and the Glory*), Querry (*A Burnt-Out Case*), Plarr (*The Honorary Consul*), Father Quixote (*Monsignor Quixote*), and Castle (*The Human Factor*, 1978) are men on the run. The hunted-hunter motif, which Greene explores in the early entertainments *A Gun for Sale* (1936), *The Confidential Agent*, or *The Ministry of Fear*, is the most explicit representation of this narrative device. In these three novels, characters who act heroically are mistakenly hunted as criminals (Anne, D., and Rowe), so that their mission becomes a double one: not only do they have to achieve their initial goal (to help Raven find Davis's boss and stop a world war in *A Gun for Sale*; to discover Dr. Forester's plan in *The Ministry of Fear*; to sign the coal deal with Lord Benditch in *The Confidential Agent*), but they also have to escape from the authorities and prove their innocence.[18] In the novella *The Third Man* (1950), Greene played with this narrative pattern and gave it a twist with the character of Rollo Martins, who sets out to prove the innocence of his childhood friend Harry Lime while trying to escape from police surveillance, only to discover that he was actually involved in serious criminal activity. The comic counterpart for these characters would of course be Wormold in *Our Man in Havana*, who is recruited as a spy by the British secret services and becomes involved in a mock espionage plot as a consequence of his fabricated reports.

Acts of sacrifice – of oneself or another – abound in Greene's novels, but they are rarely rendered as successful events in the defense of oppressed communities. They may end in failure (Eagleton 114–15) or death, but they are always followed by an ironic aftermath. Greene tends to add a coda or epilogue to the story, in which the reader learns how different communities have appropriated the hero's act to fit their purposes. Normally, all such interpretations are proven wrong by a witness who stands for a persistent skepticism. Thus, for example, in *A Burnt-Out Case* Querry's murder by Rycker is misinterpreted as a crime of passion by the locals and as a religious sacrifice by the priests, and in *The Quiet American* Fowler's betrayal of Pyle is seen as a personal revenge by the police and a political act by the Vietnamese communists. Father

Paul and Inspector Vigot, respectively, appear as the representatives of the ultimate narrative stance, according to which no commitment is permanent and no sacrifice can be fully integrated into meaningful communal narrative. Such epilogues upset the legitimacy of the communal claims made by the different groups, and complicate the redeeming narratives they tend to impose on individual failure and death. Still, as I claim in the final section of this book, contingent acts of compassion and commitment in the face of another's suffering persist as an inevitable need on the part of Greene's characters. This seems to evince, as has already been hypothesized in this introduction, that the ethical is a sort of emotional imperative in Greene, though it cannot be brought to have permanent or universal effects.

Keywords in Greeneland

The analysis of the narrative pattern in Greene's fiction entails an assessment of the semantic reinvestment of the ethical vocabulary at work in the texts. Before setting out to analyze them in depth, this introduction sketches an outline of the keywords which articulate the narrative pattern in Greene's work. Like Raymond Williams' cultural vocabulary, the terms discussed in what follows provide the lexico-conceptual basis for what critics have recurrently called "Greeneland" (Falk; Bosco 24; Baldridge; Watts 142).[19] It is through this vocabulary that the narrative dramatization of the ethical is shaped in his fictional universe. In trying to articulate a reduced vocabulary for the analysis of Greene's work, I have followed a double criterion: On the one hand, the salience of particular terms in the novels. It is clear for any reader of *The Heart of the Matter*, for example, that the word "pity" is not only recurrent in the text statistically, but also essential to the understanding of the conflict dramatized by the novel. On the other hand, I have looked for terms whose potential for the textual articulation of narrative conflict could be applied to several works. In other words, I have tried to identify "keywords" around which narrative conflict tends to be articulated, the ones which channel "formations and distributions of energy and interest" (Williams 9). The selection of terms, then, as well as the order in which they are presented, is not casual. In their capacity to generate narrative situations of an ethical kind, they tend to work as narrative functions, "stable, constant elements in a tale, independent of how and by whom they are fulfilled" (Propp 21). The sequence they constitute appears normally in the order proposed, even if some of the elements are missing in a particular text.[20] From a narratological point of view, they constitute a lineal syntagmatic structure (Dundes xi–xii; Greimas 222) leading to irreversible changes of state. The hero's life, in other words, is changed forever in the course of the story. The stories may be narrated retrospectively – as in *The Third Man*, *The Quiet American*, or *Dr. Fisher of Geneva* – but their sequentiality is dramatized in the transformation undergone by the main characters and their storyworlds.

As has been mentioned before, Greene's use of recurrent terms in his work like "pity" or "peace" is idiosyncratic. The reading and interpretation of Greene's novels necessarily entails a semantic readjustment of our habitual understanding of those terms. Entering "Greeneland," it could be argued, means accepting a different "episteme" – borrowing Foucault's term – that will allow us to understand the nature of the conflicts dramatized in Greene's novels. From this perspective, the main purpose of my study can be formulated, in Foucaultian fashion, as an investigation on "the fundamental codes of culture – those governing its language, its schemas of perception, its exchanges, its techniques, its values, the hierarchy of its practices – establish for every man, from the very first, the empirical orders with which he will be dealing and within which he will be at home" (Foucault xxii). In what follows, the major terms of Greene's vocabulary are explored and discussed, in the attempt to point to those aspects where his usage of these terms proves to be determinant for the articulation of the narrative pattern sketched above.

The narrative starting point for Greene's heroes is the need to attain a state of peace, once they have lost all hope of leading meaningful lives in their original contexts. A Graham Greene story begins after the point where nineteenth-century novels would have ended: once the hero has been integrated into society through an adjustment of his individuality into familial, professional, and national communities (Armstrong 8). Most of Greene's novels begin *in media res*, with the main character undergoing personal crisis and seeking to alleviate it through emotional numbness. Readers are never told what unleashed such crises, but we become witnesses to the hero's need to find rest. The need for "peace," moreover, directs the narrative toward a false end: were it to be achieved, the character would enter a state of quietism that would bring narrative development to an end.

The lexical recurrence of the term "peace" in Greene's work is notable; it appears in most of his novels, as well as in many of his autobiographical writings. The desire for peace often expressed by his characters may be tentatively described as a form of quietism, of getting rid of the sense of responsibility and guilt, wanting to do nothing, to be involved in nothing. As Norman Sherry notes in the second volume of his *Life of Graham Greene*, "peace seemed to him the most beautiful word in the language" (237; see also 91). Stephen K. Land describes Greene's use of the idea of peace as freedom from human emotion (45).

A second keyword to be analyzed in this book is "bargain." The term "bargain" is specifically used by Greene in several texts to narrate what could be described as moments of "negotiation," normally between a character and God. The kind of situation thus defined entails a transaction between two parties, the result of which involves a specific course of action to be followed as a consequence of the agreement reached. In Greene's fiction, the two parts involved are normally the hero and God. The nature of the deal is related to salvation, and the transaction usually works as a substitution. In spite of its evocation of economic language, this term actually points to a recurrent narrative motif that has a distinctly religious character. In his play *The Potting Shed* (1956), as well as in *The Power and the Glory*, *The Heart of the Matter*, *The End of the Affair*, and *The Quiet American*, a bargain is struck in which the protagonist offers his own salvation – sells his soul, admittedly in Faustian fashion – in exchange for someone else's life. In *The Power and the Glory* we find one of the earliest examples of this kind of "bargaining" in Greene's fiction. In this novel, the Whisky Priest negotiates his own damnation in exchange for others' salvation. His problem is further complicated by the fact that his bargain is divided between two interests: his own child, and the community for which he is spiritually responsible. Feeling love for one individual to the point of offering oneself in sacrifice, like Granger does for his son in *The Quiet American*, is not enough in the moral universe inhabited by the Priest. While in *The Quiet American* the bargain motif is arguably a minor one, in some other novels, particularly in *The Heart of the Matter* and *The End of the Affair*, the bargain constitutes a narrative crux, a kernel event that makes the plot advance through transformation (Chatman 53). We are led to think that everything happening after it is a direct consequence of God's acceptance, so to say, of the deal offered by the characters in each of the two novels.

Despair can be described as another false end in Greene's novels. In his vocabulary, it is often described as "the unforgivable sin." "Despair" offers a reversed version of quietism, one in which the individual stops moving or fighting for lack of projection into an external motivation which may have worked as trigger for action. In Greene, however, falling into despair is frequently a precondition for the establishment of some form of commitment to others. Greene's understanding of the term, in this sense, comes very close to the existentialist philosophical articulation of such a notion as the basis for human action and freedom. Greene's use of the term, therefore, manages to conflate religious and philosophical concerns that have often been perceived by critics as mutually exclusive. Additionally, he often makes despair a narrative crux in his novels, using it as a turning point for psychological characterization and plot development.

The two paired terms "pity" and "compassion" articulate a crucial distinction in Greene's vocabulary related to ethical behavior and narrative pattern. There are two novels in which Greene deals explicitly with the problematic distinction between pity and compassion: *The Ministry of Fear* and *The Heart of the Matter*. In both, Greene creates a moral opposition where two apparently synonymous terms acquire respectively a negative and a positive value. This is not, however, the kind of moral opposition in which sin is clearly opposed to virtue. Here, both terms belong to the realm of the virtuous, but one is given pre-eminence over the other. The two-level structure he creates in the realm of morality may be said to render visible a pattern whereby, in his novels, morals and ethics interact. Whereas the first term – "pity" – is associated with the kind of behavior considered morally acceptable in a social context (in controlled situations, subjected to normative regulation), the second term – "compassion" – acquires a greater value by comparison, and it is said to spring from the individual's capacity to relate to other human beings in terms of equality.

In the narrative pattern under analysis in this book, the two terms stand not only in a relation of opposition, but also as a narrative sequence. Many of Greene's heroes undergo a process of transformation that pivots on their capacity to feel for others, or to suffer with others. This transformation is articulated as a passage from pity to compassion. Therefore, the two terms serve the purpose of dramatizing ethical resolution. In Greene's works, ultimate ethical action involves feeling compassion for others, usually directed toward specific individuals rather than addressed to all humanity in Weil's fashion.

As has already been mentioned, the narrative turning point in Greene's novels may be described as a passage from detachment or indifference to commitment to a cause or ideal. The first question one may ask regarding Greene's use of the idea of commitment as a narrative crux (Chatman 53) is: To whom or what do his characters commit? What is the nature of the commitment they reach, and how does it affect their lives, and the novels' plot?

In texts like *England Made Me* (1935), *A Gun for Sale*, or *The Third Man*, the Greenean hero acts out of a vague commitment to what is perceived as ethical behavior in a given situation. For instance, Anthony Farrant, in *England Made Me*, may be said to act against the stock markets mogul Krogh out of a mixture of patriotic feeling and genuine ethics. Similarly, Rollo Martins' motives in *The Third Man* are never fully discussed in the novel, perhaps because Greene considered them too obvious to be noted. However, a quick overview of Greene's fiction allows for a preliminary classification that has undoubtedly influenced critical perception. Broadly speaking, two main specific causes for commitment seem particularly recurrent in his fiction: first, a religious one, expressed through the language of Catholic faith, and enacted in charitable action directed to others. In varied modulations, this version of commitment appears in *The Power and the Glory*, *The End of the Affair*, and *A Burnt-Out Case*. In the first and the third of these, the religious commitment paradoxically entails a deviation from Catholic orthodoxy, a mechanism of correction which leads back to an original community with a peculiar understanding of religious practice. The second framework in which commitment is established in Greene's novels is of an openly political nature, and it implies taking sides in some form of conflict in which the character is not directly involved when the story begins. That is, the motives for commitment result from the unfolding of the narrative plot and of the characterization, but they are not a narrative premise. One of the earliest versions of this pattern could be said to appear in *The Confidential Agent*, although here, as in *The Power and the Glory*, the moment when commitment takes place has already happened when the novel begins, and readers can only perceive it, in the course of their reading, through analepses showing the character's life *before committing*. More elaborated versions of the same pattern of political commitment appear in *The Quiet American*, *The Comedians*, *The Honorary Consul* and *The Human Factor*. In all these novels there are two sides involved in competition for power over a collectivity. In *The Human Factor*, the pattern is that of Cold War bloc politics, represented by Soviet and British intelligence services competing for secret information and for control over Maurice Castle. In *The Quiet American*, the same pattern was anticipated in the context of 1950s Vietnam, with French, American, and Communist interests competing for power over the Vietnamese people. In *The Comedians* and *The Honorary Consul*, the parts in conflict are rebel groups fighting, respectively, Papa Doc's regime in 1960s Haiti and Alfredo Stroessner's Colorado regime in Paraguay between 1954 and 1989. The protagonists of these three novels are emphatically described as outsiders to these conflicts: Fowler and Brown are British citizens living as expatriates in Vietnam and Haiti, Eduardo Plarr has mixed ancestry (British and Argentinian) and is drawn over the border to Paraguay by old schoolmates.

From the perspective of the relationship between individuals and communities, the transition to commitment may be perceived as (a) a shift from isolation or extreme individuality to engagement in community, (b) a change of allegiance from one community to another, and (c) an enhancement of the ties attaching the individual to an original community whose existence had been taken for granted or despised. In all three cases, the passage from detachment to commitment entails a symbolic reinvestment of models of community as sites of spiritual or ideological – ultimately ethical – replenishment.

A further question is: What does commitment, once assumed, entail for the characters? What actions are demanded from the hero, once he has become engaged? What are the consequences of these actions? The answer to this last question is probably the easiest, in the sense that Greene's novels point once and again in the same direction: commitment involves the logic of sacrifice, and the consequences of one's actions often lead to death; it involves risking one's personal security, which we often see would remain intact if the commitment had not taken place, for the sake of others. The religious dimension of this logic is explored in depth in *The Power and the Glory*, where the problematic nature of martyrdom is embodied in the Whisky Priest. In a private, reduced situation, *The End of the Affair* reproduces the same schema, with Sarah risking her life to keep her vow never to see Bendrix again, walking in the rain, getting ill, and dying of pneumonia. From the religious perspective, her apparent cruelty toward Bendrix – as perceived from *his* point of view, as the main narrator of the story – is reinscribed with the logic of sacrifice aimed at saving not herself, but Bendrix, from sin and damnation.

Greene's characters' commitment is rarely to themselves, almost always to someone else, and, as has been mentioned above, to a specific form of community. The expression of this commitment usually takes the shape of what Baldridge has called "Greenean caritas" (124). The use of this term – meaning "benevolent goodwill or love for humanity" – marks a specific connotation in Christian discourse: "*caritas*" is not just "love" in this sense, but "Christian love." It refers specifically to one of the three theological virtues, and hence the religious meaning of the term is emphasized by those authors who use it in connection to Greene's work. Greene's own rendering of this term is invested with the semantics of love, friendship, and solidarity.

In the context of Greene's fiction, this understanding of love exceeds the forms of institutionalized communities where love seems to be the rationale – love for one's family, for a lover, for one's country or people. In all these models of communal organization, the bond is established on the basis of all its members having something in common, and it is reinforced by reciprocal affirmation of identity on the basis of this common element (Esposito *Communitas*; Nancy *Inoperative*). The notion of *caritas*, as explained by Murdoch or Simone Weil, implies the "application" of love not to those with whom you have something in common, but to each and every one in need. It requires, in Murdoch's terms, a process of "unselfing" (*Sovereignty* 82) or suppression of the self (65) prior to the recognition of the existence of something else, someone in need (58).[21]

This notion of universal love as a moral ideal is constantly dramatized in Greene's fiction as a problematic, even paradoxical notion. Characters aspire to universal love, but they remain at the level of particular, contingent situations. They blame themselves for loving just one individual over the rest of the universe, as happens both in *The Power and the Glory* and *The Heart of the Matter*. In *The Power and the Glory*, the Priest's love for his own child is opposed to the love owed to the whole world: "This was the love he should have felt for every soul in the world: all the fear and the wish to save concentrated unjustly on the one child" (206). Echoes of the same idea can be found whenever characters oppose particular emotional ties to "higher" ideals encompassing world projects in either a religious or political sense. This happens in *The Quiet American*, where Fowler's egotism is set against the backdrop of Pyle's idealism, but also in many of the entertainments like *England Made Me*, *A Gun for Sale* (in Mather's dilemma between saving his girl and solving his case), *The Confidential Agent*, or *Our Man in Havana*. The universal and personal dimensions of love are thus entangled and set in opposition through plot devices that force the hero into a course of action that remains obscure for the rest of the characters. Still, it is through those acts of misreading of characters' ethics that Greene successfully dramatizes the paradoxical nature of *caritas*.

A note on the scope of this book

The selection of texts chosen for analysis in this book aims at providing ample material for the exploration of the pattern sketched in this introduction. It should be noted, however, that not all texts here discussed enjoy the same critical status. While some of the novels included have been incorporated into the academic canon of Greene's work and have received wide critical attention, others have never been sufficiently analyzed and discussed. Among the first group, *The End of the Affair*, *The*

Heart of the Matter, and *The Quiet American* may be cited. They belong to what critics have called Greene's "middle period," and they are usually considered his "masterpieces." Inevitably, the bibliography devoted to them is abundant. As for the second group, *A Burnt-Out Case* and *The Comedians* are two good examples of novels to which hardly any critical attention has been devoted. An index of this is the fact that few monographic books on Greene include them as part of their corpus for discussion. An interesting case is, perhaps, *The Power and the Glory*, a novel which was widely read and discussed immediately after its publication, but which is often excluded from contemporary research work on Greene. The novels written in the early years of Greene's career, like *The Man Within* or *England Made Me*, have received much less critical attention, partly because they are restricted by the generic conventions of the thriller and espionage fiction. Yet, many of the elements openly dramatized in later novels, like betrayal or the conflict between personal interest and ethical commitment, are already present in them. The same could be said of intermediate texts that Greene called "entertainments," like *The Ministry of Fear* or *Our Man in Havana*. The novels written in the last period of his career, mainly *Travels with my Aunt* (1969) and *Dr Fischer of Geneva* (1980), mark a tendency toward comic registers, which some critics have argued comes close to *grand guignol* (Allott and Faris 11, 208; Parkinson xxiv) and its taste for the macabre and the grotesque.

This study is not presented as an exhaustive chronological overview of Greene's work, but as a series of specific readings focused on particular concepts. The research conducted draws on all of Greene's fictional and non-fictional texts, including early thrillers like *A Gun for Sale*, entertainments like *The Confidential Agent*, novels like *The Quiet American* or *The End of the Affair*, autobiographical works and essays like *A Sort of Life* and *Ways of Escape*, and travel diaries like *In Search of a Character* (1961) or *The Lawless Roads* (1939). The chapters devoted to the detailed analysis of individual concepts expand and develop the narrative pattern sketched in this introduction, exploring the lexico-conceptual articulation of ethical situations in several texts at once, in the attempt to demonstrate the persistence of such recurrence throughout Greene's oeuvre.

1
Peace

In a crucial scene from *The Tenth Man* (1985), in which Carosse tries to seduce Therese in Charlot's presence, Greene provides a definition of "peace" that could well serve to qualify his idiosyncratic understanding of this term. From Charlot's perspective, we read: "the restless playboy [Carosse] knew how to offer *what most people wanted more than love –* peace" (151; emphasis added). For Greene, peace is the most desirable of emotional and psychological states. In a different context, he described peace as "the most beautiful word in the language" (Letter to Catherine Walston, June 27, 1947; qtd. in Sherry *Life* 2, 233). Greene's personal desire for peace is frequently expressed in his autobiographical works, suggesting a series of associated meanings that often find their way into his fiction. From a narrative point of view, peace is the zero degree position for his characters: a starting point, a state they wish to return to, and the situation against which all narrative events develop. Except for a few individuals like Alfred Jones in *Dr Fischer of Geneva*, who succeeds in finding it against his will, peace is something Greene's characters long for but rarely attain. For most of them, peace only comes with death, which is in some contexts a closely associated term in Greene's vocabulary. Thus, absence of peace becomes in his fictional universe the condition upon which narrative develops, and also the cause of much distress. In *The Lawless Roads*, Greene expressed most clearly this understanding of the world as "a valley of tears" in which peace is unreachable: "The world is all of a piece, of course; it is engaged everywhere in the same subterranean struggle, lying like a tiny neutral state, with whom no one ever observes his treaties, between the two eternities of pain and – God knows the opposite of pain, not we [...] *There is no peace anywhere where there is human life*" (33; emphasis added). Lack of peace, moreover, is related to the impossibility of remaining detached from a situation or a person in an ethical sense. Peace and responsibility, or commitment, are antagonistic concepts in Greene's usage. In this chapter, the semantic peculiarities of "peace" will be explored, and the ethical import of the term will be analyzed in terms of its potential as a narrative trigger.

The meanings of peace

In Graham Greene's fictional universe, most characters long for peace. In *Brighton Rock*, Pinkie constantly repeats the mantra "Dona nobis pacem" ("give us peace") (54, 103, 248, 261), which is also used in *The Comedians* (248). The desire for peace is present also in many other novels, expressed as an unattainable dream: "Peace was a sanity which he did not believe that he had ever known" (*Man* 43); "he dreamed of peace by day and night" (*Heart* 50); "Do you never have a desire, Mr. Wormold, to go back to the peace?" (*Havana* 145). Greene's understanding of peace may be read along four discursive lines, connected in the ethical pattern dramatized by his novels: peace as redemption, peace as quietism, peace as freedom from decision, peace as death.

The most obvious expression of this longing for peace that most Greenean heroes share is the idea of spiritual or religious redemption, in which peace appears in opposition to sin and guilt. Being at peace, in this sense, would equal being in a state from which the disturbing presence of guilt has been erased. Greene's characters rarely enjoy this state, but they desire it as they see it reflected in others. It is in this indirect way that we may learn about its meaning. In *The Heart of the Matter*, Scobie attends a church service from which he feels estranged, his own guilty conscience separating him from the community of those at peace with God: "An immeasurable distance already separated him from these people who knelt and prayed and would presently receive God in peace. He knelt and pretended to pray" (207). In the Catholic context, this is the kind of peace that comes with confession. In *The Power and the Glory*, the Whisky Priest expresses his longing for peace in terms of comparison with others who have attained it precisely by confessing to him: "Perhaps it was his duty [...] to discover peace. He felt an immense envy of all those people who had confessed to him and been absolved. In six days, he told himself, in Las Casas, I too ... But he couldn't believe that anybody anywhere would rid him of his heavy heart" (170).

Pinkie, in *Brighton Rock*, shares this notion of peace as forgiveness in a religious sense. In the early moments of the story he thinks he may attain it after all; by the end of the novel he is sure of his own damnation. Here, peace has a strong religious meaning of redemption. Compare two moments of the narrative: "then, when he was thoroughly secure, he could begin to think of making peace, of going home, and his heart weakened with a faint nostalgia" (116); "he'd learnt the other day that when the time was short there were other things than contrition to think about. It didn't matter anyway ... he wasn't made for peace, he couldn't believe in it. Heaven was a word: hell was something he could trust" (248). The skepticism about the idea of peace denoted in the second passage is related to Pinkie's own course of action, which has taken him beyond redemption according to his own peculiar religious standard.

Extending it beyond the strictly religious realm, however, it is easy to discover how the same envy for others' peace is present as well in other characters. What they all have in common is a feeling of guilt that provokes a double sense of estrangement: from their past lives, and from the communities to which they belong. Characters who feel guilty about something they have done in the past, and need to atone for it, are recurrent in Greene's oeuvre. Possibly the clearest example would be Arthur Rowe in *The Ministry of Fear*, whose entire life is dominated by the guilt he feels for having killed his sick wife out of mercy. As a consequence, Rowe does not recognize himself as the man who was once happy, and he doesn't consider he may ever be at peace again. It is also as a consequence of this act that he has become estranged from those who constituted his community, isolating himself from friends and family – "there had been a time when he had friends" (75). His isolation, the narrator states, has made him a peculiar man: "Like all men living alone, he believed his own habits to be the world's; it never occurred to him that other men might not eat biscuits at six" (23).

The remorseful hero could be said in fact to constitute an archetype in Greene's work. At this point, however, it would be necessary to establish a distinction in terms of the narrative sequences created by Greene. Some of his remorseful heroes have regrets about something belonging to their past life. Querry feels guilty about the dehumanizing dissolute life he led as a celebrity architect in *A Burnt-Out Case*, Wormold feels guilty about his divorce from his wife in *Our Man in Havana*, and the already mentioned Arthur Rowe is consumed by his mercy killing. In some other cases, however, guilt develops as a consequence of the influence that characters' actions have on others in the course of the narrative. This is the case with D. in *The Confidential Agent*, who feels responsible for Else's death: "It was as if he had been given a glimpse of the guilt which clings to all of us without our knowing it.

None of us knows how much innocence we have betrayed. He would be responsible ..." (54). Like him, Andrews is responsible for the harm done to Elizabeth by Carlyon in *The Man Within*, Greene's first novel.

In some cases, that guilt is not only an internal psychological phenomenon, but one brought about by external forces persecuting the hero. For the Whisky Priest in *The Power and the Glory*, finding peace is not only a spiritual matter, but also one related to security, derived from his status as a persecuted individual. Like him, other haunted characters in Greene's work express the same desire for safety.[1] In *The Man Within*, Greene depicted Andrews as a persecuted man whose decision to betray the smuggler Carlyon provokes both his guilty consciousness and a manhunt aimed at taking revenge on him. Thus, his desire for peace acquires a double character as he tries to escape from himself and from others: "his desperate longing for peace returned, a peace which would be empty of caution and deception" (106).

These texts share a narrative perspective from which the possibility of peace has been eradicated; it belongs to a past that cannot be recuperated. In this sense, they are set in a post-lapsarian world. These novels can only tell about the character's reality after the fall; whatever happened before remains outside the limits of the narrative, and it can only be recalled through the filter of guilty consciousness. The two novels where Greene experimented with first-person narrators constitute in fact narrative exercises on guilty consciousness. Both Fowler in *The Quiet American* and Bendrix in *The End of the Affair* must give account of themselves precisely because they feel guilty about the damage they have done to others – to Pyle in Fowler's case, and to Sarah in Brendrix's. Their narratives may be read as confessions, and they establish in the diegetic present a post-lapsarian state from which the narrators/characters feel there is no way out. Like Pinkie, they feel they are beyond redemption. The damage they have provoked is irreversible, and peace is untenable for them.[2] Their respective identities as narrators, moreover, may be said to emerge precisely from the realization that they are the cause of an irreparable injury to others (Butler *Giving* 85).

Even in this situation, however, a sort of peace may be found, if only of a temporary and illusory character. This second sense of peace is closer to the sort of ethical quietism famously identified by Jean-Paul Sartre as "quietism of despair" (345) in "Existentialism Is a Humanism" (1946). It could be characterized as lack of action, non-involvement, a refusal to make decisions or choices. It is articulated in *A Burnt-Out Case* in the following terms: "If no change means peace, this certainly was peace, to be found like a nut at the center of the hard shell of discomfort" (1). This understanding of peace may be said to spring from the realization that being alive means suffering and making others suffer. Here, Greene's understanding of the ethical finds its best philosophical expression in Sartre's understanding of responsibility and commitment. For the novelist, as for the French existentialist, anguish is the condition of ethical action, and its absence can only mean a renunciation to what makes us human, which is precisely the anguish of responsibility and commitment. In this context, if peace is to be attained, it can only come through the annihilation of the will and the subject's withdrawal from the realm of the ethical in which individual action inevitably affects others. Characters like Querry (*A Burnt-Out Case*) and Scobie (*The Heart of the Matter*) seem particularly sensitive to this conception. In both cases, their longing for peace is also related to their guilty feelings about how their actions have provoked others' suffering: "I can't bear to see suffering and I cause it all the time. I want to get out, get out" (*Heart* 216); "Her pain struck at my pain: we were back at the old routine of hurting each other. If only it were possible to love without injury" (*Quiet* 110).

Their aspiration comes close to what Greene wrote in connection to Evelyn Waugh in *Ways of Escape*: "Peace he was not granted – only a long despair which he passed off with the lighter word, boredom" (264). *Monsignor Quixote* offers a clear articulation of how the interchange with other human beings may disrupt the peace that comes with routine and boredom: "The presence of Professor Pilbeam, whose second visit to Osera this was, had removed Father Leopoldo from the peace of a routine to a more confused world, the world of intellectual speculation" (227). In this novel, the monastery appears as the ultimate location where peace is to be attained through isolation from the outside world. And yet, as shown in the novel, even this monastic peace is a precarious one: "They wanted in a romantic way to sacrifice their lives. But he had come here only to find a precarious peace" (ibid.).

A further dimension of Greene's understanding of peace may be found in how this "quietism of despair" relates to the idea of decision making. In terms of the ethical predicament in which most of Greene's characters find themselves, peace may be defined as lack of decision, not having to deliberate, to act. The idea goes back to early modern political thought, in which citizenship is defined in terms of how the individual decisions of many may be conjugated (Locke). In Hobbes's *Leviathan*, decision means "deliberation" (probably a false etymology), "putting an end to the *Liberty* we had of doing, or omitting, according to our own Appetite, or Aversion" (*Leviathan* ch. 6, 44). One stops being free the moment one makes a decision, and acts out an irrevocable choice. In this context, decision making is understood as an action that puts the individual in connection with others, affecting others.

In the context of Greene's fiction, the implications of this idea are explored in terms that come close to an existentialist framework. Greene's characters tend to identify in the moment of decision the embodiment of ethical action, and in the retreat from situations that demand decision making a liberation from responsibility. Sartre uses the example of a military leader sending his soldiers to death to illustrate his view of what human responsibility over others entails:

> In making the decision, he cannot but feel a certain anguish. All leaders know that anguish. It does not prevent their acting, on the contrary it is the very condition of their action, for the action presupposes that there is a plurality of possibilities, and in choosing one of these, they realize that it has value only because it is chosen. Now it is anguish of that kind which existentialism describes, and moreover, as we shall see, makes explicit through direct responsibility towards other men who are concerned. Far from being a screen which could separate us from action, it is a condition of action itself. (Sartre "Existentialism" 352)

For someone who has adopted a commitment, peace is therefore impossible. This is the case of the Whisky Priest in *The Power and the Glory*, for whom peace is a temptation to liberate himself from his commitment, abandoning himself to death: "Would they shoot him out of hand? A delusive promise of peace tempted him [...] Death was not the end of pain – to believe in peace was a kind of heresy" (73). Repeatedly throughout the novel, peace is presented as a mirage: "The oddest thing of all was that he felt quite cheerful; he had never really believed in this peace. He had dreamed of it so often on the other side that now it meant no more to him than a dream" (177). The entire novel could be read as a series of failed attempts at finding peace and security in a succession of scenarios – the hotel room, his lover's village, the little girl's farm, the prison cell, the Lutherans' house – a peace that can eventually come only with death.

Fowler (*The Quiet American*) may be seen as the epitome of the Greenean hero who has found an illusory peace in his detachment, one from which he will be shaken out in the course of the narrative. Like him, several others point to a constant in Greene's fictional universe: peace can only be attained by removing all links to other human beings, by avoiding responsibility over others' lives and wellbeing. These characters have "deliberately withdrawn to the sidelines, out of the conflict, to be in a position from which they may be spectators but which isolates them from involvement" (Land 77). In *The Comedians*, Brown stands as the only character who seems to be able to remain "a comedian," a fluid identity not attached to others. The key to his peace of mind comes precisely from his lack of responsibility toward others: "somewhere years ago I had forgotten how to be involved in anything. Somehow somewhere I had lost completely the capacity to be concerned" (183). Crane, in *Rumour at Nightfall* (1931), makes a very similar point: "I am on the borders now of that cold inhuman land: I have only to relinquish pain, to know the truth and not to care, and I need never fear again" (155). This is the zero responsibility position that a character like Scobie seems to find impossible to attain. In *The Heart of the Matter*, the character who represents a position equivalent to Brown's would be the merchant Yusef, who gives Scobie advice on how to deal with women: "The way is not to care a damn" (225).[3]

At the other end of the ethical spectrum we find those characters who have realized that peace is just a form of despair, and have found in action a way out of quietism. This is particularly noticeable in some of the thrillers, where the genre convention calls for a narrative structure in which the succession of events must be frenetic. The most direct connection between the thriller convention and this longing for action can probably be found in *The Confidential Agent*, where D., the main character, progressively gains control over the situation he finds himself in: "It occurred to him that never once yet had he been allowed the initiative. He had been like a lay figure other people moved about [...] it seemed to him that at last the initiative was passing into his hands; he wished he had more vitality to take it, but he was exhausted" (80–81). In *The Ministry of Fear*, Rowe's progressive involvement in the espionage plot is described as a coming back to life after a period of numbness: "he was happily drunk with danger and action. This was more like the life he had imagined years ago" (159). When the novel begins, he is paralyzed by guilt, and his incapacity for action is contrasted with his excessive thoughtfulness: "You want to do great deeds, not dream them all day long" (8). When he temporarily loses his memory during the London Blitz, liberated from the burden of guilt, involvement and action become possible again.[4]

A final expression of the idea of peace in Greene's work is to be found in its association to death. It could be depicted as the desire to put a stop to suffering derived from the sense of responsibility over others, and it is normally characterized by Greene as egotistic, defeatist. Although this desire for death as a way out of the ethical imperative and the ensuing suffering will be explored in depth in the next chapter, it is interesting to mention how death is sometimes contemplated by Greene's heroes as a desirable state, the only one that can bring peace: "the most enviable possession a man can own – a happy death" (*Heart* 213). Two of Greene's characters seem to be particularly prone to consider the association between peace and death: Scobie in *The Heart of the Matter* and the Whisky Priest in *The Power and the Glory*. Both of them contemplate the possibility of suicide as a way of achieving the peace that is denied to them in life, only to conclude that not even death can bring them the peace they long for.[5] For the former, suicide is contemplated as the only way out of an ethical dead end, the triangle of responsibility and deceit into which he has got with his wife and his lover. In his final confession to God, he assumes his damnation: "I'm not pleading for mercy. I am going to damn myself, whatever that means. I've longed for peace and I'm never going to know peace again. But you'll be at peace when I am out of your reach" (258). For the latter, not even death can bring an end to the suffering, as "death was not the end of pain" (73). None of Greene's heroes, it should be noted, seems to find a peaceful death, although many characters' deaths – Sarah Miles, Querry, Jones – will be reinterpreted by the communities around them in terms of redemption and even sanctity.

Beginnings and ends

Stephen K. Land has argued that Greene's heroes are "on the brink of action" at the beginning of the novels (266). In his study of narrative pattern in Greene's fiction, Land claims that the desire for peace lies always in the past of characters' lives (38), establishing a "definitive circumstantial divide between the remembered life of innocence and the unhappy present" (39). Rather than a Romanticized nostalgia for childhood innocence, however, the divide Land identifies in the pattern of Greene's characterization of his heroes may be related to the turning point of a moment of decision that, in many of his novels, tends to be displaced out of the limits of the story time. Indeed, several of Greene's characters seem to fulfill the pattern established by Land. For them, peace belongs to the past, and was destroyed by some irrevocable act in which they have varied degrees of responsibility. Characters who lost their peace a long time ago include Pinkie (*Brighton Rock*), who is beyond remorse, Scobie (*The Heart of the Matter*), who is already restless when the novel begins, even if he has not yet committed adultery, Querry (*A Burnt-Out Case*), the Whisky Priest, and D. (*The Confidential Agent*), who is already involved in political struggle and was removed from his peaceful life as an academic long before the story begins. For these, living with others is a form of slavery to their service; it is an unavoidable duty, but also the cause of pain and suffering. Perhaps the text in which Greene explored in greater depth the moment of such "fall" from peace and, therefore, from an innocent lack of responsibility, is the short story "The Fallen Idol," published for the first time in 1935 with the title "The Basement Room." The story focuses precisely on how the main character, the child Philip Lane, starts to acquire a consciousness of the lives of others, the secrets and lies of the adult world: "It wasn't fair, the walls were down again between his world and theirs; but this time it was something worse than merriment that *the grown people made him share*; a passion moved in the house he recognized but could not understand" (121; emphasis added). As this passage mentions, Philip's entrance into the world of adults is not voluntary, but rather forced upon him. His reaction is fierce, as he desperately tries to go back to the state of affairs before he became involved in the lives of those around him: "That was what happened when you loved: you got involved; and Philip extricated himself from life, from love, from Baines with a merciless egotism" (128). The end of the story, with an elderly Philip still haunted by his childhood memories, constitutes yet another instance of the impossibility of peace for Greene's characters.

On the other hand, there are many characters in Greene's oeuvre for whom peace is the beginning, who are awakened to a sense of ethical commitment: Wormold in *Our Man in Havana*, whose life has fallen into torpor after years of feeling guilty about being abandoned by his wife; Arthur Rowe, whose situation is almost exactly the same as Wormold's; Plarr, Henry Pulling, and Alfred Jones from *The Honorary Consul*, *Travels with my Aunt*, and *Dr Fischer of Geneva*, respectively, who live immersed in routine as an anodyne to avoid the pain of being in contact with others; and, to some extent, Fowler as well, when his story begins (after a long stay in Vietnam) and before Pyle arrives. For them, the awakening to ethical consciousness, as well as their return to life and feeling and pain, comes with the arrival of someone who alters the routine of a peaceful life. There is no nostalgia for a pre-lapsarian innocence or peace projected out of the text into the past lives of characters, but the resistance to abandon the position of detachment from commitment to other human beings they have acquired. A different kind of situation is sketched in *Travels with my Aunt* and *Dr Fischer of Geneva*, which, according to some critics, mark a tendency toward dark comedy in Greene's later fiction. For both Henry Pulling and Alfred Jones, their initial peace is signaled by their loneliness, the absence of a familial community. That peace will be upset through the establishment of family ties (with a mother and a wife, respectively) that they seem happy to accept. One may add that Alfred Jones' trajectory in *Dr Fischer of Geneva* goes back and forth: after his wife's death, he returns to the state of numbness in which he was said to live before he met her. This state of numbness is, as it happens in other cases already mentioned, an illusory peace: "I felt at peace and an odd sense of near-happiness moved in me. It seemed to me that I could spend hours, even days, like that, just watching the elixir of death in the glass. [...] As long as the glass was there I felt safe from loneliness, even from grief. It was like the interim of relief between two periods of pain, and I could prolong this interim at will" (98).

This need for peace on the character's part, moreover, directs the narrative toward a false end: were it to be achieved, the character would enter a state of quietism that would bring narrative development to an end. The risk of narrative paralysis, through the lack of action – that is, *peripetiae* – that this kind of peace would provide is frequently counteracted in Greene's novels by the introduction of characters who upset the tranquility they may have attained. The narrative pattern thus sketched may be said to be inherited from Joseph Conrad, who used it in novels like *Under Western Eyes* (1911) or *Victory* (1914). In both texts, a character who has managed to isolate himself from an outside world full of complications sees his peace of mind disturbed by someone who acts precisely as a reminder of that world they had run away from. Like many of Greene's heroes, the main character from Conrad's *Victory* sets out to live untouched by the grief which comes from being with others: "In this scheme he had perceived the means of passing through life without suffering and almost without a single care in the world – invulnerable because elusive" (86). In the end, however, "the outer world had broken upon him, and he did not know what wrong he had done to bring this on himself" (212).

Either of the two positions sketched above makes characters unhappy and perpetuates their suffering: they cannot live with others without feeling pain, but living apart and numbing their ethical sense of obligation to others is merely a form of surviving, not of living as a full human being. The figurative language used by Greene in this context often reveals the extent to which he distinguishes between the state of peace and a state of commitment/suffering in terms of a hierarchy that would see the first as a lesser form of life, and the second as its full expression. Alfred Jones, Arthur Rowe, D., Wormold … they all *awaken* to suffering when they abandon their peace, which is described as a sort of lethargy, or a dream-world of inaction. Thus, for example, at the beginning of *The Ministry of Fear*, we read: "You want to do great things, not dream them all day long" (8). Similarly, in *Our Man in Havana*, Wormold's passivity becomes the object of his wife's reproach, just before she leaves him: "Why don't you do something, act some way, any way at all? You just stand there …" (26). The association between peace and dream recurs also in *The Confidential Agent*: "only in sleep did he evade violence; his dreams were almost invariably made up of peaceful images from the past" (39).

This pattern of opposition between the authentic but unattainable peace and the illusory refuge in a momentary peace is constantly underscored in Greene's work. In some of the early novels, like *The Man Within* or *Rumour at Nightfall*, the heroes find a temporary relief from suffering in their meeting with a woman symbolically marked as an "angelic" figure. Both Francis Andrews and Crane find in Elizabeth and Eulelia, respectively, a refuge from persecution. Andrews describes his situation in terms of the discovery of a domestic peace identified with Elizabeth:

> He had a sudden wish to tell her everything, from what he was fleeing and for what cause, but caution and a feeling of peace restrained him. He wished to forget it himself and cling only to this growing sense of intimacy, of two minds moving side by side, and watch the firelight gleam downwards into the dark amber of the tea. (*Man* 56)

The fire and the tea offered by Elizabeth equally symbolize the domestic realm that Andrews identifies with "peace, security, women, idle talk" (ibid.).

As Andrews is soon to learn, this kind of peace is incompatible with the state of persecution in which these characters often find themselves. The solace found in a woman's arms has a fleeting character in this and other novels that follow the same storyline. The closest case may be *Rumour at Nightfall*, where Michael Crane also seems to find peace in the company of Eulelia. His depiction of those moments of peace is permeated with a mystical tone: "he remembered with a sort of homesickness the peace he had found that morning. That peace had lasted for seconds only, but he could recognize in it a quality of timelessness, which flight could not possess. Those seconds might have never ended; they might have become eternity ... he had become conscious of the existence of peace, but the peace had been there always" (174).[6]

Robert Hoskins has explored in detail this aspect of Greene's understanding of the notion of peace (12–15). In his reading, peace is normally associated with love, with the quasi-mystical fusion of the lovers, in which the Greenean hero seeks "the prospect of an enduring peace" (13). The ultimate archetype for this pattern is to be found in *The End of the Affair*, in Bendrix and Sarah's love relationship. Bendrix's narration gives powerful expression to the mystical component of physical love, an idea that was anticipated – although poorly executed – in the earlier *Rumour at Nightfall*. His depiction of Sarah's abandonment to love echoes the connection with eternal peace from the earlier novel: "She had no doubts. The moment only mattered. Eternity is said not to be an extension of time but an absence of time, and sometimes it seemed to me that her abandonment touched that strange mathematical point of endlessness, a point with no width occupying no space" (39). In his memories of the happy moments with Sarah, Bendrix admits having felt what he refers to as "the little peace" (36). Even in the desolate present from which he tells his story full of resentment, he acknowledges: "And yet there was this peace ..." (ibid.). For him, however, this is just an instant in the midst of constant suffering, as Bendrix does not partake of Sarah's experience of eternal peace: "She had so much more capacity for love than I had – I couldn't bring down that curtain round the moment, I couldn't forget and I couldn't *not* fear. Even in the moment of love, I was like a police officer gathering evidence of a crime that hadn't yet been committed" (40).

Although Hoskins is right in pointing out how many of Greene's heroes seek a lasting peace through women, it should be noted that they never manage to find it on a permanent basis. As Alfred Jones mentions in *Dr Fischer of Geneva*, the kind of peace produced by love is only a parenthesis between two periods of pain: "Even love changes its character. Love ceases to be happiness. Love becomes a sense of intolerable loss" (64). Thus, his relationship with Anna-Louise is presented in the novel as a brief interlude: "we were left in peace, and what a peace it was that winter, deep as the early snow that year and almost as quiet" (ibid.). Love is just another form of suffering, as Bendrix constantly expresses in *The End of the Affair*, inextricably linked to life itself. In the text, the motifs of suffering as an index of life and the desire to find peace in death are repeated: "For a month or two this year a ghost had pained me with hope, but the ghost was laid and the pain would be over soon. I would die a little more every day, but now I longed to retain it. *As long as one suffers one lives"* (113; emphasis added). The last section of this chapter takes its cue from this idea, and focuses on the metaphorical articulation of peace as death in life, an idea articulated most explicitly in *A Burnt-Out Case*: "first there had been this peace. *Consummatum est*: pain over and peace falling round him like a little death" (123).

Peace and awakening

There are two novels by Greene that have often been read as being contiguous in their treatment of the topic under analysis: *The Heart of the Matter* and *A Burnt-Out Case*.[7] At the beginning of *A Burnt-Out Case*, Querry seems to have reached that state of peace for which Scobie longed, by simply not caring about anyone. Being unable to feel for others was, in Scobie's mind, a liberation from the impossible duty to assist anyone in need of help. Querry, it could be said, has reached that state of indifference, just to discover that not caring equals being dead. In *A Burnt-Out Case*, therefore, Greene explores the way back to life, to feeling and caring and, inevitably, to suffering for others. The question remains, of course, whether it is possible to return to a meaningful life in which caring for others does not involve infinite pain.

When the novel begins, Querry is in the process of leaving behind his old identity: urban, dissolute, and marked by his professional and social success as a "great Catholic architect" (45). He is on his way from being an individual defined on the basis of his public fame – "*the* Querry," as other characters in the novel repeatedly call him (34, 37, 38, 41 etc.) – into a redefinition of his identity in a new location according to a narrative of fall and redemption that tends to see him as a repentant sinner. In Luc, the Congolese colonial town he arrives at, Querry's attempts to disengage from the different identity tags that the other characters attach to him is recurrently expressed in the use of negative forms: "I'm not a writer" (28), "I'm not a photographer" (28), "I've committed no crime" (28), "I'm not a sociable man" (29), "I am not working" (37), "I have no talent" (37), "I wouldn't call myself that" (39), "I'm not qualified to talk about that" (39).

Querry begins where many of Greene's characters end: he has the numbness and indifference toward others that would have saved Scobie and the Whisky Priest so much suffering. He has the "peace" the others long for: "a delusive promise of peace tempted him" (*Power* 73); "he had nearly everything, and all he needed was peace [...] For he dreamed of peace by day and night. Once in sleep it had appeared to him as the great glowing shoulder of the moon heaving across his window like an iceberg" (*Heart* 49–50). Peace in Greene is defined in ascetic terms, as the *via negativa*: peace is the absence of conflict, of passion, of pain. Both in *The Heart of the Matter* and *A Burnt-Out Case*, it is symbolically represented in the nakedness and austerity of the character's dwelling. In the former, the drabness of the bathroom is said to be the only space which Scobie considers "home," precisely because he can be alone: "The rest of the room was all his own. It was like a relic of his youth carried from house to house. It had been like this years ago in his first house before he married. This was the room in which he had always been alone" (30–31). In the latter, Querry's room bears witness to the absence of anchorage to the outside world: "It was the only one in the place completely bare of symbols, bare indeed of almost anything. No photographs of a community or a parent" (74).[8]

Being free to move away from his old life – something that Scobie and the Whisky Priest definitely cannot do – he has become a wanderer (Hill *Wanderers* 56), a monad without attachments to any place or any person: he does not feel (*Burnt-Out* 31), he does not believe (92), he wants nothing and suffers from nothing (16). Querry is introduced as totally alienated from any human community: "Human beings are not my country" (51), he claims. His initial aim would be the total quietude that comes only with death: "So you thought you could just come and die here? Yes. That *was* in my mind" (46). A recurrent expression for this notion in the novel is to come to the end of everything: "I've come to an end. This place, you might say, is the end" (110).

As the reader knows, however, this is not the end, but the beginning. In the diary that recounts the writing process of the novel, conspicuously entitled *In Search of a Character*, Greene mentions his decision to have the story begun before Querry arrives at Luc (*Search* 7, 13), making Querry's river journey part of the narrative. Apart from reinforcing the parallel with Conrad's Marlow and his journey along the Congo River in *Heart of Darkness*,[9] this anticipation reinforces the idea that Querry has left behind his previous identity in the eyes of the reader. The character introduces himself at the end of chapter 2: "My name is Querry" (19). Before that, the narrator refers to him as "the passenger" as he travels toward the heart of the Congo (9, 10, 11, 12, 13, 14). As the passenger ascends the river that will take him to the leper village where he is to stay, the natives sing a song about him, or rather, about his undefined identity: "Here is a white man who is neither a father nor a doctor. He has no beard. He comes from a long way away – we do not know from where – and he tells no one to what place he is going nor why" (11–12). The same indeterminacy as to the passenger's identity is expressed when he introduces himself to Doctor Colin, "speaking in an accent which Colin could not quite place as French or Flemish any more than he could immediately identify the nationality of the name" (19–20). When the captain asks him the reason for his journey he answers: "The road was closed by floods. This was the only route" (12). His avoidance of any explanation suggesting intention or motivation bespeaks a desire to shun psychological scrutiny. Similarly, when Doctor Colin asks him, upon his arrival at the leper village, whether he intends to stay, he answers: "The boat goes no further" (20). In both cases, topography or conditions of transport are given as an explanation instead of psychological motivation. His negative use of language, his refusal to comply with the social role others try to impose on him, and his overall alienation and passivity contribute to make Querry a Bartleby-like character. Unlike the protagonist of Melville's story, however, Querry is not as static and adamant in his passive resistance.

Although at the beginning of the novel we are led to think that he has given up any hope of recovery, the fact that he has not committed suicide – in Greene's idiom, that he has not fallen into despair, "the unforgivable sin" (*Power* 57) – suggests that there may be a possibility of renewal or rebirth for him. According to Richard Kelly, this is a key difference between Querry and Scobie: "Unlike previous Greene heroes, however [Querry] does not contemplate suicide. [...] Instead of death he seeks the land of childhood innocence, symbolized by Africa" (Kelly 76). The narratives of physical and spiritual redemption projected on him by the rest of the characters have such evocative power that the reader cannot help participating in them somehow, and reading as signs of healing any traces of sympathetic behavior on Querry's part.

In Greene's work, there are characters who go through similar processes, coming to life again after a period of numbness and near despair. Rowe and D., the heroes of the entertainments *The Ministry of Fear* and *The Confidential Agent*, may be said to undergo similar transformations, as has already been mentioned. However, in their case, it is a romantic element that makes the trick, in the shape of a heroine – Anna and Rose Cullen respectively – who brings the hero back to life. A similar pattern is found, in comic key, in *Travels with my Aunt*, in which Henry Pulling's initial interest in funerals may be said to work as symbolic expression of his death-in-life state at the beginning of the novel: "I have never married, I have always lived quietly, and, apart from my interest in dahlias, I have no hobby. For those reasons I found myself agreeably excited by my mother's funeral" (9). The same kind of pun over death and funerals is found in *The Honorary Consul*, in which Plarr's mother comments on her husband's refusal to stay at peace even in his coffin: "she talked to him in her usual vein of complaint, telling him how his father would not rest like a respectable man of property in the interior of his coffin. They had constantly to shuffle him back inside, and that was no way for a *caballero* to enjoy his eternal peace" (178). In all these cases, it is suggested that being at peace is in fact like being dead, and sometimes not even the dead rest in tranquility.

The key metaphor used in *A Burnt-Out Case* to express Querry's search for peace and his subsequent acceptance of suffering as an intrinsic part of the human condition is to be found in the figure of the leper. The correspondence between physical and psychological burnt-out states is stressed throughout the text: "he had always to remember that leprosy remained a psychological problem" (18). Leprosy works, in *A Burnt-Out Case*, as a metaphor of spiritual exhaustion (Bergonzi 153).[10] The equivalence between the physical and spiritual dimensions is articulated in the novel through the parallels between the charac-ters of Querry and Deo Gratias, one of the lepers treated by Dr. Colin (Bergonzi 153; Brennan 115; Kulshrestha 134). Querry and Deo Gratias are both "burnt-out cases," and, according to Michael G. Brennan, "Deo Gratias and Querry come to parallel one another, as the former's physical mutilations and numbness correspond to the latter's spiritual condition" (Brennan 115). Deo Gratias is actually the vehicle through which the meaning of the expression is explained for the first time in the text (*Burnt-Out* 21). Later, the parallel between the former's spiritual numbness and the second's physical one is established in the text:

> Querry had asked Doctor Colin before engaging [Deo Gratias] whether he suffered pain, and the doctor had reassured him, answer-ing that mutilation was the alternative to pain. It was the palsied with their stiffened fingers and strangled nerves who suffered – suffered almost beyond bearing (you heard them sometimes crying in the night), but the suffering was in some sort a protection against mutilation. Querry did not suffer, lying on his back in bed, flexing his fingers. (25)

According to the argumentative logic of the above quoted passage, feel-ing pain means you are alive and, in opposition, the fact that "Querry did not suffer" (25) indicates that he is closer to death. The epigraph chosen by Greene for the novel defines the character's state: "Io non mori, e non rimasi vivo" ("I did not die, yet nothing of life remained"). The reference is significant in connection to the main metaphor used by

Greene to describe his character. As a "burnt-out case," he is beyond the physical pain that indicates, in patients with leprosy, that a limb can be spared mutilation: "the suffering was, in some sort, a protection against mutilation" (25). Lack of suffering is translated as lack of interest in life: "I have no interest in anything any more, doctor. I don't want to sleep with a woman nor design a building [...] The palsied suffer, their nerves feel, but I am one of the mutilated, doctor" (46).

Querry's reawakening will be articulated in the novel in metaphorical terms consistent with the medical metaphor of numbness. His interest in another human being will be depicted as the recovery of sensitivity: "Interest began to move painfully in him like a nerve that had been frozen. He had lived with inertia so long that he examined his 'interest' with clinical detachment" (56). As mentioned before, *A Burnt-Out Case* and *The Heart of the Matter* end with similar epilogues, in which the cast of characters comments on the hero's death and passes judgment on whether he is saved or damned. In *A Burnt-Out Case*, Doctor Colin and the Superior conclude that Querry has effectively been cured: "'You spoke just now as though he had been cured'. 'I really think he was'" (*Burnt-Out* 198). The assessment of his healing, however, is made on different grounds by each of the two characters. Doctor Colin states it in terms of Querry's renewed capacity to relate to others: "He'd learned to serve other people, you see, and to laugh" (198). The Superior, on the other hand, reads Querry's rebirth as a religious awakening: "I though perhaps you meant that he was beginning to find his faith again" (198). Both positions, in Greene's view, actually come to be the same thing.[11]

Querry's "recovery," moreover, can be read along the lines of the pattern of detachment–commitment–sacrifice in terms that bring this novel close to Fowler's evolution in *The Quiet American*. Both Querry and Fowler define themselves as egotists, and claim to have no interest in great causes or spiritual master narratives. The first's confession, "I haven't enough feeling left for human beings to do anything for them out of pity" (*Burnt-Out* 50), echoes the latter's statement in *The Quiet American*:

> I know myself, and I know the depth of my selfishness. I cannot be at ease (and to be at ease is my chief wish) if someone else is in pain, visibly or audibly or tactually. Sometimes this is mistaken by the innocent for unselfishness, when all I am doing is sacrificing a small good – in this case postponement in attention to my hurt – for the sake of a greater good, a peace of mind when I need think only of myself. (114)

Both of them are misinterpreted in their words and actions by those around them, who tend to attach a moral value to their behavior. Finally, both of them will become involved in the affairs of the people around them, despite their initial resistance. The key moment in both novels happens when the character is forced to abandon his passivity and lack of involvement and comes in contact with a reality which makes him adopt an active role, in which decisions are made and actions undertaken. Accepting to abandon peace, the characters enter the realm of ethical responsibility and, hence, suffering. The following chapters will explore in depth the transformation undergone by Greene's characters, once they acknowledge the impossibility of taking refuge in a peace that offers little more than death in life.

2
Bargain

As noted by several critics, one religious motif reappears in Graham Greene's fiction with particular recurrence: the hero is faced with the imminent death of another human being, and in a moment of religious rapture, he offers a pact to God whereby his own death or damnation is offered in exchange for that of the other person. Cates Baldridge describes these moments as "scenes of soul-wagering" (68). David Lodge has referred to this as a "Greenean obsession" with "mystical substitution" (Foreword xii). The term used by Greene himself when this narrative situation is presented in *The Power and the Glory* is "bargain": "He was striking yet another bargain with God" (130). This chapter explores Greene's idiosyncratic use of the term "bargain", with particular attention to the way it introduces an economic dimension into the apparent religiosity of this type of scene. Critics have traditionally tended to see this as a problematic aspect of Greene's depiction of religiosity in his novels (Baldridge, Sharrock *Saints*, Chapman, Sherry). It could be argued, from the perspective of the narrative pattern explored in this book, that the scenes in which characters appear to be negotiating with God for the sake of someone else's life represent imperfect forms of attention to others, diminished versions of the true *caritas* that may eventually emerge in the texts. Thus, what is perceived as a deviation from Christian orthodoxy may in fact be regarded as one of Greene's attempts to have his characters rehearse a true ethical commitment to others. Whereas most critics who have analyzed this motif have focused on the theological problem of the existence of evil and the possibility of the dialogue with God, I consider that the third part involved in the transaction these scenes depict has often been neglected. Therefore, I would like to consider the nature of the exchange portrayed by Greene in terms of the interaction between the praying individual and the dying one. Taking cue from Alphonso Lingis, I would like to consider these scenes under the logic of communal identification: "community forms when one exposes oneself to the naked one, the destitute one, the outcast, the dying one" (12). These scenes, I contend, offer a scenario for an encounter with the other, an opening into the possibility of communal fusion and an example of what René Girard called "the sacrificial crisis".

The bargain motif

The first novel in which Greene introduced the motif of the bargain with God is *The Power and the Glory*. In this text, the unnamed persecuted Priest is caught in an ethical impasse from which there seems to be no way out. The alternatives for him are to escape and abandon his sacramental mission and his community of believers, to continue hiding and trying to stay alive to be able to administer the sacraments to the people, and to give up all effort at resistance and let himself be killed. Throughout the story, the Whisky Priest asks God to kill him, as he perceives this is the only way to put a stop to his suffering: The possibility of finding peace through death, however, is stubbornly negated by God. The Priest comes to realize that if God keeps him alive, it is only because he continues to be instrumental for His Grace:

> If God intended him to escape He could snatch him away from in front of a firing squad. But God was merciful. There was only one reason, surely, which would make Him refuse His peace—if there was any peace—that he could still be of use in saving a soul, his own or another's. (127)

The Priest asks several times for God's intervention, for liberation from his obligation by being captured: "Let me be caught soon... let me be caught" (13). Then he asks for liberation literally, praying for God's help to escape from prison:: "he was striking yet another bargain with God. This time, if he escaped from the prison, he would escape altogether" (130). It could be said that for the Priest, the act of bargaining appears as an aspect of his praying practice. However, whereas in most of the above quoted passages the Priest is asking for his own peace, a crucial difference exists between those situations and the one in which a bargain is offered to God in exchange for someone else's salvation. In the previous cases, the Priest is pleading for his own well-being. When he meets his natural daughter, Brigitta, he starts to be concerned by her lack of spiritual consciousness and innocence—"the world was in her heart already" (78)—and prays for the salvation of her soul. It could be argued that, in this case, he is acting as any father would do, putting her well-being before his own. What he offers in exchange for his daughter's salvation is his own damnation: "Oh God, give me any kind of death—without contrition, in a state of sin—only save this child" (79). This is repeated near the end of the novel. As he is about to die, he has a last memory of his daughter: "his remembered his child. Coming in out of the glare: the sullen unhappy knowledgeable face" (206). Once more, he asks for his damnation in exchange for her salvation: "Oh God, help her. Damn me, I deserve it, but let her live for ever" (206).

The Catholic context is maintained in the next novel in which Greene uses the same motif, *The Heart of the Matter*. Throughout this story, the protagonist Scobie is haunted by the same feeling of failed responsibility toward others. He tends to see everyone around him as in need of his assistance. The expression of this is the feeling of pity that he constantly displays. The asymmetry intrinsic to a relationship based on pity, which will be explored in depth in Chapter 4, is recurrently expressed in the text in the way Scobie thinks of most people around him as children in need of protection. It could be said that the image of Scobie's own dead child—whose death in England he did not witness, being in Africa at the time[1]—is being invoked in all these instances. Nevertheless, these surrogate "children" may be said to be anticipations for the moment when Scobie will perform the act of substitution involved in sacrifice through his encounter with a dying child. After the shipwreck scene, he is asked to take care of a dying little girl. Immediately before meeting her, Scobie appears to be lost in his thoughts about the immensity of his burden. This is one of the most often quoted passages from the novel: "If one knew, he wondered, the facts, would one have to feel pity even for the planets? If one reached what they called the heart of the matter?" (111). Scobie is shaken out of his musings by Mrs. Bowles, the wife of a local missionary, and he feels he cannot share his concerns with her: "He couldn't describe to Mrs. Bowles the restlessness, the haunting images, the terrible impotent feeling of responsibility and pity" (ibid). It is Mrs. Bowles who asks him to accompany her into one of the rooms where the injured are being taken to, and says: "if you want to be useful [...] stay here a moment" (ibid). The contrast between Mrs. Bowles practical approach to the shipwreck and Scobie's tendency to passive contemplation is quite striking, but it tends to be ignored by most critics who have analyzed this passage. In the room, Scobie is taken to the bedside of "the six-year old girl with the dry mouth" (ibid). Scobie's pity is then transferred from the general horror of the shipwreck into the particular existence of one of its victims: "He could hear the heavy uneven breathing of the child. It was as if she were carrying a weight with great effort up a long hill: it was an inhuman situation not to be able to carry it for her" (112). It is at this moment that Scobie offers a bargain to God: "Father, look after her. Give her peace [...] Take away my peace for ever, but give her peace" (ibid).

From a psychoanalytic perspective, one feels tempted to read Scobie's compulsion to take care of all the vulnerable and child-like as a compensatory mechanism meant to atone for his primary sense of guilt: the one that emerges from his absence at the moment of his own child's death.[2] His pity, and his need to see all others as children, would thus be attempts to substitute his original failure to fulfill his responsibility as a father (Bergonzi, 148). The idea is quite explicitly suggested in two moments of this scene. Upon first seeing the child, Scobie thinks: "When he looked at the child, he saw a white communion veil over her head. It was a trick of the light on the mosquito net and a trick of his own mind [...] He had been in Africa when his own child died. He had always thanked God that he had missed that" (112). A few lines later, Scobie acknowledges that this girl's death is actually "what I thought I'd missed" (ibid).

The passage of the dying child, nevertheless, serves another relevant function in the story. It was described by Lewis as "the book's major turning point" (Trilogy 214). It is one of those archetypal scenes in Greene's fiction, in which a character assists a dying individual and offers to make a bargain with God (Sherry, *Life* 2, 300). The Mephistophelean nature of this bargain was noted by Lewis, who claimed that when Scobie asks God to take away his peace in exchange for hers, "We are to understand, I believe, that God does exactly that" (Lewis, *Trilogy* 214). From here on, Lewis argues, Scobie's sense of peace is lost forever, his guilt grows until it becomes unbearable, and his road to perdition is rendered as the inexorable fulfillment of tragic fate.[3] Scobie will end his life sure of his own damnation, which he has offered in exchange for others' peace: "O God, I offer up my damnation to you. Take it. Use it for them" (209). As noted by Gangeshwar Rai, "Scobie's conduct appears to fulfil the Pauline doctrine of the extreme form of human love, a willingness to save others through one's own damnation" (51). Like the Priest in *The Power and the Glory*, Scobie pleads for death to bring him peace, only to realize that God is not going to let him go easily: "kill me now, now. My God, you'll never have more complete contrition. What a mess I am. I carry suffering with me like a body smell. Kill me. Put an end to me. Vermin don't have to exterminate themselves. Kill me. Now. Now. Now" (235).

The End of the Affair takes this idea to its ultimate consequences. This novel picks up the question already explored in *The Heart of the Matter*: what if God hears your prayer and performs the miracle you ask for? It will inevitably tie you forever to whatever promise you have made, or to whatever course of action you have committed to undertake. Here, the turning point comes in the moment of Sarah's prayer for Bendrix's life, which creates an obligation from which she cannot escape.

We read for the first time about what happened on the day when Sarah and Bendrix's hideaway apartment was bombed during the Blitz in Sarah's diary, which is in turn being read by Bendrix. A bomb falls on the front side of the house, Bendrix is injured and lays unconscious across the room floor. It is then that Sarah reaches for his hand, and thinks him dead: "I touched his hand: I could have sworn it was a dead hand. [...] I knew that if I took his hand and pulled it towards me, it would come away, all by itself, from under the door" (76). In this passage, Sarah claims that she has been tricked into believing that Bendrix was dead: "I was cheated. He wasn't dead" (75). This statement points to the idea that Sarah's offer to God has been conditioned by her situation of extreme distress. In fact, all the characters who undergo similar experiences with the dying may be said to act while in a similar state of mental disturbance. Sarah then starts her process of negotiation with God. She kneels on the floor, an act she regards as irrational, for she is not a religious person: "I was mad to do such a thing, I never had to do it as a child—my parents never believed in prayer, any more than I do. I hadn't any idea what to say" (75). At this stage, she reiterates the idea that Bendrix *was* dead: "Maurice was dead. Extinct. There wasn't such a thing as a soul" (75). First, she asks God for faith: "make me believe" (76). Then, she establishes a condition, and offers a deal: "Let him be alive, and I *will* believe" (ibid). This first deal is considered then as insufficient, as if the price to pay was too low for Bendrix's life. In Sarah's reasoning, this is measured in terms of suffering, a kind of "no pain, no gain" logics is established: "But that wasn't enough. It doesn't hurt to believe" (ibid). It is then that she makes a second offer, one that involves extreme suffering on her part. Her happiness is offered in exchange for Bendrix: "So I said, I love him and I'll do anything if you'll make him alive, I said very slowly, I'll give him up for ever, only let him be alive with a chance" (ibid). This second offer has immediate effects: "then he came in at the door, and he was alive, and I thought now the agony of being without him starts" (ibid). The moment of Bendrix's return to life is juxtaposed with the beginning of Sarah's suffering. Her realization of the binding character of her promise is immediate, and her reaction is to repent from having made it: "I wished he was safely back dead under the door" (ibid).

A lot has been written on the ambiguity of the "miracle" which occurs in this passage, and whether Greene intended Bendrix to be dead and resuscitated, or simply recovering from a concussion. Critics have traditionally read it trying to ascertain whether Greene was actually narrating a miracle or not. In my view, what matters is not so much whether Bendrix is dead or not at this moment—that is, whether the conditions for a miracle are fulfilled—but the fact that Sarah does believe he was dead. The terms of Sarah's bargain, in this sense, do not change in relation to objective reality, because they are established from the standpoint of Sarah's subjective perception of it. Moreover, Sarah's own interpretation of the event as a miracle is not as important, I'd claim, as the inescapable nature of the responsibility she has acquired from the moment she offered her commitment to faith in exchange for Bendrix's life.

The next entry in Sarah's diary emphasizes the notion that a life has been exchanged for another, implicitly pointing to the romantic notion that being alive, for Sarah, means being with Bendrix. In the next few lines, she will refer to herself as being dead: "It is horrible feeling dead. One wants to feel alive again in any way" (ibid). From this chapter on, the diary will become a continued form of prayer, a textual construction meant to remind her of her promise.[4] Throughout the diary, she returns to the moment of her first prayer in an attempt to reason her way out of the promise made: "Is one responsible for what one promises in hysteria? Or what promises one breaks?" (75). In subsequent entries, her initial sacrifice is replicated and amplified in numberless echoes of the initial deal with God, in which her sacrifice was offered. Sarah's willingness to sacrifice herself for others is patent in the diary sections of the novel, where she frequently expresses her desire to avoid others' suffering by offering hers instead. In the text she writes, it is easy to observe that bargaining with God is a habitual practice: "I don't mind my pain. It's their pain I can't stand. Let my pain go on and on, but stop theirs" (96); "When I ask You for pain, You give me peace. Give it to him too, give him my peace—he needs it more" (99). She takes her sacrificial role so far as to offer herself in exchange for the figure of Christ: "Dear God, if only you could come down from your Cross for a while and let me get up there instead. If I could suffer like you, I could heal like you" (96).

As Michael Gorra has argued, this novel explores the consequences of adultery not as a social challenge—a pattern typical of nineteenth century fiction—but "as a question of private conscience, a matter of individual betrayal" (120). The element enforcing Sarah's decision to end her affair with Bendrix is not the fear of social rejection, which is barely considered as a threat in the novel, nor the risk of spiritual damnation, which Sarah seems to embrace (Gorra 121). Rather, it is the inviolable nature of her promise, an extreme form of commitment which cannot be undone at all, even by denying the existence of the entity upon which that promise was made. According to Monica Ali, the central question for the reader is "why does she persist in keeping her vow not to see Bendrix again, made at a moment of crisis to a God in whom she does not believe?" (xii). In my view, however, this is not the book's central question. I'd rather claim it constitutes the kind of inviolable commitment that stands at the center of many of Greene's novels, like *The Power and the Glory, The Quiet American, The Comedians* or *The Honorary Consul*. It is not the act of commitment itself that remains mysterious—it is made plain both in this and the other novels that for the characters this is not a matter of choice. What remains unexplained, enigmatic, is their incapacity to share, to communicate or justify that commitment on rational grounds. All the novels mentioned above meander around the justification of character's decisions, explained in terms of religious and social commitment (*The Power and the Glory*), the sense of humanity inextricably attaching one to other human beings (*The Quiet American*), social justice and a vague notion of communal identity (*The Comedians* and *The Honorary Consul*). The main difference between *The End of the Affair* and these other novels regarding this issue is, I would say, that whereas in the others the idea of commitment is necessarily associated to some representation of communal life that eventually drives the character's sense of commitment (respectively, the victimized Mexican, Vietnamese, Haitian and Paraguayan people), in *The End of the Affair* Sarah's commitment is related to no one but herself and her lover. Her vow is the expression of personal obligation to an idea for its own sake, directed exclusively toward one individual: Bendrix, whose life is the object of her bargain with God.

After *The End of the Affair*, Greene used the narrative motif of the bargain with God in two more works. In both of them, the main details of the motif may be said to have been rehearsed in this earlier novel. *The Quiet American* features a situation similar to the one presented in *The End of the Affair*: a nonbeliever, the cynical journalist Granger, receives the news that his eight-year-old son has got polio.

His immediate reaction, as Sarah's, was to turn to a God he does not believe in: "'I was praying. I thought maybe if God wanted a life he could take mine'. 'Do you believe in a God, then?' 'I wish I did,' Granger said. He passed his whole hand across his face as though his head ached, but the motion was meant to disguise the fact that he was wiping tears away" (185). This passage happens near the end of the novel, shortly after the narrator, Fowler, has made a statement about the capacity of human beings to suffer for one another: "Suffering is not increased by numbers: one body can contain all the suffering the world can feel" (183). Granger's reaction, in the light of this statement, illustrates Fowler's point. In this novel, however, we never get to know about the effects of the suggested bargain: Granger is not mentioned again in the text, nor is his child.

Just one year after *The Quiet American*, Greene wrote the play *The Potting Shed*. The plot revolves around a moment in the past of the Callifer family, whose main protagonist, James, does not remember about. As the play reaches its dramatic climax, the audience learns of James' attempted suicide in the family's potting shed, and how he miraculously survived after having laid dead for a while. His uncle's prayer is introduced into the play as a form of bargain with God, a deal to save young James' life. As in *The End of the Affair*, Father Callifer is also convinced of his nephew's death when he starts his prayer: "How could you have been dead? Oh, Potter thought so. And so did I, perhaps. I put a leaf on your lips and it didn't move" (92). His identification with James is total in this moment: "When I had you on my knees I remember a terrible pain—here. So terrible I don't think I could go through it again. It was as though I was the one who was strangled—I could feel the cord around my neck" (93). This identification is what facilitates the exchange offered by the priest, for as in Sarah's case, James' return to life signifies the beginning of his spiritual death: "I had to pray in my mind, and then your breadth came back and it was just as though I had died instead" (96). "I'd have given my life for you—but what could I do? I could only pray. I suppose I offered something in return. Something I valued—not spirits [...] But what had I got to give Him? I was a poor man. I said 'Take away what I love most'" (94). The priest, then, offers his own faith (94), and James comes back to life: "He answered my prayer, didn't He? He took my offer" (95).

Trading souls: the religious background of bargaining

After examining separately the recurrence of the bargain motif in several of Greene's novels, it seems inevitable to consider this narrative device in terms of the religious dimension it necessarily introduces into the stories. Once the false ends offered by peace and despair are disclosed as impossible solutions for Greene's heroes, these moments of "negotiation" offer a path out of the narrative paralysis that the other two elements provoke. Negotiating with God works as a turning point in the narrative pattern pursued in this book, one through which the characters involved perform an act of "unselfing" that turns them toward ethical action. Therefore, although the religious dimension of these moments should be underscored, the ethical and the communal aspects of what this motif entails should not be neglected.

In the five cases analyzed in the previous section, the bargain is a deal with God, and in four of them—all except *The Quiet American*, in which the outcome of Granger's prayer is unknown—God may be said to respond affirmatively by granting whatever the supplicant has asked for. The logic of bargain may entail a substitution of one life for another, or one character's peace of mind for someone else's life. It happens whenever an innocent's life is seen as unnecessarily wasted. The term "bargain" evokes the ideas of interchange and agreement, but it also involves an element of asymmetry, as a bargain is necessarily more advantageous to one of the parts involved than to the other.[5] In other words, the idea of bargaining suggests buying something at a price which is previously identified by both parts as being lower than its actual cost. In Greene's fictional universe the object of such exchange is normally a human life. The kind of situation thus defined entails a transaction between two parts, which involves a specific course of action to be followed as the result of the agreement reached. In Greene's fiction, the two parts involved in negotiation are normally the hero and God, and the business is done over a third party, another individual in a situation of extreme physical or spiritual peril, whose life or soul is going to be traded.

In several of the cases where bargaining with God is dramatized in Greene's novels, the hero offers to exchange his/her own peace of mind for the sake of someone else who is in a position of extreme vulnerability (*The Heart of the Matter, The Power and the Glory*). In three cases, it is a child who becomes the object of the transaction (*The Power and the Glory, The Heart of the Matter, The Quiet American*); in the fourth one, it is a (supposedly) dead man (*The End of the Affair*). The child, as seen through the eyes of the heroes who offer to give their lives for her, is the emblem of innocence. Additionally, it represents a recurring thought in Greene's religious vision: the random death of a child casts doubt over the idea that moral law rules over the universe, and eventually dramatizes the problem of evil, for what kind of God would allow an innocent child to die while sinners walk the earth? In *The Living Room*, Greene has one of the characters, Michael, state this explicitly: "Can you believe in a God who lets that happen?" (121). This point has also been made by some critics, like Judith Adamson, who describes Scobie's plight in *The Heart of the Matter* in the following terms: "He cannot give himself over to a God who allows the innocent to suffer" (83).[6]

Together with the idea of negotiation, the articulation of the logic of the bargain sets in motion other associated vocabularies in Greene's work. Bergonzi, for example, has noted how this motif involves a process of substitution (148). This may be read along anthropological-symbolic lines, in the context of sacrifice and the figure of the scape-goat (Girard, Derrida). Jean-Luc Nancy has argued that "all sacrifice is a traffic in victims and indulgences" (*Inoperative* 135). The theological problem of the existence of evil may be linked, in its dramatization in Greene's novels, to the problem of how the stability of a community of believers may be restored through the identification of a sacrificial victim recognized by this community as a redeemed sinner. In *Violence and the Sacred*, René Girard outlined the anthropological and mythological bases for what he called "the sacrificial crisis", the scenario in which acts of sacrifice are demanded on the part of individuals who are meant to put a stop to social unrest through their death (8). Although Greene may be said to follow this pattern quite explicitly in some of his novels—particularly in *A Burnt-Out Case*—the bargaining motif could be considered as a subtler version of the same scenario. It should be noted, firstly, that the moments of bargaining happen to all characters in contexts in which the religious order is put at risk through different events or catastrophes, situations in which believers may well ask: How can God allow this to happen? The shipwreck in *The Heart of the Matter*, the process of religious persecution in *The Power and the Glory* and the London Blitz in *The End of the Affair* may be seen as different embodiments of crisis leading to doubt. One of the side effects of the bargains made by Greene's characters is that they affect other people's beliefs, either by returning to them a faith that had been temporarily lost, of by granting it to the non-believers. The outcome of the sacrifice performed by the protagonists of these novels enacts, therefore, a reinforcement of the religious community, offering confirmation to Thomas Aquinas' idea that "God allows evils to happen in order to bring a greater good therefrom" (3674).

Putting themselves in the place of the innocent and offering themselves as sacrifice works for these characters as an acknowledgment of their position as sinners. This is quite explicit in *The End of the Affair*, where Sarah constantly refers to herself as "a bitch and a fake" (75). They identify themselves clearly as being of an inferior worth than the individual at risk, and they claim that it would be much fairer if they were to be sacrificed deservedly. By asking God to remove from the innocent ones the sacrificial role, the sinner tries to restore an order he perceives to have been threatened by a random decision. The death of the innocent child, in this sense, works as the narrative excuse for the hero's commitment, for his/her self-identification as a sinner, and subsequent impulse toward good. As I argue in the final section of this chapter, the bargaining scenes are also scenes of attention to the dying, moments in which Greene's characters are exposed—sometimes for the first time, as it happens with Sarah Miles—to the absolute vulnerability of another. From this perspective, ethical action may be said to spring directly from the contemplation of the suffering of others. In a religious sense, Greene's understanding of evil seems to be related to Irenaean theodicy, which justifies the existence of evil as being necessary to provoke the spiritual improvement of human beings.[7] This idea is expressed for example in the play *The Living Room*, where the function of human suffering in the delivery of the soul to God is explicitly pointed out: "Suffering is a problem to us, but it doesn't seem a big problem to the woman when she has borne her child. Death is our child, we have to go through pain to bear our death" (123).

A further aspect of the bargain with God recurrently portrayed by Greene is that God seems to accept the offer made by the supplicant. We are led to think that everything happening after it in these texts is a direct consequence of God's acceptance, so to say, of the deal offered by the characters. Both in *The Heart of the Matter* and *The End of the Affair*, the moment of bargaining works as a narrative trigger; it sets in motion a series of events that confirm the idea that the transaction has effectively taken place. The narrative role of the bargain, in this sense, is close to Propp's articulation of the narrative function in which the hero reacts to the action of a future donor (Propp 42).

In some texts, this is codified in terms of a miraculous intervention that makes the dead come back to life. This is what happens in *The End of the Affair* and *The Potting Shed*. In both cases, the individual whose life is made the object of the bargain is explicitly said to be dead, only to be "resuscitated" after the prayer is performed. The two texts offer afterwards a rational explanation for what is deliberately presented at first as a miracle in the eyes of the supplicant: James was in a coma, not dead; Bendrix was unconscious, but not dead. Nevertheless, these explanations do not diminish the effects of the bargain on the subject. Sarah's commitment to her promise is adamantly kept; and Father Callifer truly loses the faith he had traded for his nephew's life. More than the allegedly miraculous effects of the bargain, however, what Greene tends to underline is the ironic way in which the offer made by the supplicant ends up binding him/her tightly. Scobie asks God to take away his own peace and to bring rest to the dying child, and never again does he have a moment of rest. Similarly, Sarah offers to live in agony in exchange of Bendrix's life, and agony is what she gets. Except for Granger, who offers his life—in a generic sense—in exchange for his son's, all the other characters who strike a bargain with God are actually trading their peace of mind, the tranquility of their own souls. In this sense, it may be argued that there is always a Faustian overtone to these scenes, and one cannot avoid the feeling that Greene's portrayal of God is based on the idea of a divinity willing to take advantage of human beings on the verge of despair in order to offer them a path toward salvation that is filled with suffering. This was noted by R.B.W. Lewis in his seminal discussion of Greene's "Catholic trilogy": "God moves in a singular Mephistophelean manner, His wonders to perform—a deity with whom one bargains away one's peace or love or beliefs, for the life of someone else" (214).

As Baldridge argues in *The Virtues of Extreme*, Greene's introduction of these scenes into many of the so-called "Catholic novels" is problematic in that the logic of the pact with God does not seem to be compatible with Catholic orthodoxy (Baldridge 67). In connection to this, Raymond Chapman has wondered: "Greene has provided a bigger stumbling block which has tripped up some of his greatest admirers. What can be said of the bargaining prayer, the bartering which God seems to accept?" (92). Chapman concludes that this "stark bargain" (92) is as troubling to believers as to nonbelievers: "the Christian sees [it] as blasphemy and the unbeliever as proof of the inadequacies of professed faith" (93). Discussing the central use of this motif in the play *The Potting Shed*, Norman sherry identifies it as a "gambit" that raises more questions than it answers (Sherry, *Life* 3, 30). Indeed, *The Potting Shed* is probably the text in which Greene made a most explicit and melodramatic use of this motif. Nevertheless, as Roger Sharrock has pointed out, it is a problematic one in its religious meaning: "The idea of a bargain with God makes for strong drama but doubtful theology" ("Unhappy" 77).

These perceived deviations from Christian orthodoxy may in fact be regarded in the light of the narrative pattern this book explores as the starting point for ethical commitment to others. They do have the inaugural character of ethical action, which according to Derrida can only spring from the perspective of imminent death: "It is from the perspective of death as the place of my irreplaceability, that is, of my singularity, that I feel called to responsibility" (*Gift* 42). In order to introduce this ethical dimension into the apparently religious motif of the bargain, I would like to conduct a detailed analysis of its constituent elements that brings into consideration not only the dialogue between man and God that seems to have absorbed critics' attention, but also the interpersonal relationship established between the supplicant and the dying individual.

Morphology of the bargain

The first element to consider in the analysis of this motif is the identity of the individual who offers the bargain. In *The Power and the Glory*, it is the Priest who spends most of his time trying to establish some kind of pact with God. The praying priest, pleading to God, was to reappear in *The Potting Shed*, a text where, as it has already been mentioned, the moment of bargaining is central to plot construction. Later, in *The Heart of the Matter*, a restless Scobie makes a similar gesture in an early moment in the novel. In his case, he is a Catholic, so his pleading to God takes place within a context of prayer that is part of the character's everyday routine. In *The Quiet American*, in which a non-religious character is made the subject of the bargaining through prayer, it is the cynical journalist Granger who will undergo a moment of religious inspiration. Yet, the most determinant dramatization of this device appears in *The End of the Affair*, where Sarah offers a pact to a God she does not believe in. As in *The Potting Shed*, the motive of bargaining is transformed into a narrative of religious conversion. In Sarah's case, it could be claimed that her action illustrates a point made by the Father Superior at the end of *A Burnt-Out Case*: "a man who starts looking for God has already found him" (198).

Reviewing Greene's use of the term, the main distinction that could be drawn between all cases in which he uses it is the status of the subject as a believer/non-believer. Whereas the Whisky Priest and Scobie are believers praying to God on a constant, day-to-day basis, for Granger and Sarah bargaining appears as a desperate attempt in the face of impotence. For most of them, particularly Scobie and Sarah, the outcome will be similar, in the sense that both will be asked in exchange to perform a great sacrifice, by renouncing what they love most.

In the second place, it is necessary to consider the identity of the individual who becomes the main object of bargaining: Who do the supplicants pray for? As it has already been hinted at in the previous section, childhood and death combined tend to be the triggers of the act of bargaining. Several of the characters involved in such situations pray for their own loved ones, particularly their children. Such is the case for Granger, who prays for his own sick son, and also for the Whisky Priest, who prays for the soul of his daughter. Scobie prays for a dying little girl, who is not his own daughter. However, this moment of the story is echoed later when we learn about Scobie's feeling of guilt for having been absent at the moment of his daughter's death. Finally, Sarah prays for her lover, apparently dead. In several cases, the object of prayer is a human being who, to all appearance, is already dead. Bendrix is said to be dead when Sarah prays to God for him. Similarly, James Callifer is supposedly dead in *The Potting Shed* when his uncle prays for him.

In those two cases, the miraculous nature of the bargain is dramatized in the fact that both individuals apparently come back to life after the prayer has been performed. In *The Quiet American* and *The Power and the Glory* we never get to know whether the children who are the object of pray actually get to be saved or not. This could be taken as an index of the fact that in these narratives, what matters to Greene doesn't seem to be the effect that prayer has on the external world, but its transformative power for the individual who performs the praying. Two cases seem worthy of note, nevertheless, in that the prayer is not so much oriented toward the saving of life as such, but of spirit. When the Whisky Priest and Scobie pray for their respective children, they ask God to save their souls. For one thing, Scobie already knows the dying girl is beyond physical salvation, and therefore his prayer is directed to bring spiritual rest to her. Similarly, the Whisky Priest offers his own damnation in exchange for his daughter's spiritual salvation, which he believes to be at stake.

A third element to be taken into consideration is the nature of the price to be paid in exchange for the victim's life or soul. In order words, what do the supplicants offer to God? It is curious to note that each of the characters involved in a bargain with God tends to offer in exchange whatever is most precious to them. Here, the distinction as to whether the praying characters are believers or not becomes relevant in a second sense. The Whisky Priest, Scobie and Father Callifer offer their spiritual virtues: the first offers to be damned, the second offers his spiritual peace, and the third, in what actually constitutes a reversal of Sarah's act in *The End of the Affair*, offers his faith. Granger, whose vision is more prosaic than any of the other characters', offers simply his life. As for Sarah, she offers to make the sacrifice of her own love for Bendrix by renouncing him if his life is preserved.

Considering the two kinds of "goods" involved in the bargain, the victim's life or soul, and the supplicant's peace, life or faith, a further question may arise as to the choice of the term "bargain" rather than any other one associated to the realm of business or purchase. If the term bargain involves the mutual recognition that a price lower than the actual one is being paid, then one may wonder for whom is this a bargain, for the supplicant or for God? Bargaining emphasizes an asymmetry in the commercial interchange that is after all a reflection of the asymmetry between God's omnipotence and man's impotence in the face of death. In all the cases where Greene uses this narrative motif, it is suggested that the price paid by the supplicants is too high for what they get in exchange. Their suffering is melodramatically aggrandized in the subsequent narrative—particularly so for Sarah and Scobie, I would claim—and the narrative itself is bent on hinting at the idea that the sacrifice made has been futile at best, for those for whose sake it was done do not recognize it as a gift.

But one may also reverse this line of thought and, from a religious standpoint, claim that if God is letting a soul go (the victim's) for the sake of another, this is just a sort of cat-and-mouse game on his part as, after all, don't all souls already belong to him? As Shakespeare wrote in the second part of *Henry IV*, "we owe God a death". This understanding of the exchange of souls turns the deal into a sort of divine hustle in which God would pretend to pay a price for something that is already his, thus leading once more to the theodicist argument about how the suffering undergone by characters is just a series of necessary obstacles put in their way toward salvation.

Watching the pain of others

As it has already been anticipated in earlier sections of this chapter, a central dimension of the bargain motif in Greene's work is how it relates to the pattern of individual turn toward ethical action through the substitution mechanism entailed. In *The Quiet American*, the narrative establishes, through textual proximity, a moral comparison between Granger and Fowler himself. Although Granger had been described earlier in the text in unfavorable terms, his humanity and capacity for love are underscored in this passage, hence implying that even an apparently soulless man like him is able to show compassion. Pyle's and Fowler's capacity to abstract the humanity of those around them—evident in Pyle's treatment of the dead as "casualties", and in Fowler's instrumental role in the elimination of Pyle—is opposed to Granger's willingness to exchange himself for another individual, to his "unselfing" for someone he genuinely loves. This constitutes, I'd argue, the first step toward commitment for Greene's characters.

Nevertheless, feeling love for one individual to the point of offering oneself in sacrifice, like Granger does for his son in *The Quiet American*, is not enough in the moral universe inhabited by the Whisky Priest. His obligation extends to all humanity, for the simple reason of their being human, as Simone Weil would argue: "There exists an obligation towards every human being for the sole reason that he or she is a human being, without any other condition requiring to be fulfilled, and even without any recognition of such obligation on the part of the individual concerned" (Weil, *Need* 5).

If true ethics, in Greene's perception, should be born out of the idea that "the dying of people with whom we have nothing in common [...] concerns us" (Lingis x), then these scenes of pleading for a beloved one may be said to represent an early step toward attention to others. In several texts the moment of prayer for a beloved one will be mirrored by a further moment in which prayer has extended toward others, with whom the praying individual has nothing in common. These second acts of prayer are what actually mark the ethical commitment adopted. The Whisky Priest and Sarah undergo similar processes, first praying for their beloved ones—his daughter, her lover—and later praying for perfect strangers—the people in the prison cell, the Parkis boy. From a religious point of view, these characters have attained what in the Christian framework would be identified as sanctity. Detective Parkis' narration about the miraculous cure of his son at the end of *The End of the Affair* is intended to suggest this idea: "I don't mind telling you, Mr. Bendrix, that I prayed very hard. I prayed to God and then I prayed to my wife to do what she could because if there's anyone in heaven, she's in heaven right now, and I asked Mrs. Miles if she was there, to do what she could too" (148). Although three miraculous agents are mentioned in this passage—God, Parkis' wife and Sarah—it is the third one whom the narration identifies as being responsible for the cure, in a passage evoking a Christological image: "he told the doctor it was Mrs. Miles who came and took away the pain—touching him on the right side of the stomach" (149).

In the ethical paradigm created by Greene in his texts commitment is expressed as "attention to others" (Murdoch *Sovereignty* 33). Maurice

Blanchot has written on the ethical implications of such deathbed moments in terms that may throw light on the significance they have in the novels:

> What, then, calls me into question most radically? Not my relation to myself as finite or as the consciousness of being before death or for death, but my presence for another who absents himself by dying. To remain present in the proximity of another who by dying removes himself definitively, to take upon myself another's death as the only death that concerns me, this is what puts me beside myself, this is the only separation that can open me, in its very impossibility, to the Openness of a community. (Blanchot *Unavowable* 9)

In Blanchot's formulation, it is only by being put beside oneself that a genuine connection to others can be achieved. This is the ground on which Greene's understanding of ethical commitment is to be enacted as a full recognition of the plight of others. Sarah, like the Whisky Priest at the end of *The Power and the Glory*, may be said to have overcome what according to Iris Murdoch constitutes the major difficulty of ethical behavior: "The difficulty is to keep the attention fixed upon the real situation and to prevent it from returning surreptitiously to the self with consolations of self-pity, resentment, fantasy and despair" (89). This is precisely what happens to Scobie, who undergoes an opposite process from attention to others to exacerbated attention to himself. From a promising moment of prayer for an unknown child, he may be said to fall into the depths of self-centered despair. His last attempts to bargain with God are strikingly marked by their egocentrism. He does not "see" others anymore, and is consumed with self-pity at the thought of his own damnation.

3
Despair

In the narrative pattern under scrutiny in this book, the impossibility of finding peace has its opposite trope in the notion of despair. For Greene's characters, who often fail to buy their peace through bargain, despair is depicted as a state of ethical and narrative paralysis. It interacts with the dialectics between peace and action sketched in the first chapter, dramatizing the moment when the individual "gives up" to whatever situation he or she is in. The logic of despair is closely related to the semantic field of struggle: to despair is to stop fighting, or to stop believing. It is an interruption of action and, in a religious sense, of faith. From the point of view of narrative structure, despair is often regarded by characters and narrators as a situation in which one loses the sense of direction, thus provoking a deviation from a – narrative and vital – path that the character should be following in a straightforward manner. In Greene's novels, moreover, the idea of despair often appears in close association with suicide. As has been noted by several critics (Bergonzi 120; Donaghy *Graham Greene* 23–24; Friedman *Fictional* 232), the recurrence of suicide in his fiction is striking, and should not be simply explained through reference to the author's biography. In terms of narrative development, the main character's suicide puts an end to the plot constructed around the ethical dilemmas he experiences. Greene's use of the notion of despair is informed by two lines of philosophico-religious discourse. On the one hand, there is the Catholic doctrine that considers suicide as "the unforgivable sin."[1] In *Brighton Rock*, Rose, who is tricked by Pinkie into a fake suicide pact, considers: "it was said to be the worst act of all, the act of despair, the sin without forgiveness" (249). The same idea is expressed in *The Power and the Glory* (57) and in *The Heart of the Matter* when Scobie is called to examine the scene of Pemberton's suicide early in the novel (50), and repeated in a later moment of the text as Scobie contemplates his own fate: "The priests told one it was the unforgivable sin, the final expression of an unrepentant despair" (174). In *Monsignor Quixote*, in a later moment of Greene's career, we read: "he felt as if he had been touched by the wing tip of the worst sin of all, despair" (174). On the other hand, the recurrence of despair in his novels may be linked with the philosophical context of existentialism, particularly the works of Miguel de Unamuno (whom Greene admired deeply and often quoted), Kierkegaard, and Sartre. From them, Greene borrows the idea that despair may be considered as the natural state of man, one from which it is possible to be redeemed only through meaningful ethical action and what Unamuno calls, in *The Tragic Sense of Life* (1913), an "effort in human solidarity" (142). Despair ultimately cuts down all communal ties between the Greenean hero and those around him, and alienates the individual from any sense of communal life.

The functions of despair

The recurrence of the term "despair" in Greene's fiction is remarkable (McCormack 268). Nearly all of his protagonists may be said to suffer from it at one point in their stories. It is a concept that invokes a spiritual dimension, since it is necessarily related, by definition, to belief and hope. Specifically, despair may be defined as the interruption of the hopes or beliefs held as the basis of human behavior in an earlier moment. Thus, the notion of despair itself seems to indicate an intermission or a disruption in a teleological master narrative, one that would be regarded as the "normal" state of affairs in spiritual, ideological, or moral terms.

In *The Human Factor*, despair is contrasted with hope, but both states are regarded as incompatible with rational action: "Hope was out of place just as much as despair. They were emotions which would confuse thought" (190); "Then he reproached himself with the thought that none of his actions must be dictated by despair any more than by hope" (199).[2] Pure rational thought, nevertheless, is rare in Greene's fictional universe, where most characters undergo extreme emotional transformations. It is interesting, in this sense, that the course of action undertaken by the majority of them is dictated from the realm of emotion rather than reason, thus pointing to the emotivist ethical stance that will be analyzed in the later chapters of this book.

For some of Greene's characters, this state of despair arises suddenly, a clearly marked breaking point in an otherwise continuous trajectory of belief. This is the case with Father Callifer in *The Potting Shed*. The priest, who has offered God his own faith in exchange for his nephew's life, is said to spend the rest of his life in a state of permanent despair. In the cases of Rowe (*The Ministry of Fear*) and Jones (*Dr Fischer of Geneva*), despair is directly linked to the loss of a loved one. In this sense, there is a turning point in their lives, a moment in which, it could be argued, they lost faith. However, for both of them, as well as for Father Callifer, despair is not a momentary state, but a life-long one. Their despair is prolonged in time, and leads them toward the kind of death in life that is often expressed as the false sense of peace explored in the first chapter of this book. Rowe is said to live in despair since his wife's death:

> Since the death of his wife Rowe had never daydreamed; all through the trial he had never even dreamed of an acquittal. It was as if that side of the brain had been dried up; he was no longer capable of sacrifice, courage, virtue, because he no longer dreamed of them. He was aware of the loss – the world had dropped a dimension and become paper-thin. He wanted to dream, but all he could practise now was despair. (73)

For many others, however, despair is often expressed not as a radical breaking point, but as a certain tiredness or weariness of life, a condition that Greene himself identified as his own emotional state (Hoskins 41). In *A Gun for Sale*, Raven is said to feel "a pain and despair which was more like a complete weariness than anything else" (168). This is closer to ennui, a state from which his characters can only escape through death. As Sinha has argued, ennui is "the human response to nothingness" (132). A case in point in this sense is Querry in *A Burnt-Out Case*. In a conversation with Father Thomas, one of the missionaries working in the *léproserie* where he seeks refuge from his existential ennui, Querry argues in terms of lack of faith: "I don't want any of the things I've known and lost. If faith were a tree growing at the end of the avenue, I promise you I'd never go that way" (92). In an earlier passage, Querry expresses his ennui as lack of interest in others: "I haven't enough feeling left for human beings" (50). It is precisely Father Thomas who introduces the interpretive key to this despair, which he reads in mystical terms: "Don't you see that perhaps you've been given the grace of aridity? Perhaps even now you are walking in the footsteps of St. John of the Cross, the *noche oscura*" (ibid.). The image of the soul undergoing a dark night has been repeatedly used by Greene, for example in

The Potting Shed, where Father Callifer compares his state of permanent despair to the mystical expression of spiritual crisis as a "dark night": "The saints have dark nights, but not for thirty years. They have moments when they remember what it felt like to believe" (92–93).[3]

Of all of Greene's characters, however, the one that best embodies his understanding of despair is Scobie in *The Heart of the Matter*. Overwhelmed by the contradictory responsibilities he has assumed regarding his wife, his lover, and his profession, Scobie falls into a dark night that is more related to a sense of ethical aporia than to lack of faith. His despair, I would argue, emerges from the impossibility of making his actions match his beliefs, from the inconsistencies in the teleological understanding of his own life as a path toward salvation. Thus, Scobie is forced to change the path of salvation for that of damnation, and commits suicide with the intention of offering his damnation to God as an act of sacrifice. Suicide emerges most clearly in this novel as the ultimate expression of despair, and, in the light of Catholic doctrine, it is presented as the surest way to achieve damnation.

Suicide may be said to be the ultimate expression of the individual's refusal to continue with the trajectory imposed by an external motivation, for, as Greene reminds us in *The Comedians*, one does not choose to live, but can choose to die: "We have chosen nothing except to go on living" (284). The recurrence of suicide in Greene's work has been observed by many critics. In *Fictional Death and the Modernist Enterprise*, Alan Warren Friedman refers to Greene as "pathologically morbid" and lists the characters who commit suicide in his works (*Fictional* 232). Indeed, the motif of suicide has been present since Greene's first novel. At the end of *The Man Within*, Andrews and Elizabeth commit suicide. The same narrative motif is also suggested in the (false) suicide pact Pinkie offers to Rose in *Brighton Rock*. Other characters who take their own lives, apart from the already mentioned Scobie, include Dr Fischer and Rose in *The Living Room*.[4]

For Scobie, the damnation encompassed by suicide is clearly stated from the beginning of the novel. It is first anticipated in the captain's letter to his daughter: "You do not know how easy it is for a man like me to commit the unforgivable despair" (44–45). Later, examining the room where Pemberton has killed himself, Scobie points out Pemberton's lack of religious consciousness: "You're not going to tell me there's anything unforgivable there, father. If you or I did it, it would be despair ... we'd be damned because we know, but *he* doesn't know a thing" (78). This anticipates what is to be expected when Scobie himself falls into that kind of despair and ends up killing himself. But even then, as some critics have mentioned, the "unforgivable" nature of suicide may be redeemed by God's mercy (Adamson *Dangerous* 85; Ker 142).

Scobie anticipates in early moments of the novel how despair may lead to suicide: "Despair is the price one pays for setting oneself an impossible aim. It is, one is told, the unforgivable sin, but it is a sin the corrupt or evil man never practices. He always has hope. He never reaches the freezing-point of knowing absolute failure" (50). This conception of despair is associated by Scobie with the complete abandonment of human links, as it prevents the sharing of any other thing but despair itself: "all he could share with them was his despair" (174). It should be noted that, although Greene's works in general, and *The Heart of the Matter* in particular, have often been read through the prism of existentialism, Scobie's understanding of despair in this passage resists Jean-Paul Sartre's conception of the same term. For Sartre, as he famously stated in "Existentialism Is a Humanism" (1946), despair would result from man's acceptance of "that which is within out wills, or within the sum of the probabilities which render our action feasible" (35). In other words, despair works for Sartre as the key to the idea that "we should act without hope" (ibid.). It could be said, in this sense, that Scobie's despair emerges precisely from his hope, from his refusal to accept that he can only adopt a course of action to be selected from a reduced number of choices. Faced with the impossibility of attaining a higher hope, he feels trapped. Sartre's final words in that essay may actually work as perfect commentary on Scobie's predicament:

> Existentialism is not atheist in the sense that it would exhaust itself in demonstrations of the non-existence of God. It declares, rather, that even if God existed that would make no difference from its point of view. Not that we believe God does exist, but we think that the real problem is not that of His existence; *what man needs is to find himself again and to understand that nothing can save him from himself, not even a valid proof of the existence of God.* In this sense existentialism is optimistic. It is a doctrine of action, and it is only by self-deception, by confining their own despair with ours that Christians can describe us as without hope. (45–46; emphasis added)

Scobie's point about evil men never losing hope – and his earlier comment on how ignorance of sin may shield an individual like Pemberton from despair in suicide – is also made in *The Power and the Glory*, but this time in connection with animals. Observing a wounded dog from his hiding place, the Whisky Priest observes: "Unlike him, she retained a kind of hope. Hope is an instinct only the reasoning human mind can kill. An animal never knows despair" (140). In both passages, the main character's despair is contrasted to others who are unable to feel it, for whom hope is inexhaustible. As with peace, however, incapacity for despair tends to be something Greene associates with the lack of an ethical standpoint. In this sense, even if it is presented as an expression of surrender, the enactment of hope abandoned, it may still be contemplated as a narrative motif that belongs to the realm of the ethical.

It is curious to note, moreover, that the number of characters who actually commit suicide is lower than that of characters who consider the possibility of taking their own lives but end up not doing it. In this second group, we may include Raven (*A Gun for Sale*), Rowe (*The Ministry of Fear*), Bendrix (*The End of the Affair*), or Jones (*Dr Fischer of Geneva*). In these cases, suicide is perceived as the natural outcome of a state of despair: "Even if a man has been contemplating the advantages of suicide for two years, he takes time to make his final decision – to move from theory to practice" (*Ministry* 87). In Rowe's case, suicide appears, as for Scobie, as a solution to a situation of paralysis, a way out of a dead end: "It would be simpler and less disgusting to die" (ibid.). Both for Rowe and Bendrix, however, despair is not as complete as it is for Scobie, and they retreat from the idea of suicide: "I began seriously to think of suicide. I even set a date, and I saved up my sleeping pills with what was almost a sense of hope. I needn't after all go on like this indefinitely, I told myself. Then the date came and the play went on and on and I didn't kill myself" (*End* 59).

In *Dr Fischer of Geneva*, Greene depicts again his main character as falling into despair. After his wife Anne-Louise's death, he immediately plans his suicide. Returning from the cemetery to the house they had shared, he says: "What to do when I was there I had decided beforehand. I had read many years ago in a detective story how it was possible to kill oneself by drinking a half pint of spirits in a single draught" (98). His failed suicide attempt is interrupted by an invitation from his father-in-law. Dr Fischer also ends up shooting himself, after having engaged his friends in a charade involving a macabre Russian roulette game with Christmas crackers. The point, though, is that Jones decides to attend his father-in-law's "bomb party" precisely because he does not wish to continue living. Although he does not die at the end of the story, he has shown the same kind of despair displayed by previous Greenean heroes.

Similarly, at the beginning of *A Burnt-Out Case* we are led to think that Querry has given up any hope of recovery from his despair. Eventually, however, the fact that he does not commit suicide suggests that there may be a possibility of renewal or rebirth for him. According to Richard Kelly, this is a key difference between Querry and Scobie: "Unlike previous Greene heroes, however [Querry] does not contemplate suicide. [...] Instead of death he seeks the land of childhood innocence, symbolized by Africa" (Kelly 76).

This distinction may be expanded into a double understanding of despair in Greene's fiction. In *Monsignor Quixote*, the main character makes a distinction between two kinds of despair. "I do sometimes despair," Sancho confesses, to which Father Quixote answers: "Oh, despair I understand. I know despair too, Sancho. Not final despair, of course" (40). One of them seems to work as fuel for life, one might say, in a sense that is anticipated by Miguel de Unamuno in *The Tragic Sense of Life*: "Whosoever believes in God, but believes without passion, without anguish, without uncertainty, without doubt, without despair-in-consolation, believes only in the God-idea, not in God Himself" (211). The other one, the "final despair," is the one presented as an abyss for many of Greene's characters. This double understanding of despair has also been read from the Catholic perspective by critics like Mark Bosco, who have noted the double function it may serve: "Doubt is thus a two-edged sword for Greene's characters: it can allow for the ineffable and mysterious workings of faith to be recognized and honored, or it can lead to a rationalistic and ultimately skeptical stance toward the 'human factor'" (Bosco 27).

In terms of the narrative pattern pursued in this book, however, this distinction between two kinds of despair is rather related to the reversibility (or not) of the characters' situation. Many of Greene's heroes are said to escape from despair, so it seems to be a reversible state from which you can return. *The Power and the Glory* dramatizes precisely this reversibility, by narrating the Whisky Priest's story as one of fall and redemption in terms of human nature: "He had given way to despair – and out of that had emerged a human soul and love" (97). The religious framework, in this sense, offers the clearest representation of the risk of despair for Greene's characters. In novels like *The Power and the Glory*, despair lurks beneath the main character's apparently unflinching commitment to his sacramental mission. In his worldview, despair is translated as lack of belief in the motivated pattern of his life as designed by God, and the refusal to act as His instrument. The hero of this novel is said to have undergone his own dark night of the soul at some point in his past life, before the narration begins. We learn about it through analepsis: "Five years ago he had given way to despair – the unforgivable sin – and he was going back now to the scene of his despair with a curious lightening of the heart. For he had got over despair too" (79).

The Priest's despair takes the shape not of a suicide attempt, but of failure to fulfill his evangelical mission in a double sense: firstly, by hiding and pretending not to be a priest so as to avoid his capture (the biblical overtones of the idea are quite evident, as the Priest is made to look like Saint Peter denying God out of fear); and secondly, by betraying his vow of celibacy and having sexual intercourse with a woman. The conception of the child, Brigitta, is depicted in the novel as an act of despair: "They had spent no love in her conception: just fear and despair and half a bottle of brandy and the sense of loneliness had driven him to an act which horrified him – and this scared shame-faced overpowering love was the result" (63). Greene uses here a narrative device which may be related to Hawthorne's discussion of Pearl in *The Scarlet Letter* (1850). The Priest's despair, even when it disappears, leaves a trace: the child he bears to one of the village women. Just as Pearl is the indelible trace of Hester's adultery, so this child is the equally indelible evidence of the Priest's despair. This child, like Pearl in Hawthorne's romance, works as a double symbol (of Hester's sin, from a social perspective, and of her freedom to love). She represents the Priest's double nature: his fallen nature and despair, on the one hand, and his capacity for individual love and his potential commitment to universal charity, on the other.

The Priest's estrangement from his partner in crime is notable in this passage. In his despair, what would have been regarded in other circumstances as an act of communion with another human being is depicted as a lonely act. Despair is expressed in Greene's work precisely through images of alienation from others. In *A Burnt-Out Case*, Querry writes in his diary: "Human beings are not my country" (51). It is an emotional state that prevents any kind of attention to others, an aspect emphasized in the existentialist framework by Unamuno or Sartre. In all the cases explored above, falling into despair also means breaking one's links with the rest of humanity. The point has been repeatedly made in existentialist readings of Greene. In reference to *The Honorary Consul*, Sunita Sinha writes a description of Plarr that could be extended to other characters as well: "He despairs, and lives without hope, stranger to the world, holding out in solitary confinement within the impervious walls of his individuality. He is locked up within himself. So estrangement also involves disintegration from society. By virtue of absolute despair man becomes an 'existing' individual" (133). Consequently, the possibility of recovering from despair, as happens for Querry or the Whisky

Priest, is attached to the re-establishment of a communal dimension embodied in the attention demanded by a vulnerable individual like Deo Gratias or Brigitta.

Existentialist and religious views on despair

Jean-Paul Sartre famously stated: "man's dignity lies in his despair" (*Bariona* 108). In his existentialist articulation, the notion of despair is a starting point for man. Adopting despair, abandoning hope, are essential gestures toward the assumption of responsibility and freedom. "With despair," he writes, "true optimism begins: the optimism of the man who expects nothing, who knows he has no rights and nothing coming to him, who rejoices in counting on himself alone and in acting alone for the good of all" ("Characterization" 159). This position, as he clearly stated in "Existentialism Is a Humanism," tries to counteract the nefarious influence of Christian conceptions of man as dependent on God's will, which often results in human beings who are incapable of assuming their responsibility toward others. The Christian view, on the other hand, would see despair as the abandonment of faith. In this conception, despair deprives human action of any significance, by eliminating from it the teleological dimension sustained by religious discourse. Giving up to despair would turn human beings into mechanical agents performing random actions, or make them retreat into quietism in the absence of any moral certainty. Irreconcilable as they may seem, these two frameworks find their way into Greene's idiosyncratic conception of despair.

Indeed, those two views have laid claim to legitimacy in interpreting and appropriating Greene's work in antagonistic ways. One of the earliest examples of a critical reading of Greene's fiction that enacts this clash between existentialist and Catholic views is François Mauriac's 1951 short essay on *The Power and the Glory*, where we can read: "To the young contemporaries of Camus and Sartre, desperate prey to an absurd liberty, Graham Greene will reveal, perhaps, that this absurdity is in truth only that of boundless love" (77).

The tension between existentialist and Catholic readings of Greene's understanding of despair may be observed throughout the history of Greenean criticism. On the one hand, critical accounts of Greene's interest in the notion of suicide have often been put in connection to the philosophical context of existentialism. Lynette Kohn, in an early monograph on the author, pointed out the way in which his novels may be read in an existentialist light (21). Along the same lines, the connection between Greene's ideas about despair and Unamuno's depiction of it in *The Tragic Sense of Life* has been noted by critics like Cates Baldridge (54) and Eric Ziolkowski (241–42).

On the other hand, as with his view of bargaining with God, it is easy to see that Greene's understanding of despair and specially suicide does not fit Catholic orthodoxy. This is something critics like Friedman (*Fictional* 232, 234) have observed in connection to his view of suicide as something meritorious rather than sinful (232). The consideration of suicide as the ultimate expression of despair that is so recurrent in Greene's fiction is ingrained in the logic of Catholic doctrine. As Bernard Bergonzi has noted, in reference to Scobie: "He has committed what many Catholics at that time regarded as the ultimate sin, one which, in the nature of the act, cannot be forgiven. Greene's preoccupation with suicide is evident in his autobiographical writings, and it was a motif in his fiction and drama from *The Man Within* onwards" (120).

However, there is another crucial aspect of Greene's use of the term "despair" that may be said to depart from Catholic doctrine, and it is the way in which it is often conceived in his novels as a turning point, rather than a dead end. It is through their despair that characters may begin their process of regaining an interest in others and starting a course toward ethical action and commitment. In this sense, Greene's understanding of despair comes closer to Miguel de Unamuno's. Greene's *Monsignor Quixote*, which may be said to be largely inspired by Unamuno's work on the character created by Cervantes,[5] makes doubt the point of origin for a potential community with other human beings: "sharing a sense of doubt can bring men together perhaps even more than sharing a faith" (51).[6] Common doubt eliminates individual differences, thus favoring a sort of community of uncertainty. In *The Tragic Sense of Life*, Unamuno wrote: "out of this abyss of despair, hope may emanate, and how this crucial point may serve as source for human, profoundly human, effort and action, may serve the cause of solidarity and even of progress" (142). This Christian existentialist position may be traced back to Saint Augustine's famous dictum: "Do not despair; one of the thieves was saved. Do not presume; one of the thieves was damned." Doubt and uncertainty about salvation stand at the core of Augustine's statement. From it, both Unamuno and Greene may be said to develop an ethical stance based on doubt.

For the Spanish author, despair serves the key purpose of making uncertainty the foundation of action and morality: "The reader will see that this uncertainty, the suffering, and the fruitless struggle to escape uncertainty, can be and are a basis for action and a foundation for morals" (142).[7] The idea is echoed in Greene's own writing. In *Ways of Escape*, he quotes from *The Tragic Sense of Life* in order to illustrate Querry's trajectory in the novel:

> I would not look for Querry in that waste land. I would seek him among those – Unamuno describes them – "in whom reason is stronger than will, they feel themselves caught in the grip of reason and haled along in their own despite, and they fall into despair, and because of their despair they deny, and God reveals Himself in them, affirming Himself by their very denial of Him." (257)[8]

The logic hereby sketched is the one Greene would have articulated in the process of Sarah's conversion in *The End of the Affair*. It could be argued that this line of thought would suggest that Bendrix is converted as well at the end of the novel, when he expresses his hatred for God: "I hate You, God, I hate You as though You existed" (159).[9] In fact, it is interesting to note that critics who have favored the existentialist reading of Greene's notion of despair tend to interpret the end of this novel in lines quite close to Unamuno's thought. Thus, Lynette Kohn argued, in a seminal reading of the novel: "Bendrix is led against his will to belief. When one compares Bendrix's final actions with those of Sarah as revealed in her diary, one sees that Bendrix is beginning the same reluctant movement toward belief and love of God" (27).[10]

In his analysis of *Monsignor Quixote*, Eric Ziolkowski explored the interplay of faith and despair in Greene's fiction, claiming that, while characters like the Monsignor and the mayor in that novel may be seen as vulnerable to despair (240), theirs is the kind of despair which, in Unamuno's philosophical framework, "engenders heroic hope, absurd hope, mad hope" (Unamuno 352; see Ziolkowski 241–42). And yet, Unamuno considered that too much uncertainty could lead some individuals beyond their breaking point – and so did Greene. The predicament he describes is precisely the one most of Greene's characters find themselves in. Unamuno sees suicide as a renunciation of communal life and a failure to find an incentive for life: "if any man, finding himself in the depths of the abyss, fails to find there motives and incentives for life and action, and thereupon commits bodily or spiritual suicide, either by self-destruction or by renouncing any effort at human solidarity ..." (142).

Dr Fischer's theological views on God's relationship to man may throw some light on Greene's understanding of despair, by presenting an inverted image of the dynamics between hope and despair: "The world grows more and more miserable while he [God] twists the endless screw, though he gives us presents – for a universal suicide would defeat his purposes – to alleviate the humiliations we suffer" (*Dr Fischer* 62). His marriage to Anna-Louise is what, for Jones, embodies his "present" to alleviate the temptation to commit suicide and thus escape God's humiliations. *Dr Fischer of Geneva* is probably the most Kierkegaardian novel by Greene. Dr Fischer's suggestion that human beings may rebel against God through universal suicide echoes Kierkegaard's conception that suicide is "mutinying against God" (46).

Narratological implications: Despair as a black hole in a master narrative

In *Gravity and Grace*, Simone Weil wrote about despair as that "which turns attention away from the future" (20). Considering the role despair may play in the narrative pattern under analysis, it is interesting to note the moment in which it appears in different texts, and how it contributes to narrative development. Considering Weil's statement, despair could be seen as a disruptive element in narrative sequence. Those who fall into despair stop looking into the future, and this may be said to translate into narrative paralysis. Despair, and suicide as its outcome, would be the end of narrative development. This is what Conrad narrates through the character of Decoud in *Nostromo*. When faced with existential nothingness, the character becomes unable to act, and ends up killing himself out of despair. In Greene, this is not necessarily the case. Scobie seems to be the most relevant instance of this kind of narrative structure, in which exposure to suffering would lead to despair, and this to suicide as a way of escape.

In many of Greene's novels, however, despair is not the end of the story, but the beginning of one. In "The Later Greene: From Modernist to Moralist," Frances McCormack has recently explored the narrative role of despair: "The experience of despair facilitates a pivotal point in the narrative" (268). Writing about *The Tenth Man*, she depicts the turning point in the novel as the moment when despair "turns to hope when Chavel falls in love with Thérèse, only for this hope to be again threatened by the appearance of Carosse" (272). McCormack's discussion of despair in novels like *The Tenth Man* or *Dr Fischer of Geneva* emphasizes the narrative function that this motif plays in Greene's fiction as a narrative trigger. This understanding of despair connects to the existentialist view that despair may be the point of departure for hope and action.

In *Monsignor Quixote*, despair is also perceived in connection to narrative interruption. In a dream sequence included in the novel, the priest dreams of a world in which the identity of Christ as Son of God is made self-evident, thus bringing about a situation in which "there was no ambiguity, no room for doubt and no room for faith at all" (68–69). The dream provokes the priest's despair: "Father Quixote had felt on waking the chill of despair felt by a man who realizes suddenly that he has taken up a profession which is of use to no one, who must continue to live in a kind of Saharan desert without doubt or faith, where everyone is certain that the same belief is true" (69). Commenting on this passage, Cates Baldridge has pointed out the connection made by Greene between the possibility of narrative development and the conception of the world as a force field where different beliefs are measured up. This world described in the Father's dream, without doubt or faith, would be a world "without narrative" (Baldridge 171). In a world where all struggle in the name of faith has been rendered unnecessary, there is no place for narrative, Baldridge suggests.

In novels like *The Power and the Glory*, *The End of the Affair*, or *A Burnt-Out Case*, despair is the starting point for narratives structured around the pattern of fall and redemption. Out of the abyss of despair, the main characters in these texts emerge into new hope, in the effort of contributing to Unamuno's utopia of human solidarity. The pattern stands clearly on religious discourse, as in all three cases the characters' actions are interpreted – by the Catholic community, by Parkis, and by the missionaries, respectively – as the fulfillment of God's will. These individuals, in a Jansenist reading, would be instruments in God's hands, who would have used their despair as a mechanism for redirecting their lives into a religious teleological pattern. The same logic, however, may be perceived to operate in other contexts as well, particularly in the political one, where the idea of teleological motivation by God may be replaced by a parallel narrative of struggle against a particular political situation. Despair is a threat to narrative development dramatized as political activism.

A case in point is the long captivity section in *The Honorary Consul*, where delay in the negotiation for the consul's life results in narrative paralysis, putting the entire mission at risk.[11] In this novel, about which Greene said that it meant the "logical climax of the method" (30), hiding involves a suspension of narrative development which is contrasted to action sequences. In this case, however, the effect is achieved by means of two parallel narrative sequences, one depicting the rebels hiding in a hut with the kidnapped Consul Charles Fortnum, and the other following Eduardo Plarr's efforts to resolve the situation in the city. When Plarr joins the kidnappers in the woods near the end of the novel, a moment of total narrative paralysis occurs, which precedes the catastrophic climax. This may account for the general gloomy tone of the novel, noted by reviewers like Peter Ackroyd: "There is a fatality about the narrative, a sense of privation and abandonment which invades the central characters and which generates the tone of the whole book" (344). In the passages devoted to Leon Rivas and his associates, we observe the dissolution of the bonds uniting them as engaged in the same cause. We also witness their mutual accusations, the rise of fear, and even repentance for their deed. One of the recurrent ideas in this part of the novel is the discussion as to what differentiates political action from plain criminality. It is only when Plarr assumes a leading role that the pattern is perceived to return back to its logic of commitment, and the deaths of Rivas and the others acquire significance in its light. By becoming witnesses of the way in which Plarr embodies their cause, assuming the responsibility for negotiating with the authorities outside the hut and hence putting himself at risk, Rivas may be said to regain consciousness of his own trajectory and assume the role of sacrificial victim that will restore meaning to his actions.

In *A Burnt-Out Case*, Querry's journey to the Congo is said to have been a result of his surrender to despair at an earlier period of his life. The narrative pattern Greene elaborates in this novel is one of reawakening from despair through contact with humanity and suffering. Putting the episode of Deo Gratias's rescue at the center of this pattern, Greene indicates that through Querry's moment of "unselfing," he is able to recuperate his own humanity. The structure hereby created may be described in the terms offered by Greene in *The Comedians*: "There is a point of no return unremarked at the time in most lives" (1). Brown's statement anticipates the pattern to be followed by his own narration, in the attempt to (retrospectively) identify that point of no return – from detachment to commitment for both Jones and himself. But it also works as an explanation of the way in which many of Greene's characters relate – directly, in first-person narration, or through free indirect discourse – to their own past experience and construct master narratives in which the dark spots are identified as moments of "despair." Despair, therefore, may emerge retrospectively as a "black hole" in the narrative pattern advancing toward commitment and solidarity.

4
Pity and Compassion

In *Ways of Escape*, Greene introduces an opposition between the paired concepts of "pity" and "compassion" which may serve as the basis for the conceptual articulation explored in this chapter. The distinction is first mentioned in the discussion of what Greene perceived to be a generalized misunderstanding of Scobie, the main character in *The Heart of the Matter*: "I had meant the story of Scobie to enlarge a theme which I had touched on in *The Ministry of Fear*, the disastrous effect on human beings of pity as distinct from compassion" (*Ways* 120). "Pity," he claims, "can be the expression of an almost monstrous pride" (120). Greene complains that most readers of *The Heart of the Matter* reacted to the character in a sympathetic way. This contradicted his original intention, which had been to show him as the protagonist of a cruel comedy rather than as a tragic hero (121).

This opposition between "pity" and "compassion" illustrates a recurrent method used by Greene to dramatize ethical conflict in his fictional world. The two terms invoke a framework in which one individual reacts to the pain of another. In Greene's usage, each introduces a different tone of ethical response, one of which is acceptable, but deemed insufficient or imperfect, the other portrayed as preferable in ethical terms, although very often harder to achieve. Through the conceptual antagonism between two terms he epitomizes the dialectical clash between a socially acceptable ethical behavior and an alternative, often subversive, one. This second course of action is eventually preferred, being closer to the ethical ideal endorsed by the narrator. In the case of these two paired terms, their dialectical relationship can be traced as far back as, on the one hand, Aristotelian ethics and, on the other hand, Christian ethics as expressed in the New Testament. In what follows, I would like to sketch the conceptual framework from which Greene's articulation emerges, so that it may contribute to an understanding of a recurrent narrative pattern in his work.

The ethico-philosophical framework

First of all, a brief etymological note is in order. The root of the term "pity" is *pietas*, and it is defined as "sympathetic sorrow for one suffering, in distress or unhappy." The term "compassion" in turn is defined as "sympathetic consciousness of other's distress together with a desire to alleviate it."[1] Its Latin root brings together two stems *com* (with) and *pati* (to suffer, to bear). The two definitions point to a major distinction regarding their meaning: whereas pity implies just the recognition of others' suffering, compassion involves the desire to alleviate this suffering. A more "active" role is attributed, one may argue, to those who feel compassion than to those who feel pity. Another difference regarding these terms, however, is more determinant of Greene's idiosyncratic usage. Whereas the first may be said to be unidirectional – *pietas* exerted by someone over someone else – the second involves the prefix "com-," adding a reciprocal aspect to the relationship established, a sort of mutual recognition of the same kind implied in the terms "confidence," "community," and "commitment."

The distinction thus traced between these two Latin terms was already present in Aristotelian ethics, through the use of the Greek pair *eleos* and *sym-paschō* (from which "com-passion" comes).[2] In the *Rhetoric* (II.8, 1385b13–16), Aristotle describes "pity" or *eleos* as "a feeling of pain caused by the sight of some evil, destructive or painful, which befalls one who does not deserve it, and which one might expect to suffer oneself or one of one's own, and moreover when the suffering seems close to hand" (Aristotle *Rhetoric* 113). As Friedrich Nietzsche famously noted in *The Anti-Christ* (section 7), Aristotle "saw in pity a morbid and dangerous condition" (Nietzsche 131), and he considered it an affect, but not a virtue. Immediately after defining pity in the *Rhetoric*, Aristotle expands his explanation by establishing a crucial contrast: "The people for whom they feel pity are: those whom they know, unless they are very closely connected to us – for in that case they relate to them as if they themselves are likely to suffer" (II.8, 1386a17–18). Pity, then, involves a certain distance. Compassion, on the other hand, involves "being affected together."[3]

Aristotle never addresses the issue in terms of one word's ethical superiority over the other. That is, he never claims that compassion is better than pity from an ethical point of view. As an affect, compassion and pity are equally left out of Aristotle's notion of ethical duty. This is also the ground on which the Kantian understanding of compassion stands. Kant considers that compassion is an affect, a feeling, and as such, it is left out of his moral system: "this *feeling* of compassion and tender sympathy, if it precedes consideration of what is duty and becomes the determining ground, is itself burdensome to right-thinking persons" (*Practical* 235; emphasis added). Kant implicitly traces the distinction between pity and compassion by claiming that "the feeling of pity would not be sufficient for morality" (*Lectures* 25). Our obligation toward others springs from their right to justice, regardless of our feelings for them: "even acts of generosity are acts of duty and indebtedness, which arise from the rights of others" (Kant *Lectures* 179). Compassion, however, is not part of man's moral duty, which comes from a rational, universal idea of justice (*Metaphysics* 575). Kant's understanding of duty, moreover, is strictly rationalistic: "when morality is in question, reason must not play the part of mere guardian to inclination but, disregarding it altogether, must attend solely to its own interest as pure practical reason" (Kant *Practical* 235).

Greene's dramatization of compassion in his novels is very far from Kantian moral philosophy, because his understanding of ethics is of a sentimentalist, rather than rationalist, kind. Ethical action springs in his novels from the feeling aroused by another's suffering, not from a categorical imperative of a rational kind. Greene is closer, in this sense, to Shaftesbury than to Kant.[4] Yet, Greene shares Kant's idea that goodness to another should not be perceived as voluntary beneficence, but as restitution of the other's right.

Following a different path, the dialectical logic involved in Greene's opposition of pity and compassion leads back to Christian ethics, as expressed in the New Testament.[5] Here, we do have an evaluative arrangement of the two terms. On a literal level, the Gospels are full of passages in which a pre-existing ethical order, based on keeping one's distance from those in sorrow, is subverted through the explicit erasure of physical distance (see for instance Matthew 9, on Jesus eating with sinners and publicans). The keeping of distance implicit in the notion of pity is put at stake through an investment in notions of closeness to sin and disease. As Jean-Luc Nancy has noted, "Christianity will have been the invention of the religion of touch, of the sensible, of presence that is immediate to the body and to the heart" (Nancy *Noli* 14). In this context, true compassion – enacted in the numerous passages in which Jesus is depicted with sinners, with the sick and the poor – is opposed to the false charity of the Pharisees (Matthew 6). Jesus charging against the apparent virtue of the pious, in favor of the sinful, will become a recurrent idea in Greene's work: "It is not the healthy who need a doctor, but the sick. But go and learn what this means: 'I desire mercy, not sacrifice'. For I have not come to call the righteous, but sinners" (Matthew 9:12–13); "It was too easy to die for what was good and beautiful, for home, or children or a civilization – it needed a God to die for the half-hearted and the corrupt" (*Power* 94).

This ethical order plays upon the moral polarity between virtue and sin. It redefines authentic virtue as the capacity to feel compassion for those who have fallen, as opposed to the Pharisaic understanding of virtue as abstention from sin. The new Christian virtue is performed in the acts of sitting and suffering with sinners, rather than looking down on them with pity. The idea is constantly dramatized in Greene's *The Heart of the Matter* where, as Michael Brennan has noted, "Scobie is unable to find virtue in mere absence of sin" (86).

For Greene, the Christian investment in the rhetoric of touch enacts a leveling out of social differences that pity tends to reinforce. The asymmetry implicit in the interpersonal relationship established through pity has been the object of philosophical scrutiny for a long time.[6] Alain Badiou has based his critique of Lévinasian ethics on the claim that, since the eighteenth century, ethics has been posited in terms of a relation with the other which springs from pity (*Ethics* 9). He argues then against an ethics which defines man as victim (10), a position that would reinforce the alleged condescending attitude to the person being pitied (Leighton 101). Along similar lines, Jean-Paul Sartre, in his *Notebooks for an Ethics* (1983), claimed that "the situation of the pitiable man is not unjust (otherwise it would raise to indignation), yet it is insupportable. What it represents is a *diminished* man. And it is true that the diminution of the man to whom I address my pity touches me directly" (234).

The Nietzschean argument about the dismissal of pity coincides with Greene's standpoint as expressed in *Ways of Escape*: that pity is ultimately directed toward one's own good rather than toward another's, and that it demeans the person pitied and gives a false kind of superiority to those who feel pity (Leighton 101–2). However, Nietzsche's view of Christianity, famously expressed in the idea that "pity thwarts the law of evolution [...] it defends life's disinherited and condemned" (*Anti-Christ* 130), overrides the distinction that remains crucial to Greene's work. The Nietzschean view does not allow for a positive understanding of sympathy toward others' suffering – which is always interpreted as a weakness on the part of the one offering it – thus erasing the term "compassion" altogether. Greene's ethical view, on the contrary, relies entirely upon the possibility of counterbalancing the pernicious effect of pity with the beneficial one of authentic compassion.[7]

In Greene's use of "pity" and "compassion," the key difference between the two terms, as discussed by W. H. Auden in 1949, is that the first implies a position of superiority on the part of the one who feels pity regarding those who are pitied. Compassion, on the other hand, implies a position of equality and emotional identification with the object of such compassion: "Behind pity for another lies self-pity, and behind self-pity lies cruelty. To feel compassion for someone is to make oneself their equal; to pity them is to regard oneself as their superior" (Auden 94). In Greene, the preferred term is obviously "compassion." He explains it in very similar terms in an interview with Gloria Emerson from 1978: "pity is a sense of superiority, isn't it? Unlike compassion. You have compassion for an equal but you have pity for somebody you consider to be inferior" (137).

The two-level structure he creates through that opposition provides the basis for the dramatization of ethical conflict in many of his novels. The first term – pity – is associated with the kind of behavior considered morally acceptable in a social context (in controlled situations, subjected to normative regulation), whereas the second term – compassion – acquires a greater value by comparison, and it is said to spring from the individual's capacity to relate to other human beings in terms of equality. The dichotomy between pity and compassion, then, articulates the double-depth structure of religious practice in Greene's work. On how this double religious structure operates in Greene's fiction, Murray Roston has argued: "From a close reading of this novel [*The Power and the Glory*], then, it would appear that the supposed unorthodoxies it contains were not movements away from Christianity, marking a writer dissatisfied with his adopted faith but, in the opposite direction, deviations from the official doctrines of the Church in order to re-assert or re-affirm its fundamental concepts" (Roston 64).

The opposition between "pity" and "compassion" is omnipresent in Greene's work. It constitutes the dialectical basis upon which the pattern of individual transformation – from detachment to commitment – undergone by Greene's heroes is articulated. In the next sections of this chapter I set out to explore the narrative pattern that emerges through the conceptual framework sketched above, in novels such as *The Heart of the Matter*, *A Burnt-Out Case*, *The Power and the Glory*, and *The Honorary Consul*. The main aspect to be discussed is Greene's use of the dialectical opposition between pity and compassion to dramatize a process of individual evolution from one to the other. None of Greene's characters is innately compassionate. In the early stages of narrative development, they tend to show pity for others, expressed in their tendency to infantilize and victimize those around them. Yet, in the course of the narrative, they develop the capacity to suffer with others through their exposure to extreme ethical dilemmas.

Although the passage from pity to compassion is not necessarily a religious one, it is frequently expressed in Greene's novels as a contrast between institutionalized religiosity and another, more emotional, universal, and primitive approach to religious practice meant to represent a return to "original religious values." The pattern is thus expressed with particular intensity in *The Power and the Glory*, *A Burnt-Out Case*, and *The Honorary Consul*. The three novels feature official, liturgical Christianity in opposition to subversive religious practices. In all three texts, the latter is considered to be closer to original Christian ethics, embodied in a Christ-like figure – the Whisky Priest, Querry, and León Rivas, respectively – who champions an oppressed, suffering community. In *The Ministry of Fear* or *The Quiet American*, the religious elements are removed, but the narrative pattern remains: the hero overcomes his initial detachment from a community by endorsing a line of action that runs opposite to its official ethical codes and that is expressed in acts of compassion. In those cases, the dialectical opposition between pity and compassion is embedded in medical and political discourse, respectively, rather than in a religious one.

In *The Heart of the Matter* the dialectics between pity and compassion acquires explicit religious overtones, but it is kept entirely at the level of individual consciousness. Scobie seems to have interiorized the two ethical codes which, in the other novels, have a public dimension. León Rivas in *The Honorary Consul* embodies the people's Christian ethics in opposition to a corrupt Catholic Church complicit with Stroessner's dictatorship in Paraguay. In *The Heart of the Matter*, however, both institutional religious ethics, identified with pharisaic pity, and its opposite, the primitive Christian compassion for sinners, seem to emerge from Scobie's inner consciousness, and are staged only at a private level.

Still, it is with Scobie that Greene returns to an idea that had only been sketched before in *The Ministry of Fear*: that only God can feel pity for humanity as a whole, while men can only feel true compassion for particular individuals.[8] This leads back to Aristotle's observation that one can only feel compassion for those one knows closely, by the bridging of the distance that separates us from others. As Oele has claimed (60) pity may be universal, but compassion is necessarily addressed to particular individuals. Hence, for Greene, ultimate ethical action involves feeling compassion for others, and it is directed toward specific individuals rather than addressed to all humanity. This dimension of the pity–compassion dialectic overlaps with other formulations of the particular versus the universal in Greene, affecting his understanding of notions of commitment and love that will be explored in the following two chapters.

The morphology of pity

The most comprehensive treatment of the problematic nature of pity in Greene's oeuvre appears, undoubtedly, in *The Heart of the Matter*. It is in this novel that he develops what could be called the morphology of pity, including elements such as its asymmetrical nature and its effect on the representation of the objects of pity as infantile victims.

As argued by Lynette Kohn, *The Heart of the Matter* is built around the process of decline of a man – Major Scobie – consumed by pity, an "aberration of love" (Kohn 11). In Greene's own words, he set out to prove the point that "pity is a corrupting force" (Donaghy *Conversations* 21). The nature of love according to Scobie implies an asymmetrical relationship in which one must necessarily feel pity for the other, and hence be responsible for him/her. The sense of responsibility that characterizes Scobie is determined by his attraction toward the helpless: "He had no sense of responsibility towards the beautiful and the graceful and the intelligent. They could find their own way. It was the face for which nobody would go out of his way [...] that demanded his allegiance" (147).

The true source of Scobie's obligation toward his wife Louise, for instance, lies in the pity she inspires, expressed in terms that emphasize his diminished view of her: "he was bound by the pathos of her unattractiveness" (19). For Scobie, love necessarily springs from the contemplation of the other's frailty, failure, and ugliness: "These were the happy times of ugliness when he loved her, when pity and responsibility reached the intensity of a passion" (13). The same feeling of pity produces his attraction to Helen Rolt, as Stephen K. Land has noted: "it is rather the unattractiveness and consequent pathos of these women that draws Scobie to them" (63).

The connection established by Greene between pity and weakness recalls George Eliot's argument, in chapter 17 of *Adam Bede* (1859), about the need for charity regarding the vulgar and ugly rather than the beautiful:

It is these people – amongst whom your life is passed – that it is needful you should *tolerate*, pity, and love: it is these more or less ugly, stupid, inconsistent people whose movements of goodness you should be able to admire – for whom you should cherish all possible hopes, all possible *patience*. (194; emphasis added)

The passage, though apparently building on Christian ethics – "it is not the healthy who need a doctor, but the sick" – fails to overcome the intrinsic inequality betrayed in Eliot's use of terms like "tolerate" or "patience," which involve the same kind of inequality that operates in Greene's representation of pity. While Scobie – as well as Eliot's narrator – assume they are wishing good to those pitied, the distance regarding their object of pity is textually palpable. From a Kantian perspective, Eliot's formulation falsely presents as charity what should indeed be an act of justice. It presents others as "objects of [...] magnanimity" (AK 19: 145; qtd. Wood xviii). Pity, then, is problematic from an ethical point of view, because it perceives as freely given beneficence what should be a regard for the rights of others (Kant *Metaphysics* 575). In *The Human Factor*, this vision is corrected and expressed in terms that recuperate Kant's notion of moral justice, according to which "even acts of generosity are acts of duty and indebtedness, which arise from the rights of others" (*Lectures* 179):

Why are some of us, he wondered, unable to love success or power or great beauty? [...] Perhaps one wanted to right the balance, just as Christ had, that legendary figure whom he would have liked to believe in. "Come unto me all ye that travail and are heavy laden" [...] Perhaps he had merely wanted her to feel that she was loved by someone and so he began to love her himself. It wasn't pity, any more than it had been pity when he fell in love with Sarah pregnant by another man. He was there to right the balance. That was all. (141)

Righting the balance is just a way of restoring what Kant called "general injustice" (*Lectures* 179), and it involves recognition of the equality of all human beings on moral grounds.

Taking his cue from Sartre's argument that pity is "a diminution of the human in his person" (Sartre *Ethics* 234), Hayim Gordon's existentialist reading of *The Heart of the Matter* claims that "pity, for Scobie, is a manner of distancing himself from his fellow human beings" (Gordon *Fighting* 87). Although I disagree with Gordon when he claims that the source of Scobie's problems is his cowardice and inability to confront others, I do agree with the idea that pity has a distancing effect on Scobie, who feels more and more alone as his pity for those around him grows.

A textual consequence of this conception of pity as necessarily involving inequality and condescension is the tendency to perceive others as infantile victims on the part of specific characters. The asymmetry intrinsic to a relationship based on pity is repeatedly expressed in *The Heart of the Matter* in the imagery used by the narrator to depict those characters presented as victims: Louise (34), Ali (14), the Portuguese Captain (41), Pemberton (77–78), and Helen (253) are all said to be, in one moment or other, "like a child." Through Scobie's eyes, all of them are seen as children in need of protection.

Another case in point is *The Quiet American*, where the protagonist-narrator, Fowler, reproaches his friend and rival, Alden Pyle, for this tendency to infantilize others. In this case, the pitied others are the Vietnamese people, as their country falls prey to competing political interests. As I have argued elsewhere (Martin Salván "Being" 115–19), the political setting of the novel complicates Pyle's perception of the Vietnamese as pitiful victims in a double sense: as his pity is mainly directed toward Phuong, first Fowler's lover and then Pyle's fiancée, it tends to overlap with discourses on victimization along the axes of gender and colonial relationships. Phuong is one of the frequent child-woman characters in Greene's fiction (Land 214), but her childishness is here linked to the ethnic stereotype that tends to see the Vietnamese in general as child-like: "It's a cliché to call them children – but there's one thing which is childish. They love you in return for kindness, security, the presents you give them – they hate you for a blow or an injustice" (104). Fowler keeps on trying to correct what he thinks are Pyle's prejudiced notions: "She's no child. She's tougher than you'll ever be ... She can survive a dozen of us" (133). Hence, through Fowler's perspective, we perceive how Pyle's relationship to her is based on a protective attitude grounded on pity and, therefore, condescension. Most postcolonial readings of *The Quiet American* have criticized the paternalistic tone used by the narrator to construct Phuong as a "subaltern subjectivity" (Pathak et al. 203): "the Asian woman is meant to represent relative helplessness, naïveté, inferiority, and subservience" (Christopher 159).

Nevertheless, it should be noted that Greene's representation of Phuong in this novel reaches beyond the particularities of the colonial context into a general pattern whereby the pitiful tends to be articulated as childish. The tendency is also present in other novels like *The Power and the Glory*, where the Whisky Priest refers to the peasants as "My children" (125). During the prison episode, his condescension toward them is noteworthy: "They were extraordinarily foolish over pictures [...]

He had always been worried by the fate of pious women. As much as politicians, they fed on illusion [...] It was one's duty, if one could, to rob them of their sentimental notions of what was good" (125).

Ironically, throughout the novel, children are persistently portrayed as the carriers of true compassion, which they display constantly to the Priest: it is a child, Coral, who saves him from being captured by risking her own life; and it is a child who opens the door to the last persecuted priest at the end of the novel. Unable to understand his own child, the Priest confesses his inability to relate to actual children except through the superior stance granted to him by his position: "He had never known how to talk to children except from the pulpit" (65). Through the parallelism between the infantilized peasants in the Priest's speech and the compassion shown by actual children toward him, Greene dramatizes the demeaning inflection of his pity, and the counterfeit nature of his superiority toward them.

The dialectics between pity and compassion

One of Greene's preferred methods for the textual dramatization of ethical conflict is the confrontation between opposing worldviews as epitomized in paired characters. Fowler and Pyle in *The Quiet American*, the Priest and the Lieutenant in *The Power and the Glory*, or Querry and Rycker in *A Burnt-Out Case* may be mentioned among the most salient cases. In connection to this tendency, critics have often perceived a certain inclination toward allegory in these texts.[9] The allegorical readings of the novels, however, may obscure the complexities of Greene's dialectical use of characterization.

An early example of Greene's method of characterization through the pairing of conflicting identities can be found in *The Power and the Glory.* The main characters in the novel are unnamed and are referred to only as "the Priest" and "the Lieutenant." An aspect often overlooked by allegorical readings of this novel is that the labels used to refer to the characters link them explicitly to their respective social roles, as representatives and administrators of religious and civil law. It is through their public social identities that they are made known to the reader, unlike other characters in the novel, who are labeled on the grounds of racial identity – "the Mestizo," for instance. This invites a reading of the text in a different allegorical key: each of them represents in turn an institution invoking a different model of social organization. In the novel, these are presented as mutually exclusive.

Initially, Greene characterizes the Priest and the Lieutenant by interchanging their moral attributes. The first is morally condemnable, whereas the second is virtuous. Brennan talks about the "inversion of moral polarities" (72) in Greene's creation of the two characters. However, the opposition between them is more complex than mere inversion, as each of the two main characters sets out to fulfill his personal and institutional vision.

The Lieutenant may be said to represent a quasi-Nietzschean position regarding pity. His desire is to eliminate the need for pity, echoing William Blake's verses in "The Human Abstract" (1794): "Pity would be no more, / If we did not make somebody Poor" (27). He blames the Church not only for having contributed to social inequality, but for teaching resignation to the poor while retaining its economic privileges. Turning his humanitarian vision of a poverty-free Mexico into a reality, however, requires putting into practice repressive measures and the exertion of violence over the very people he is trying to save: taking hostages and arresting people become common practices in the Lieutenant's world. Like Alden Pyle in *The Quiet American*, he seems incapable of distinguishing his zeal in the application of an idea from the consequences it may have on individual human beings. Although both characters are guided by high principles, the results of their enterprises will be bloody and inhuman. The seed for Greene's exposition of the dangers of abstract thought in *The Quiet American* may indeed be found in his portrayal of the Lieutenant in *The Power and the Glory*.

The Priest, on the other hand, undergoes a deep transformation in the course of the story. He starts out in a desperate state, trying to run away from detention, hiding his identity as a priest, and avoiding contact with other people, specifically with his former parishioners, who keep on asking him to fulfill his role as a priest. He considers himself to be unworthy of people's protection: "O God, send them someone more worthwhile to suffer for. It seemed to him a damnable mockery that they should sacrifice themselves for a whisky priest with a bastard child" (133–34). In the course of the novel, the Priest will progressively lose the tools of his profession: the breviary, abandoned in Mr. Tench's house (12); the altar stone, "too dangerous to carry with him" (57), and the chalice he had carried around for two years (68). His clothes and appearance also show the process through which he is dispossessed of all external signs identifying him as a priest. This process of abasement, however, brings him closer to the people and bridges the social gap between the clergy and the community that the Lieutenant seeks to eradicate: "For a matter of seconds he felt an immense satisfaction that he could talk of suffering to them now without hypocrisy – it is hard for the sleek and well-fed priest to praise poverty" (68).

This renunciation of his public identity is compensated for, however, by his progressive acceptance of his role, as he finally admits to being a priest halfway through the novel, and sticks to it till the end. In a parallel fashion, the Priest's understanding of religion is seen in retrospect as undergoing a process of transformation which lays bare the structure and social function of religious ritual. In fact, this process helps him to return to the primitive values of religion which, in Greene's worldview, are always close to specific forms of community progressively abandoned in the institutionalized practices of the Catholic Church. The opposition between institutionalized religion and primitive faith, associated with the vindication of the underprivileged, is a recurrent idea in Greene, particularly strong in *A Burnt-Out Case* and *The Honorary Consul*.

The articulation of this opposition in *A Burnt-Out Case* is explicitly modeled upon the account of Jesus' teachings in the New Testament, structured in terms of an opposition between the Pharisaic ethical code, based on the kind of superiority and distance identified with pity, and the Christian one, claiming to stand closer to the sufferings of others in a more authentic way. St. Matthew's account of Jesus' teachings on almsgiving and prayer (chapter 6) or the Sermon against the Scribes and Pharisees (chapter 23) are structured in terms of this opposition, to mention two well-known examples. In Greene's *A Burnt-Out Case*, Rycker embodies the Pharisaic ethics, whereas Querry undergoes a transformation leading him to acts of compassion identified as genuinely Christian. The contrast is explained in *Ways of Escape*, where Greene rejects "the piety of the educated, the established, who seem to own their Roman Catholic image of God, who have ceased to look for Him because they consider they have found Him" (257). In this text, Greene reports how he told Evelyn Waugh that, in *A Burnt-Out Case*, he "wanted to give expression to various states or moods of belief and disbelief" (Greene *Ways* 255). From his representation, a specific ethics of practical charity emerges, favoring Doctor Colin's and the Superior's attention to others over Rycker's and Father Thomas's religious ruminations. In fact, it is in the dialogues between the first two characters that the moral stance in the novel is rendered visible. Particularly in their final discussion, where their mutual accusations of never abandoning someone in need reveal them as ethical models (191), the Doctor and the Priest claim that Querry may have experienced true compassion: "You remember what Pascal said – that a man who starts looking for God has already found him. The same may be true of love – when we look for it, perhaps we've already found it" (ibid.).

According to Robert Pendleton, Greene was advocating a specific view of Christian ethics, and he talks about "the novel's wider quest to renew the connection between Christianity and everyday social life" (Pendleton 112). Through the antagonistic characterization of the Superior and Rycker, and through the rhetorical contrast between the representations of Europe and Africa, he constructs a symbolic force field in which practical Christian charity is linked to the living conditions of the Congo. Against a spiritually exhausted Europe, Africa is represented as the place of religious re-enchantment. Both the primitive character of his depiction of Africa and the primitive Christian ethics he advocates come together in the novel: "In this way, Greene builds upon the association forged in *Journey without Maps* between primitive Africa and primitive Christianity, going beyond 'intellectual faith' and returning to one of the basic teachings of the New Testament: 'love thy neighbor as thyself'" (Pendleton 111).[10]

In *The Quiet American*, this basic principle is presented in contrast to the tendency to think of human good in abstract terms. Hidden in a watchtower near a war zone, the two main characters, Pyle and Fowler, spend a night discussing their views on Vietnam and humanity under the terrified gaze of two Vietnamese soldiers who share their hiding spot. Fowler repeatedly accuses Pyle of being unable to look beyond abstract ideology into the material reality of the Vietnamese: "Thought's a luxury. Do you think the peasant sits and thinks of God and Democracy when he gets inside his mud hut at night?" (95). Against Pyle's alleged instrumentalization of the Vietnamese people for political purposes, Fowler stresses his own compassion for them, specifically directed toward the two Vietnamese soldiers: "I've no particular desire to see you [Americans] win. I'd like those two poor buggers there to be happy – that's all. I wish they didn't have to sit in the dark at night scared" (97). While the religious overtones have disappeared from this text, the dialectical structure remains the same, even if it is rendered in political terms. The foreign, abstract considerations about a native, oppressed community are shown as spurious ethics in the face of a more authentic, compassionate concern for them.

Compassion and community

Both in *A Burnt-Out Case* and *The Power and the Glory*, the recovery of a primitive religiosity is articulated through the explicit opposition of pity to compassion. For the Whisky Priest, redemption will come with the development of the capacity to feel an authentic connection to others, suffering with others in a purely Christological fashion: "he was moved by an irrational affection for the inhabitants of this prison [...] he was touched by an extraordinary affection. He was just one criminal among a herd of criminals... he had a sense of companionship which he had never experienced in the old days when pious people came kissing his black cotton glove" (125–26).

In Greene's fiction, as has previously been mentioned, the dialectics between pity and compassion serves a double purpose: on the one hand, it articulates the ethical conflict in the texts at a discursive level, as seen in the examples analyzed in previous sections. On the other hand, this dialectics allows for the dramatization of a narrative turn at the level of plot – from detachment to commitment – that is expressed as the hero's passage from pity to compassion. Using Roland Barthes's terminology, we could say that the hermeneutic code of the narrative – that of discourse – is projected over the proiaretic one, that of actions and events (Barthes 28). While most narratologists agree in defining plot as the proiaretic sequence of events producing a change in a state of affairs (Rimmon-Kenan 13–15), analyzing Greene's rendering of the passage from detachment to commitment presents a serious difficulty. No explicit kernel event shows the character's internal transformation. Rather, this change is symbolically enacted as a narrative crux in a scene representing the anointing of the sick.[11] The event itself lacks any self-evident transformative force, but it is symbolically invested in the semantics of the sacramental. The anointing of the sick is, in Greene's novels, the ultimate expression of Christian compassion, effecting a transformation of the sick individual, but also of the one who assists him/her. These moments enact "an outer framework which both occasions and identifies an inner event" (Murdoch *Sovereignty* 16). Thus, the scene depicted is static, but it is meant to illustrate an inner transformation of an ethical kind. Very similar scenes appear in *The Heart of the Matter*, *The Comedians*, and *The End of the Affair*.

The anointing of the sick is a narrative crux in Greene's fiction that is used to dramatize the transformation of a character from detachment to commitment to others. It is usually staged as a momentary, fleeting event, during which the hero comes to perceive the suffering of other individuals with striking, unprecedented intensity. According to Whitehouse, "The break in the egocentricity of their own physical and psychic life, which is clear in all the novels and which for Greene seems to be a precondition for human growth, brings with it a deeper love of others and a fuller understanding of their fellows" (48). The ephemeral nature of this kind of encounter is expressed explicitly in

The Honorary Consul: "A few minutes ago there had been a moment of closeness, of sympathy, even of friendship between them, but that moment had passed" (114). Greene tends to represent these moments in visual terms, as instants where the subject is able *to see* others with unprecedented clarity. This recalls Iris Murdoch's contention that behaving ethically is an act of "true vision" (*Sovereignty* 64). When this happens to Greene's characters, a connection to the other is established through the common recognition of mortality. This is what Jean-Luc Nancy calls a community of singularities (*Community* 27). In opposition to the earlier manifestations of pity, a true moment of compassion in Greene's fictional world involves, as explained earlier, the recognition of the absolute equality of mankind in the face of death, through which distance to the other is eliminated. Greene's rendering of this tends to explicitly highlight physical contact with the other. In a Kantian fashion, compassion is never formulated as beneficence, but as an obligation toward the other. However, this obligation is not of a rational kind, but of an emotional one. This is where Greene deviates from Kantian morality: his moral imperative is an emotional imperative, and it is often in open conflict with the dictates of reason.

The pattern here sketched may be illustrated with a specific example. In *A Burnt-Out Case*, the symbolic scene of the anointing of the sick is staged in Querry's search for Deo Gratias in the bush. Querry's transformation is represented in terms of his capacity to tend to others, overcoming his previous distance; "redemption in Greene lies precisely in ridding oneself of egotistical forms of mediating experience" (Dobozy 438). Initially, his indifference toward others had been his defining feature: "I haven't enough feeling left for human beings to do anything for them out of pity" (50).

The transformation of Querry's initial indifference toward Deo Gratias (53) into something else starts when the servant disappears one evening: "One night when the moon was full Querry became aware of the man's absence as one might become aware of some hitherto unnoticed object missing from a mantelpiece" (ibid.). At this point his departure is perceived as a physical vacancy, as illustrated in the simile equating Deo Gratias with "some unhitherto unnoticed object." Maurice Blanchot has theorized how true community emerges precisely from an exposure to absence (Blanchot *Community* 15). Deo Gratias's absence, in this sense, may be read in Blanchot's terms as the moment "in which the event begins to take place, a point where the real truth of the encounter occurs" (Blanchot *Book* 9). Querry's reaction evinces a change of attitude regarding his relation to others:

The thought of his servant lying injured in the forest waiting for the call or footstep of any human being would perhaps at an earlier time have vexed him all night until he was forced into making a token gesture. But now that he cared for nothing, perhaps he was being driven only by a vestige of intellectual curiosity. (55)

Before, helping his servant would have been a "token gesture," an external sign of his acceptance of the social obligation to charity – that is to say, an act of pity. Now, his growing curiosity is described as a process of awakening to something old: "Interest began to move painfully in him like a nerve that has been frozen. He had lived with inertia so long that he examined his 'interest' with clinical detachment" (56).[12] The passage echoes the rhetoric of "awakening" so common in Greene's work, as mentioned in Chapter 2. Yet, while Querry enters the woods in search of Deo Gratias, he repeatedly stresses the foolishness and absurdity of this "stupid errand" (55). Similarly, the Priest in *The Power and the Glory* considers himself foolish for following what seems like an irrational course of action rather than what reason dictates (209). It is against reasonable action oriented toward self-preservation that the emotional imperative imposes itself on Greene's heroes. Here, Greene comes very close to Shaftesbury's contention that compassion and self-preservation may be mutually exclusive: "This we know for certain, that all social love, friendship, gratitude or whatever else is of this generous kind does by its nature take place of the self-interesting passions, *draws us out of ourselves* and makes us disregardful of our own convenience and safety" (*Characteristics*, I.ii.1, 193; emphasis added).

When Querry finds Deo Gratias, lying near a marsh, the narrator repeatedly refers to him as a "body," a term which is used three times in the course of seven lines (56). Physical contact, but no verbal interchange, will establish the bond between the two characters: "The fingerless hand fell on Querry's arm like a hammer and held him there. [...] He took Deo Gratias's hand to reassure him, or rather laid his own hand down beside it" (57). Greene anticipates here the potential space for an alternative community in *A Burnt-Out Case*, born out of the recognition of finitude (Martín Salván "Community" 315–19). What happens between Querry and Deo Gratias in the bush is the enactment of a potential momentary compassion toward others, expressed earlier in the novel in an apocalyptic vision: "In the last cooling of the world, when the emptiness of your belief is finally exposed, there'll always be some bemused fool who'll cover another's body with his own to give it warmth for an hour more of life" (77). The relationship Querry talks about is deprived of spiritual or transcendental significance – "when the emptiness of your belief is finally exposed" (77) – it focuses on physical, material care – "cover another's body with his own" (77) – and it is not meant to last – "for an hour more or life" (77). It has no hope of survival, no purpose beyond compassion near death, and yet, it is inevitable: "there'll always be some bemused fool." Moments of compassion in Greene's fiction have a contingent, finite nature, but they effect an inner transformation in the heroes' ethical stance that constitutes an irreversible narrative turning point.

Two crucial questions are raised in the aftermath of an act of compassion. First, can this be permanent? That is, can compassion become the norm ruling individual action in Greene? Second, can it be universal? The first question is addressed in the next chapter, devoted to the idea of commitment. As Iris Murdoch stated in *The Sovereignty of Good* (1970), "the difficulty is to keep the attention fixed upon the real situation and to prevent it from returning surreptitiously to the self with consolations of self-pity, resentment, fantasy or despair" (89). Very few characters, in Greene's oeuvre, manage to keep this kind of attention on a permanent basis. The second question remains the most problematic in Greene's ethical conceptualization, as it touches upon the ultimate paradox of Christian ethics: the universal nature of *caritas*, or love. This will be the object of the last chapter in this book.

5
Commitment

This chapter explores the notion of commitment, considered as the turning point in the narrative pattern under analysis. The oppositional communitarian logic suggested by Greene's use of the concept is the critical pivot around which the chapter is organized: being committed, in Greene's novels, involves an engagement with some form of communal organization, against the influence of another, conflicting community. Therefore, an exploration of commitment in Greene's work necessarily involves an analysis of the communities with which his characters are in contact: those they try to escape from, and those they end up joining. The adoption of some form of commitment on the part of the main characters, as I argue in the next section, is normally articulated in terms of communal dynamics. Thus, they often undergo an inner transformation that springs from their acknowledgment of the values and worldviews of a "new" community (as opposed to their community of origin, of a national, professional, or familial kind). Commitment, in this sense, is for the typical Greenean hero a form of ideological or spiritual replenishment, and it is triggered by what Adorno calls an "ethics of responsibility" toward others. As was argued in the previous chapter, it is compassion for another human being that effects a crucial transformation in the Greenean hero.

Another aspect to be accounted for is the connection between commitment and action, as commitment remains a crucial factor in the hero's passage from paralysis to agency. Once committed, Greene's heroes are asked to act. Abandoning peace, as was argued in Chapter 1, is not only the condition on which narrative development is set, but also the springboard for ethical growth. The nature of characters' committed action is precisely what precipitates the narrative toward its denouement, normally involving a sacrifice.

In the last section of this chapter, a further narrative issue will be analyzed: the problematic narrative rendering of the passage from detachment to commitment, in order to illustrate how Greene's novels continually call attention to the impossibility of narrating explicitly the moment when commitment takes place.

Community and commitment

The narrative plot of *The Quiet American* epitomizes the treatment of commitment in Greene's narrative: Two characters, Fowler and Pyle, are introduced as representing diverging perspectives on the political issue of foreign intervention in Vietnam. Whereas the latter is openly committed to the cause of American interventionism to prevent the country's downfall into communism, the former expresses his reluctance to intervene in any way in the lives of others, and mocks the other's naïve commitment: "I don't take sides. I'll still be reporting, whoever wins" (96). As the story advances, Fowler's initial reluctance is transformed into a deep involvement in the conflict from which he had remained neutral, to the point that the initial dialectics between the two characters is reversed, and Fowler emerges as the most truly committed of the two: "I had become as *engagé* as Pyle, and it seemed to me that no decision would ever be simple again" (183).

The pattern thus sketched is repeated in Greene's fiction again and again. What changes is the specific designation of the cause or collectivity to which the main character commits at some point in the story. Two main causes for commitment are particularly common in his novels: first, a religious one, expressed through the language of Catholic faith, and enacted in charitable action directed to others; and second, an openly political one, which involves taking sides in some form of conflict in which the character was not directly involved when the story began. Examples of the first may be found in *The Power and the Glory*, *The End of the Affair*, and *A Burnt-Out Case*, whereas the second has characters like Brown becoming involved in revolutionary action against Papa Doc's dictatorship in Haiti, in *The Comedians*; Eduardo Plarr against Stroessner's dictatorship in Paraguay in *The Honorary Consul*, Fowler against American intervention in Vietnam in *The Quiet American*, or D. against the national side in the Spanish Civil War in *The Confidential Agent*. The political version of this pattern underscores a crucial element in Greene's understanding of commitment: it is necessarily an adversarial act; it happens always "against" an enemy faction or against the established powers.[1] However, the same oppositional nature may be observed in the so-called religious novels: in *The Power and the Glory*, commitment to religious ministry takes place in the context of political persecution of church members by the Mexican government; in *A Burnt-Out Case*, Querry's commitment to the missionary community in Congo clearly upsets the balance of the colonial community epitomized by Rycker; even in *The End of the Affair*, probably the most "domestic" of Greene's novels in this sense, Sarah's commitment to her newly acquired faith contains this adversarial element, since it emerges against the desire of her lover and narrator, Bendrix.

A further category may be considered, including several texts by Greene in which characters apparently escape the realm of the political, or rather try to disentangle themselves from the complications of political allegiances. *England Made Me*, *The Third Man*, and *Our Man in Havana* may be cited as examples. However, in all these cases we find characters acquiring a sense of ethical responsibility as a consequence of their experience as victims of larger, established powers, of an economic or political kind. Their decisions to act will have disastrous consequences for those structures, and they may be said to spring from the need to respond to what is perceived as an ethical imperative.

The character's commitment, therefore, involves his becoming attached to a community of partisans against another, normally hegemonic one. At the outset, the hero may be said to have been (unwillingly) included in a community without clear goals or ideological stance, a neutral community. In some cases, as for Fowler, a cynical detachment from the situation, or at best neutrality regarding it, is demanded. A liberal individual, an ethical monad untouched by others, the Greenean hero moves freely in a territory where the powerful abuse the weak before his very eyes. Many of Greene's heroes could be depicted in the terms used to describe Anthony Farrant in *England Made Me*: "he was free as she could never be free; he had no responsibilities, other people would always do the fighting for him" (166). Characters representing the possibility of a permanent neutrality in situations of conflict constantly appear in Greene's fiction: Rycker in *A Burnt-Out Case*, the cowardly renegade priest in *The Power and the Glory*, the cynical and drunkard journalist Granger in *The Quiet American*. One of the side effects of the hero's commitment in all these cases is the discovery of an authentic community whose existence had been dismissed before, and the realization that the previous situation of detachment was a lesser form of life. The passage from detachment to commitment, therefore, entails a symbolic reinvestment of models of community as sites of spiritual or ideological – ultimately ethical – replenishment. The terminology used by Greene to dramatize this activates the organicist metaphors of roots, home, and brotherhood.

The communal logic of commitment is in fact inscribed in the word itself. The "com-" in community is the "com-" in commitment. The etymology of the word refers to the Latin verb *committere*, meaning "to connect, entrust," from *com + mittere*, to send. Notions of loyalty, promise, obligation, purpose, and action are invoked in dictionary definitions of the term. The passage from isolation to commitment involves allegiance to a community of people that is already constituted. In Greene's fiction, characters commit to people, not to abstract ideas. In his texts, an oppositional dialectics is often established between two kinds of commitment: a fake or naïve one, in which an individual may be said to commit to an ideal, and an authentic one, in which the individual commits to others. This notion is most clearly formulated in *The Ministry of Fear* in connection to Dr Forester, whose "abstract love of humanity" is identified as the basis of his depravity: "One can't love humanity. One can only love people" (166).

The same criticism is present in Fowler's opinions about Pyle's conviction in *The Quiet American*. From the beginning of the novel, we are told that Pyle's desire to become involved pre-exists his arrival in Vietnam, and that it is not specifically addressed to human beings: "He was absorbed already in the dilemmas of Democracy and the responsibilities of the West; he was determined – I learnt that very soon – *to do good, not to any individual person but to a country, a continent, a world*" (18; emphasis added). As we will learn in the course of the story, this commitment to abstract principles will have disastrous consequences, because it leads to a consideration of the Vietnamese as little more than pawns in a chess game, easily rendered as collateral damage in the larger geopolitical field. Thus, from Fowler's perspective, Pyle's actions exert a kind of violence on reality to make it fit a preconceived political stance: "He gets hold of an idea and then alters every situation to fit the idea" (167–68). Throughout the novel, and particularly during their conversation on the night they are forced to spend together hiding in a watchtower near Tanyin, Pyle's abstract political convictions are contrasted to Fowler's concern with individuals. First, he argues that the Vietnamese are not interested in the ideas of progress, democracy, and individuality implicit in Pyle's political project for the country: "You and your like are trying to make a war with the help of people who just aren't interested" (94). Pyle's idealism is opposed to Fowler's materialism. When the former tries to argue that "they don't want Communism" (94), the latter replies that "they want enough rice" (ibid.). When Pyle argues about freedom of thought, Fowler replies "Thought's a luxury. Do you think the peasant sits and thinks of God and Democracy when he gets inside his mud hut at night?" (95).

Fowler's rejection of "isms and ocracies" (95) is echoed in many of Greene's novels. In general terms, his characters tend to distrust totalizing and organized ideological systems of a political or religious kind. Thus, in *A Burnt-Out Case* Querry rejects Rycker's apparent religious virtuosity as pharisaic with the same strength with which, at the end of *Our Man in Havana*, Wormold refutes national allegiance as a motive for commitment in favor of a smaller model of community: "I can't believe in anything bigger than a home, or anything vaguer than a human being" (226). In fact, it is curious to note that two of Greene's best espionage novels – the aforementioned *Our Man in Havana* and *The Human Factor* – in which Cold War political polarizations provide the force field in which the stories are to be developed, feature protagonists who become involved in bloc dynamics only to discover that true allegiance is only possible to individuals, not to countries. At the end of *The Human Factor*, Sarah remembers Castle: "He said once I was his country" (263).

The nature of commitment in Greene's work, I would claim, is ultimately ethical. Even when it is articulated or framed in terms of political or religious discourse, the legitimacy of these discourses is explicitly linked to their ethical import. Thus, Fowler's decision to interfere in the political affairs of Vietnam is not so much triggered by an ideological conviction but by the way in which he has been shaken by the horror of seeing the Vietnamese killed in a set-up terrorist attack orchestrated by the US government. Similarly, Querry is awakened to charity and love for others not through Catholic doctrine but through his emotional involvement with the lepers at the Congo mission.

Greene's understanding of commitment implies that it is not possible to find rational justification for it, but that commitment is rather a matter of personal and emotional preference. In *Ways of Escape*, he included a quotation from Herbert Read that summarizes this view: "At certain moments the individual is carried beyond his rational self, on to another ethical plane, where his actions are judged by new standards. The impulse which moves him to irrational action I have called the sense of glory" (44). His, it could be argued, is clearly an emotivist ethical stance that takes as its departure point the idea that claims to objectivity and impersonality in the field of moral action are no longer possible (MacIntyre 22–23). As Bosco has claimed, for Greene's characters "actions motivated by love and not law are the moral compass" (144). The ethical realm in Greene unfolds as a process of discovery that beneath the exhausted moral framework of liberal England stands a truer, irrational but more authentic dimension of individual action grounded on meaningful ethical terms that have a necessary adversarial and inaugural character. The moment of engagement or commitment in Greene's fiction is usually codified as the acknowledgment of an ethical imperative through which those terms like "compassion" or "commitment" are meaningfully reinvested in the communal logic of attention to others (Weil, Murdoch). Moreover, as will be argued in the last section of this chapter, the lack of rational justification for commitment is a key feature of Greene's textual representation of the ethical dimension, in which lack of understanding of one's own motives becomes the starting point for the concern for others:

> To take responsibility for oneself is to avow the limits of any self-understanding, and to establish these limits not only as a condition for the subject, but as the predicament of the human community [...] reason's limit is the sign of our humanity [...] My own foreignness to myself is, paradoxically, the source of my ethical connection to others. (Butler *Giving* 83–84)

In *The Quiet American*, Fowler underlines the idea of a personal transformation: "I *had become* as engagé as Pyle, and it seemed to me that no decision would ever be simple again" (183; emphasis added). Fowler's account of himself is, in this light, an attempt to explain this transformation. In the course of the story, Pyle's innocent commitment to his cause will be contrasted to Fowler's awakening to responsibility. I consider that Adorno's distinction between an ethics of conviction and an ethics of responsibility is apposite in this context (*Problems* 7), and it could illuminate the key aspects of Greene's view of what constitutes a genuine ethical commitment. Pyle is a genuine moral subject in the Kantian sense, someone for whom morality is a matter of conviction, who acts out of his own free will, independently of the empirical circumstances surrounding a particular situation (Adorno 84). Fowler's ethics, on the other hand, spring from his sense of responsibility to others in specific circumstances. He refuses to have principles that may be applied on a universal basis, but is rather guided by an emotional response to the specific case. There is a sense of obligation that impels him to act in a certain way, that binds him to external conditions and external consequences that make him dependent on something which is not reason (Adorno 85).

In Greene's view, the only possible ethical commitment is the one springing from individual, emotional attachment. The experience in

Tanyin may be said to have changed Fowler, in that he realizes that involvement is not necessarily the outcome of individual will, the product of a conscious decision on the part of the subject. The progress of his involvement, however, is represented as a complex one in the novel. On the one hand, it may be said to relate to the key idea of *responsibility*. By the end of the night, when Pyle has saved Fowler's life, the latter realizes that their presence in the watchtower may have resulted in the two soldiers' death (their escape has called the Viets' attention to the tower, and hence to the hiding soldiers): "I was responsible for that voice crying in the dark: I had prided myself on detachment, on not belonging to this war, but those wounds had been inflicted by me just as though I had used the sten, as Pyle had wanted to do" (113). Fowler draws a connection here between responsibility, commitment, and the pain caused to others.[2] A little later, the same point is made in connection to personal relations, which he compares to war: "I thought 'how much you pride yourself on being *dégagé*, the reporter, not the leader-writer, and what a mess you make behind the scenes'. The other kind of war is more innocent than this. One does less damage with a mortar" (119). Immediately before, he had compared the pain he inflicts on Phuong by lying to her about his wife's decision to refuse his petition of divorce to the pain he had indirectly inflicted on the soldier from the tower: "Unfortunately the innocent are always involved in any conflict. Always, everywhere, there is some voice crying from a tower" (119).

On the other hand, Fowler's assumption of responsibility regarding the death of the soldier and later Phuong's potential suffering is given an explanation which seems to contradict any attempt to interpret Fowler's behavior in the course of the novel as a conversion to ethical commitment. He explicitly relates his desire to help others, to see them happy, to his own selfish peace of mind:

> I know myself, and I know the depth of my selfishness. I cannot be at ease (and to be at ease is my chief wish) if someone else is in pain, visibly or audibly or tactually. Sometimes this is mistaken by the innocent for unselfishness, when all I am doing is sacrificing a small good – in this case postponement in attention to my hurt – for the sake of a greater good, a peace of mind when I need think only of myself. (114)

Greene's taste for moral paradox may be said to work at its best here. The events in the novel seem to suggest that this selfishness is actually the source of an ethics of responsibility: is it possible to claim that only through the attempt to eliminate one's guilt can one really attend to the other? The key is offered by one of the secondary characters in the novel, Captain Trouin, who sees Fowler as more engaged than he would admit. When the latter states for the nth time "I'm not involved" (151), the other's answer is: "You will all be. One day" (151). Like Querry resisting Rycker's attempts to attach a label or a definition to him in *A Burnt-Out Case*, Fowler also rejects Captain Trouin's view that "one day something will happen. You will take a side" (ibid.). The Captain anticipates one crucial aspect of the notion of involvement advocated by Greene in the novel, the fact that it is not the result of a rational decision: "It's not a matter of reason or justice. We all get involved in a moment of emotion and then we cannot get out. War and love – they have always been compared" (152). The logic of Trouin's argument is anti-Kantian, in the sense that he traces the source of commitment and ethics to the emotional, the irrational, to what cannot be accounted for in rational terms, nor related to the universality of a categorical imperative. Commitment, in the view espoused by Greene in the novel, emerges from emotional attachment and from attention to the particular human being: "Suffering is not increased by numbers: one body can contain all the suffering the world can feel" (183).

The need for roots

It is generally agreed among literary critics that the frequency with which characters in Greene's work tend toward some form of commitment is one of his most persistent narrative plotlines. They diverge as to the nature of the cause – religious or political – to which the hero commits. Against the grain of these readings, my understanding of Greene's conception of commitment puts the stress on the "com-," that is, on the communal dynamics involved in any act of commitment. In Greene's work, I'd claim, characters do not commit to causes or ideologies, but to communities, to people. The question as to what it is that the Greenean hero commits to needs to be rephrased, then, in the following terms: To whom do Greene's characters commit? From the point of view of the characters themselves, this may be formulated as "Who am I with?"

In a celebrated passage from *The Quiet American*, the Communist leader Mr Heng tells the protagonist: "One has to take sides. If one is to remain human" (174). The sentence calls attention to another fundamental aspect of Greene's understanding of commitment: in every "com-" there is also an "anti-" involved. In other words, commitment in his novels always involves the existence of another community, opposed to the one chosen by the hero, so to speak, against which it constructs its communal identity and whose existence is antagonistic to the first one. This entails that the collectivity to which the typical Greenean hero commits is engaged in an oppositional communitarian logic. Furthermore, the community to which the hero becomes attached is normally at a disadvantage regarding the other, hegemonic one. In many cases, we are thinking about an ethnic minority, an ideological resistance group of rebels or terrorists, a persecuted religious group, or simply a collectivity of social outcasts. In this context, the act of commitment is also one whereby the hero becomes explicitly dissociated from the hegemonic institutional framework or the social norm. Until the moment when commitment is dramatized in some act of compassion, the hero remains neutral or ethically detached from the oppositional dialectics developing between the two. In most cases, he is expected to remain neutral while implicitly being claimed by the realm of social normality as one of its own. After becoming *engagé*, it becomes impossible for him to remain unnoticed by the antagonistic community. The committed hero then becomes an enemy of the state, or an enemy of the class/country/race that claimed him as one of its own. Thus, the hero is turned into the antagonist of the establishment, and will often be persecuted for this reason.

Although his rendering of commitment rarely reproduces the discourse of national allegiance per se, it is curious to note how Greene's articulation of its logic tends to draw on the rhetoric of nationalistic myths of identity, brotherhood, and authenticity. The discursive model on which Greene seems to draw is close to Frantz Fanon's articulation of the native communities as opposed to colonialist liberal individualism:

> The colonialist bourgeoisie hammered into the colonized mind the notion of a society of individuals where each is locked in his subjectivity, where wealth lies in thought. [...] Involvement in the organization of the struggle will already introduce him to a different vocabulary. "Brother," "sister," "comrade" are words outlawed by the colonialist bourgeoisie. (Fanon 11)

Greene's understanding of commitment invokes a discourse of allegiance to organic communities expressed in the two key metaphors of "home" and "roots." These two terms are used prominently by Greene in many of his novels, and through them the nationalistic schemata are brought to the realm of romantic theories of organic community.

In *The Captain and the Enemy*, Greene articulates explicitly the issue of individual allegiance in terms of the identification of what is "home."

Throughout the story we see how Victor, abducted by the Captain and renamed Jim, reassigns this term to the house where he has come to live through a long process of adaptation: "I had never thought of my aunt's flat as home" (34); "So I went to the place they so wanted me to call home" (40); "what I had learned to call home" (72). Victor, like most characters in Greene's fiction, is a displaced, homeless individual in search of a place that he can call home.

The Captain and the Enemy keeps the discourse on home at the domestic level, but most often in Greene's work, the search for home will have a larger, national dimension. Such is the case in *England Made Me*, where the twins Kate and Anthony Farrant, British subjects living in Stockholm, discuss their homelessness: "'I'm going home', Anthony said. 'Home?' He said with irritation: 'I mean London – I don't suppose my room's still free. I know we haven't a home. It's a manner of speaking'" (184). While Anthony still claims his allegiance to London as "home," Kate has been struggling to make a new home in Stockholm and bring her brother closer to her: "It was the culmination of all her plans, to have him here, making himself at home beside her desk, 'a home from home'" (138).[3] In *The Quiet American*, the hero's attachment to Vietnam is expressed in terms of his abandonment of an earlier notion of home (in London, with his estranged wife) for the sake of a new one:

> When I first came I counted the days of my assignment, like a schoolboy marking off the days of term; I thought I was tied to what was left of a Bloomsbury square and the 73 bus passing the portico of Euston and springtime in the local in Torrington Place. Now the bulbs would be out in the square garden, and I didn't care a damn [...] I wanted Phuong, and *my home had shifted its ground eight thousand miles*. (25; emphasis added)

In addition to the well-known case of *The Quiet American*, there are two other novels by Greene in which the narrative pattern under discussion in this book is predominantly formulated in terms of a character's passage from the condition of émigré or exiled to that of integrated member of a national community immersed in a struggle for its identity and political freedom.[4] These are *The Comedians* and *The Honorary Consul*. The characters of the two novels, Jones and Eduardo Plarr, may be said to become loyal members of a national community to which, at the beginning of their respective stories, they did not belong. The political background against which both stories are set underscores the communitarian articulation through which commitment is expressed in them. Thematically, both novels display a series of recurrent elements which can in turn be traced back to other Greene novels. The foreign setting is the most evident of these, showing Greene's knowledge of the situation in several American countries during the 1960s and 1970s: *The Comedians* is set in Haiti during "Papa Doc" Duvalier's regime, after the creation of the Tontons Macoute in 1959; *The Honorary Consul* is set on the Argentina–Paraguay border during Alfredo Stroessner's dictatorship, after the 1967 constitution which gave him full power over Paraguay. The political changes in Cuba are also described by the narrator in the opening pages of *Our Man in Havana*, which also features an émigré as protagonist: "Tourists were sadly reduced nowadays in number, for the Presidential [last stages of Batista's regime] was creaking dangerously towards its end. There had always been unpleasant doings out of sight ..." (21). The oppressive regimes in the three countries are set against the backdrop of a resistance movement or a counterforce trying to overcome those in power. A political polarization is thus established, around which secondary characters are classified according to their position regarding power.

In the three novels, the main character has foreign origins, and the fact that he has established himself in that particular country is said to be the product of chance rather than any other motivation. In *The Comedians*, Brown wonders: "Why was I here? I was here because of a picture-postcard from my mother which could easily have gone astray" (224). Neither Brown nor Plarr feel any kind of attachment to the place they live in. Curiously, however, they both have landed in their respective adoptive countries through their parents. Although he hardly likes his medical practice in northern Argentina, Plarr stays there because it helps him keep his mother, who lives in Buenos Aires, at a convenient distance. Brown, like Henry Pulling would do later in *Travels with my Aunt*, is requested by his mother to visit him on the other side of the world.

The main characters in these novels may be described in terms of what Stephen K. Land has called "final phase heroes," whose main characteristic is their withdrawal from conflicts around them. The protagonists of at least five of Greene's novels may be placed in this category: *The Quiet American*, *A Burnt-Out Case*, *Our Man in Havana*, *The Comedians*, and *The Honorary Consul*. All of them are set in sites of political conflict and humanitarian disaster in which they do not want to take part: Vietnam, Congo, Cuba, Haiti, and Paraguay, respectively. Like Fowler, Querry, or Wormold, they are "deliberately withdrawn to the sidelines, out of the conflict, to a position from which they may be spectators but which isolates them from involvement" (Land 77).

Both Brown and Plarr display the same lack of attachment from what is happening around them as Fowler does in *The Quiet American*. Brown's detachment, for instance, is contrasted with Smith's capacity to empathize with others' causes through a shared vocabulary: "'I wonder if we ought to involve ourselves any further'. 'We are involved', Mr Smith said with pride, and I knew he was thinking in the big terms I could not recognize, like Mankind, Justice, the Pursuit of Happiness" (112). Brown, this dialogue implies, lacks the belief in the terms that could help him to feel a deeper sympathy toward those involved in the resistance against the Tontons Macoute.[5] What Greene's novel explores is to what extent involvement can happen in the absence of such belief. As has been said, this is something he already hinted at in the final pages of *Our Man in Havana*, where the languages of political allegiance and personal loyalty to a family or to another individual are confronted: "I can't believe in anything bigger than a home, or anything vaguer than a human being" (226). Earlier in the novel, Beatrice reports to Wormold what she has told the Chief: "A country is more a family than a parliamentary system" (225). The familiar/personal is here given precedence over the interests of a political system. "Home," a key term in both passages, is used as the rationale against which to measure any communitarian articulation.

As suggested above, Greene's deployment of the discursive tools of nationalism may remind the reader of Fanon's arguments when he claims that when peoples unite in struggle against oppression, "the community has already triumphed and exudes its own light" (12). However, whereas Fanon describes the unifying effects that political consciousness may have on the native peoples involved, and talks about communities resembling "a religious brotherhood, a church, or a mystical doctrine" (84), Greene is much more skeptical about the kind of communal calling that may eventually demand from the individual a total surrender to the cause.

Considering the interaction between the languages of family and politics, particularly in the development of a nationalist vocabulary, one may think of Tönnies' claim, in *Community and Civil Society* (1887), that "the archetype of all community-based unions is the family itself, in all its manifestations" (204). Tönnies' romantic sociology of the political community links it to the organic elements of "blood, soil and spirit" (ibid.).[6] The town, village, and nation are, in this articulation, structures "contained within the idea of the family, and all proceed from it as the universal expression of the reality of Community" (Tönnies 36). The echoes of this rhetoric can be found in the abundant imagery, in Greene's novels, related to "cords" (evoking the biological link of blood), "roots" (evoking the vegetal attachment to the soil), and "love" (whereby spirits are supposed to commune). As I will try to illustrate in what follows, Greene explores the conjunction of the languages of nation and family ties, and the difficulties experienced by characters who seem to be immune to this rhetoric. His two main characters in *The Comedians* and *The Honorary Consul*, Brown and Plarr, are the sons of two exiles – the French Resistance heroine Yvette and the British liberal Henry Plarr – who managed to become *engagé*, even at the cost of their own family. Unlike them, however, their children seem incapable of nationalist identification with a land or a people: "I should never have come to this country, I was a stranger. My mother had taken a black lover, she had been involved, but somewhere years ago I had forgotten how to be involved in anything. Somehow somewhere I had lost completely the capacity to be concerned" (*Comedians* 183). The constant references to broken families in both novels – as both Plarr and Brown were abandoned by their heroic parents – seems to imply, in terms close to Tönnies' argumentation, that in the absence of family ties, any other model of community is not possible.

The opening passage in *The Comedians* sets the tone regarding Brown's skepticism about the nationalist rhetoric of "homeland" by contrasting the obscure death of Jones with the public monuments to generals and statesmen commemorating national pride:

> When I think of all the grey memorials erected in London to equestrian generals, the heroes of old colonial wars, and to frock-coated politicians who are even more deeply forgotten, I can find no reason to mock the modest stone that commemorates Jones on the far side of the international road which he failed to cross in a country far from home. (1)

The passage reminds us of Joseph Conrad's similar skepticism about public monuments in *Nostromo*, and successfully introduces Jones as a Byronic figure, who gave his life for a foreign homeland: "At least he paid for the monument – however unwillingly – with his life, while the generals as a rule came home safe and paid, if at all, with the blood of their men" (*Comedians* 1). Brown, with an irony that will only be appreciated as we read further into the story, concludes: "Whenever my rather bizarre business takes me north to Monte Cristi and I pass the stone, I feel a certain pride that my action helped to raise it" (ibid.). Two key issues in the novel are announced in this passage: the questioning of the notion of home and the idea of sacrifice inherent to commitment.

In *The Comedians*, Greene insists on drawing distinctions between two kinds of people: those who have a sense of home, who may be said to have roots linking them to a specific place and a set of ideas associated to how people should live in that place, and those who don't.[7] Borrowing the terms used by William Thomas Hill in the monograph *Graham Greene's Wanderers* (1999), the novel distinguishes between "dwellers" and "wanderers."[8] Brown, the narrator of the novel, declares himself to be one of the second kind: "my roots would never go deep enough anywhere to make me a home or make me secure with love" (223). Brown's statement suggests the idea of "roots" in connection to the realms of place and community, the contiguous feelings of home and love. Roots may link you to a place or to a people. In the novel, several characters, such as Philipot or Magiot, illustrate how in nationalist discourse both – land and people – come to represent exactly the same thing, through an assimilation of the community to the land they inhabit that has clear romantic resonances.[9] Against the sense of stability implicit in the idea of being attached to a territory, Brown highlights his lack of anchoring to a place: "Perhaps there is an advantage in being born in a city like Monte Carlo, *without roots*, for one accepts more easily what comes" (283; emphasis added). When, early in the novel, he describes the dawn at the Hotel Trianon, the sense of permanence he associates with the place is contrasted to the lack of it in himself: "The first colours touched the garden, deep green and then deep red – transience was my pigmentation" (223). The lack of a sense of "home" is expressed again as a lack of pigmentation later in the novel: "*We – the uncoloured –* were all of us too far away from home" (161; emphasis added).

Beyond the nationalistic overtones, Greene's use of the term "roots" may also be read in wider ethical terms, expressing the need to commit to other human beings. In *The Need for Roots*, Simone Weil uses the vegetal metaphor to explain the concept of obligation of one human being regarding others. This obligation, she explains in her introduction, is directed toward the fulfillment of man's earthly needs, either physical or moral (7). If those needs are not satisfied, she claims, "we fall little by little into a state more or less resembling death, more or less akin to a purely vegetative existence" (7). Read in the light of theories of community, Weil's notion of obligation may be said to be the constituting force of any communitarian articulation. Community, she claims, is the structure through which reciprocal obligations are enacted, feeding basic human needs: "We owe a cornfield respect, not because of itself, but because it is food for mankind. In the same way, we owe our respect to a collectivity, of whatever kind – country, family or any other – not for itself, but it is food for a certain number of human souls" (8).[10] The problem in Weil's understanding of roots as the representation of reciprocal obligations shaping community models, however, is that she doesn't offer a solution for the potential conflict arising when the same individual is attached to different obligations, or when the obligations of different individuals regarding their respective communities clash against one another. About this possibility, she admits: "Unfortunately, we possess no method for diminishing this incompatibility. We cannot even be sure that the idea of an order in which all obligations would be compatible with one another isn't itself a fiction" (*Roots* 10–11). This is precisely the terrain of Greene's fiction, which repeatedly focuses on situations in which the incompatibility between different obligations, or the conflict between different individuals' obligations, is exposed.

On the other hand, as Greene also repeatedly illustrates, withdrawing from our obligations to others does not work as a solution. In this, he coincides with Weil, who claims that "whoever, so as to simplify problems, denies the existence of certain obligations has, in his heart, made a compact with crime" (*Roots* 10). The absence of any sense of obligation toward others, Weil argues, makes us less than human. Her conclusion comes very close to Mr Heng's words to Fowler at the end of Greene's *The Quiet American*: "One is to take sides, if one is to remain human" (174). This diagnosis is shared by critics who have noted how Brown's new job as an undertaker at the end of *The Comedians* may work as a metaphor for the idea that he does not belong to the realm of the living: "There is no commitment to anything, not to love, not to religion, not to God, not to innocence. It is right that at the novel's end Brown becomes Fernandez's partner in the undertaking business [...] He belongs to the world of the dead and not that of the living" (De Vitis "Hollower" 136; see also Kulshrestha).

Brown's most explicit reflection on this issue in the novel comes near the end, in his attempt to justify his lack of attachment as a paradoxical form of attachment itself, proposing what may be termed, echoing Alphonso Lingis, a community of those who have nothing in common (Lingis 4), a "community of the rootless":

> The rootless have experienced like all the others, the temptation of sharing the security of a religious creed or a political faith, and

for some reasons we have turned the temptation down. We are the faithless; we admire the dedicated, the Doctor Magiots and the Mr. Smiths, for their courage and integrity, for their fidelity to a cause, but through timidity, or through lack of sufficient zest, we find ourselves the only ones truly committed – committed to the whole world of evil and of good, to the wise and to the foolish, to the indifferent and to the mistaken. We have chosen nothing except to go on living. (283–84)

Brown's repeated use of the first-person plural in this passage – "we are the faithless," "we admire the dedicated," "we find ourselves," "we have chosen" – reinforces the sense of belonging to a community of those who are together not in their sharing religious or political ideas, but in their lack of such belief. Moreover, the dichotomy operating in the passage is presented in morally ambiguous terms: whereas the committed are praised for their courage and integrity, the possibility of committing is described by Brown as a "temptation," as if it were indeed a weakness on the part of those who commit. The last part of the passage duplicates the structure of commitment by paradoxically stating that, in fact, those who are not committed are really "the *only* ones *truly* committed." But committed to what? Brown seems to imply, in his references to "the whole world of evil and of good, to the wise and to the foolish, to the indifferent and to the mistaken," that only those who are not blinded by any totalizing discourse are capable of perceiving the imperfect nature of the world and of human beings. Instead of limited versions of faith in specific causes, he seems to propose an ultimate form of universal commitment to survival, to life itself. Brown's relationship with Jones fits exactly into this pattern. Whereas in the course of the novel Brown insists on distinguishing himself from others – for instance when Marta tells him he is like her father, and he replies "what could I possibly have in common with a war criminal responsible for so many unidentified deaths" (231) – at the end he admits his kinship with Jones in terms of their commitment to survival: "It was like meeting an unknown brother [...] We had both been thrown into the water to sink or swim, and swim we had – we had swum from very far apart to come together in a cemetery in Haiti" (269).

As De Vitis notes, Brown is the only one who remains uncommitted till the end ("Hollower" 135). Moreover, as the narrator of the story, he makes great efforts to convince the reader that other characters' causes for commitment are naïve or unjustified, showing a distance from other people's concerns which reflects his own incapacity to commit to anything except, in his own words, staying alive. Greene's ethical stand-point, however, may be said to legitimate the actions of those who com-mit, by skillfully playing with the unreliability of the narrative voice, a technique he had already experimented with in *The End of the Affair* and *The Quiet American*, where the ethical positions established through Bendrix's and Fowler's narratives are called into question in the light of the events we learn from them. In *The Comedians*, as Maria Couto has argued: "The narrative validates Philipot's action in a paradoxical rep-resentation. Greene's art consists in his ability to reveal the validity of Philipot's consciousness through his narrator, who keeps himself clearly outside the framework of struggle" (181). Similarly, the Smiths are shown to have the same innocent belief in their cause that Pyle exhib-ited in *The Quiet American*, even if Brown makes them look ridiculous and blind to the Haitian reality of which they are witnesses.[11] Jones, finally, who had been suspect in Brown's eyes from the beginning, is said to have spurious motives in wanting to help the rebels with their training in the mountains. In the end, however, he will sacrifice his life in order to help them to escape to the Dominican Republic. Thus, he provides a secular version of the Whisky Priest's double nature, suggest-ing that it is his actions that matter, independently of his motivation.

The fluidity of identities in *The Comedians* is thus resolved through a plot that forces characters to take a stance. The question "Who am I?" is here explicitly reshaped in communal terms as "Who am I with?" Similarly, in *The Honorary Consul*, the issues of identity, community, and commitment are dramatized as one single problem. David J. Leigh has argued that *The Honorary Consul* is not only a political novel, but one about a man who "searches for his identity" (13). The first few pages of the novel trace his personal evolution from childhood to adult life in a double key: in terms of his attachment to his mother and father, and in terms of his nationality. The languages of family and nation interweave constantly in the novel. The opening passage portrays a breaking point in Eduardo Plarr's family life: the moment when his father said goodbye to him and his mother, sent to Argentina to escape from Stroessner's dictatorship. At that time, we are told, Plarr seemed to have no doubts about his identity: "Doctor Plarr had considered himself in those days quite as Spanish as his mother, while his father was very noticeably English-born" (1). In those early years, the character clearly identifies himself with his Paraguayan nationality, whereas his British ancestry is regarded with the same distance attributed to his relation-ship with his father: "the legendary island of snow and fog, the country of Dickens and of Conan-Doyle [...] When Doctor Plarr as a boy read a novel of Dickens he read it as a foreigner might do" (2). It will be only as an adult that he will feel the need to put some distance between his mother in Buenos Aires and himself, as he confesses to his mistress: "I left Buenos Aires to get away as far as possible from my mother" (4). Once in Corrientes, in northern Argentina, he starts to seek the company of Englishmen: "Doctor Plarr, who every ten years, without quite knowing why, renewed his English passport, felt a sudden desire for company which was not Spanish" (4). Therefore, Plarr's search for identity may be said to oscillate between "his Paraguayan mother, a mother whose character embodies all the vices of the urban bourgeoisie so that her self-indulgence, both emotional and material, contrasts with the austere idealism of her English husband who stayed back in Asunción to help in the struggle against repression" (Couto 186).

Read in the light of this family structure, Plarr's involvement in the rebel struggle against Stroessner entails an attempt to reconnect with his memories of his father and to understand his actions. As David Leigh has noted, "The image of *father*, in fact, ties together the entire novel" (17). Perhaps the moment when his personal memories are projected into current events comes most clearly when he starts to see in Charley Fortnum, accidentally kidnapped by the rebels, a father figure: "When he tried to substitute Henry Plarr's face for Charley Fortnum's he found his father's features had been almost eliminated by the years" (162).

As in *The Comedians* and *Travels with My Aunt*, the turning point in these characters' lives comes through the recovery of family links thought to be broken. In *The Honorary Consul*, the moment is given explicit attention, described as the act of stepping into uncharted territory, a common metaphor in Greene's work: "He couldn't move one step in either direction without falling deeper into the darkness of involvement or guilt" (172–73). In *The Comedians*, Brown discovers that his mother, whom he thought was a "comedian," detached from the serious issues that usually move other people, had in fact been awarded a medal for her involvement in the French resistance during World War II. Plarr is confronted with the truth about his father that he had been ignoring since he was a child: the fact that despite being an Englishman, he was deeply involved in the resistance movement against Stroessner, and that he had died in jail trying to escape. In both cases, parents are said to have been involved in a struggle to which they were both, strictly speaking, foreigners. Commitment for Brown and Plarr will be shaped in exactly the same way: they will become involved in the struggle of a people with whom, at least in principle, they have nothing in common.

This means, among other things, that allegiance is not given as part of an innate sense of belonging to a place. Rather it is constructed. The process whereby this transformation is described, however, draws on the language of nationalism: finding one's roots, finding a home. In the case of *The Honorary Consul*, moreover, this is formulated in political terms which are explicitly linked to Ernesto Guevara's doctrine against the fragmentation of American nationalities, in favor of a single pan-American discourse: "South America is our country, Eduardo. Not Paraguay. Not Argentina. You know what Che said: 'The whole continent is my country'" (*Guerrilla* 100).[12] This idea is expressed again by Leon Rivas, pointing to the mutual trust between people from different American countries: "El Tigre [the rebel leader] never thought of us as foreigners here in Argentina. He does not think in terms of Paraguayans, Peruvians, Bolivians, Argentinians. I think he would like to call us all Americans" (207).

Realizing that the only way out of the situation with Fortnum and the rebels is probably death, Plarr still resists admitting his bond with his own father's destiny: "His own death might be one of the errors, for afterwards people would say *he had followed his father's steps*, but they would be wrong – that had not been his intention" (207–8; emphasis added). This realization coincides with his change of attitude regarding the child Clara is expecting – presumably his own son:

> He thought of the tangle of his ancestry, and for the first time in the complexity of that tangle that child became real to him – it was no longer just one more wet piece of flesh like any other torn out of the body with a cord that had to be cut. *This cord could never be cut.* It joined the child to two very different grandfathers – a cane-cutter in Tucumán and an old English liberal who had been shot dead in the yard of a police station in Paraguay. The cord joined it to a father who was a provincial doctor, to a mother from a brothel, to an uncle who had walked away from the cane-fields to disappear into the waste of a continent, to two grandmothers … (208; emphasis added)

As in many of Greene's novels, commitment is fully attained through personal sacrifice: in the attempt to save the lives of Rivas and the rebels, negotiating with Colonel Perez and his men, Plarr is shot by the police. The epilogue to this dramatic climax, with Rivas and Plarr agonizing in the jungle, is the latter's funeral in Corrientes. His final act of commitment is deliberately concealed by the British and American diplomatic corps, who fabricate an official version according to which Plarr would have been "shot down without mercy by a fanatic priest" (253). Doctor Saavedra's obituary ironically acknowledges Plarr's sacrifice, on the basis of this falsified official version:

> My friend, you spoke that night of how best to deepen the ties between the English and the South American communities. How little either of us knew that in a matter of days you would give your own life in that cause. You surrendered everything [...] in the attempt to save those misguided men and your fellow countrymen. (254)

Borrowing Girard's terms on the analysis of sacrifice, Plarr would be the scapegoat through which the community reinstates its stability after the threat represented by the rebel group's action: "The elements of dissension scattered throughout the community are drawn to the person of the sacrificial victim and eliminated, at least temporarily, by its sacrifice" (Girard *Violence* 8). The actual sacrifice of Plarr's life is as important, I would claim, as the official narrative through which it is presented to the community as an act meant to bring concord to "the English and South American communities" (*Honorary* 254).

Similarly, in *The Comedians*, Jones's final sacrifice, which allows the Haitian rebels to cross the border to the Dominican Republic while he stays behind, is wrapped in a heroic narrative of courage concealing the truth about his pretended military record. Instants before the Tontons Macoute attack them, he confesses to Brown that he was never a war hero, but literally a comedian, sent to entertain the troops: "I'm an awful liar, old man [...] I've never been in a jungle in my life – unless you count the Calcutta zoo [...] I was at Imphal, in charge of entertaining the troops" (267–68).

In this sense, both novels are accounts of acts of commitment on the part of people whose real motives remain concealed. Both unveil the fabricated nature of narratives of heroic sacrifice, by pointing to how those sacrifices are often the consequence of "a chain of errors" (*Honorary* 207). This, again, is a recurrent *topos* in Greene's fiction: the crimes at the end of *The Quiet American* and *A Burnt-Out Case*, as well as the political mess at the end of *Our Man in Havana* are incorporated into the hegemonic community through fabricated narratives that conceal the hero's actions, or manipulate them in order to absorb them into a different ideological framework. Thus, the crimes in which Fowler and Querry are involved are labeled as "crimes of passion," hiding the complex motivations behind them. Similarly, the traces of Wormold's actions in Havana are concealed by the secret services in the attempt to maintain the status quo of the political situation in Cuba.

Commitment and narrative ellipsis

In narratological terms, the passage from detachment to commitment on the hero's part may be considered the major narrative crux in Greene's fiction, the kind of event called "kernel" by authors like Seymour Chatman: "They are nodes or hinges in the structure, branching points which force a movement into one of two (or more) possible paths" (Chatman 53). This crucial transformation, however, is rarely articulated in the novels as an explicit change in the characters' attitude motivated by external circumstances or internal thought processes. Rather, it emerges retrospectively in most cases, as something whose exact point of origin is untraceable. Sometimes, commitment is evoked as a form of awakening to a knowledge already contained within the individual but forgotten or buried in the recesses of the mind.

The clearest case of such retrospective unveiling of commitment may be said to appear in *The Quiet American*, the novel in which Greene explored the problem of political commitment in most explicit fashion. Famously, the cynical British reporter Fowler, who spends half of the novel claiming to be "not *engagé*" (96) in the political struggles of 1950s Vietnam, will end up betraying Pyle, the American mentioned in the title, an act that will bend the political situation toward the Communist side. Fowler's passage from detached reporter to engaged political agent may be initially attributed to the triangular love relationship involving the aforementioned Pyle, Fowler, and the Vietnamese girl Phuong. Denouncing Pyle to the Communist leaders is a way of getting rid of his rival, as Inspector Vigot suggests in the novel. The textual rendering of this transformation, however, reveals that there is much more to it than mere jealousy.

We learn of Fowler's decision to intervene in the situation through a statement that makes his commitment appear as a path of no return: "I had become as *engagé* as Pyle, and it seemed to me that no decision would ever be simple again" (183). But when did this happen? Apparently, in the transition between parts 3 and 4 of the novel. Part 3 ends with the carnage of the Place Garnier massacre, from where Fowler leaves unharmed. He has witnessed what his quiet American friend Pyle is willing to do to ensure political control of Vietnam. Part 4 begins apparently without textual ellipsis of any kind, and yet it narrates how Fowler goes directly to visit Mr Heng and asks him: "What can I do, Heng? He's got to be stopped" (173). Heng offers him alternatives: (1) to publish the truth about the American responsibility in the bombing in his newspaper, or (2) to tell the police. Both options are rejected by Fowler as useless, and it is only then that Heng asks him for direct action: "Would you be prepared to help us, Mr Fowler?" (174).

The moment that actually would mark the shift in Fowler's mind, the passage from lack of commitment to direct involvement, is absent from the narration as such. It is left unexplained, and uninterpreted, except through a retrospective account generated in the context of an official truth-exacting process, Fowler's interrogation by Inspector Vigot at the beginning of the fourth part of the novel. The previous chapter ends with the bomb explosion, and with Fowler's reflection on the anonymous dead: "what I remembered was the torso in the square, the baby on its mother's lap" (163). The death of innocent individuals is once more opposed to the ideology that would justify such acts for the sake of a greater good: "How many dead colonels justify a child's or a trishaw driver's death when you are building a national democratic front?" (ibid.). The emphasis on bodies harmed by the bomb is dramatically juxtaposed with the abstract notion of a "national democratic front." What is most interesting about this passage, though, is that it ends with an apparently unrelated note indicating Fowler's subsequent movement: "I stopped a motor-trishaw and told the driver to take me to the Quai Mytho" (163). There is no textual or temporal transition between the above-quoted question and the following sentence. An implicit gap, however, may be said to exist between one and the other, during which a decision has been made, a course of action decided.

When part 4 begins immediately after, we are again in the midst of Fowler's conversation with Vigot, who is speculating on the former's motives for being involved in Pyle's death. One main motive appears to be the most probable: the personal one, led by the frustration of having lost Phuong – "Do you imagine it was revenge for losing one?" (167). When Vigot suggests that he may have got as "mixed up" as Pyle was, Fowler remembers Captain Trouin's words, "What was it he had said? Something about all of us getting involved sooner or later *in a moment of emotion*" (168; emphasis added). I would claim that a moment of emotion is precisely what happens to Fowler in the square, watching the dead and injured by the bomb. His decision is really not a decision, as he feels compelled to act out of love for these people, to respond to a calling placed on him by the people who are not considered to be "sufficiently important" (163) in the schemes for the control of Vietnam.

The strength of Fowler's decision to act, against the grain of his previous neutral stance throughout the story, has seemed so overwhelming to some critics that quite often they have argued that his initial detachment was not sincere, but only a professional façade. In an early reading of the novel, Kenneth Allott and Miriam Faris suggested that Fowler "has never, in any real sense, managed to remain uninvolved" (196).

I'd rather claim that the ethical nature of such passage from detachment to commitment remains a blind spot in the narrative, and that it can only be recognized retrospectively in the attempt to make an account of one's actions. Looking back into a specific moment of the past foregrounds its importance retrospectively, confirming the idea introduced by the narrator Mr Brown in a later novel, *The Comedians*: "There is a point of no return unremarked at the time in most lives" (1).

The same gap in the narration appears in other novels as well. In some cases, it is because the moment of commitment has already happened when the narration begins, so that it is never told in the novel – as in the case of *The Power and the Glory* – whereas in others the point of no return goes unnoticed until after its consequences have become evident, as in *A Burnt-Out Case*. In both kinds of narrative situation, the moment of decision itself seems to be left out of the narration, and it is only understood retrospectively, either in the diegetic present narrating previous events, or in the typical epilogue scenes that Greene often included in his novels.[13] One may speak here about "an effect of retroversion" (Žižek 115; derived from the Lacanian concept of "*point de capiton*") or the Freudian *Nachträglichkeit* or retroactivity: "people become aware of the dynamics of some new system, in which they are seized, only later on and gradually" (Jameson *Postmodernism* xix). I'd argue that the transition from lack of commitment to commitment cannot be represented in an explicit way in Greene's novels, in much the same way as, according to J. Hillis Miller, "Trollope cannot show the transition from not being in love to being in love" (Miller and Wolfreys "Why" 419).[14]

Similarly, in *The Power and the Glory*, Greene creates a double temporal structure in which the story time combines with a series of analepses or flashbacks, meant to provide the reader with information about the Whisky Priest's past life. The novel begins *in media res*, once a life-changing decision has been made, and the Priest has already begun a life of pilgrimage and become a fugitive of Mexican justice. There is a narrative discontinuity created between the analepses telling us about a plump young priest pampered by the bourgeoisie, and the main storyline, where we read about a lean and shabby priest who takes refuge among the lowest classes. This underscores an interpretation of narrative development divided into before and after, a clear schism signaling that, at some point before the novel begins, the Priest made the decision not to run away or to accept new laws and become instead a martyr for the people. From the perspective of how the two parts of the storyline connect, this represents a deviation from expected social behavior in terms of what the other priests living in the region are said to have done. Most importantly, nothing of what we have been told about this plump young priest could have helped readers predict his future conduct, as there is no textual evidence suggesting a psychological transformation or a spiritual or ethical awakening. And yet, the main body of the text focuses on telling the story of a man who has embraced his commitment to others and is carrying it out to its ultimate consequences. Once more, the moment of decision itself, that is to say, the moment when the Priest chose to sacrifice his life of comfort among the bourgeoisie for a life of penury among the poor, is never represented in the novel. This constitutes a gap not only in the narrative timeline, but also in terms of the character's psychological motivation, which is left open by the author.

The problem of representation linked to the moment of commitment seems to be a textual one, not only an ethical one. In the ethical sense, as it has been explored in earlier sections of this chapter, the moment of commitment is a moment of transgression in social-communitarian terms, in which the character overcomes his initial detachment and starts a course of action that contradicts his previous stance regarding the communal tensions portrayed in the novel. In Derridean terms, one could argue that true ethical decisions necessarily have this transgressive character, as they always break with previous moral law and are in this sense singular occasions not regulated by general norms. As expressed by J. Hillis Miller: "Ethical prescription may claim to have a universal basis, but is likely to be no more than the reassertion of unconscious ideological assumptions peculiar to a given society or person at a given time. All situations demanding ethical decision, it may be, are singular, not assimilable to general rules or evaluations" (Miller "How" 271).

From the point of view of the literary conventions of realism, these moments of commitment are also transgressive, in that they upset the psychological construction of character as a coherent textual device. As has been suggested, there seems to be a certain mismatch between the retrospective portrayal of a character like the Whisky Priest and what we read about him in the novel's diegetic present. In several of Greene's novels, this incoherence is dramatized as a conflict between the (old) identity of the character as projected by the community that recognizes him/her as one of its own and the (new) committed identity evinced by his/her actions. In *A Burnt-Out Case*, the journalist Pendleton embodies the frustrating efforts of the community to identify Querry as "*the* Querry*,*" the famous architect, an identity that the character refuses to adopt anymore. In *Our Man in Havana*, the incoherence between the communal construction of individual identity and the individual's self-fashioning is given a comic stance. Wormold is constantly labeled in the text as a fraud by others – "you are a fraud" (200) – and by himself – "I am no secret agent, I'm a fraud" (137) – as he fails to live up to the identity others have created for him. Fabricated narratives superimposed on individual identities are frequent in Greene's novels, and they suggest that the process of communal re-affiliation on the part of the individual tends to lead to discursive strategies covering for apparent psychological inconsistencies. In other words, it is quite frequent on the part of the communities of origin of many of Greene's characters to resist acknowledging these characters' "new" committed selves, and to interpret them as eccentric or abnormal. The colonial communities making up "official versions" of what has happened in *The Honorary Consul* and *A Burnt-Out Case*, or Bendrix reacting to Sarah's diary for the first time in *The End of the Affair*, may be good examples of such communities developing discursive strategies meant to reappropriate individuals who are felt to be falling into the margins of what they would consider "normal" behavior on the part of such individuals.

Moreover, because the committed character contradicts the previous version of the same character offered by the novel, Greene seems to be unable to explain in psychologically consistent terms the thought process leading him/her to such transformation. Fowler, the Whisky Priest, Querry, Jones, Plarr, or Sarah do not progressively come to the conviction to endorse a cause, but are suddenly compelled to become part of a community. Rational causality cannot explain, in the Greenean context, the psychological motivation of commitment. Rather, it is a matter of emotional reaction to the suffering of others that instantly effects this transformation in them. The moment of witnessing the suffering of another human being is juxtaposed with the characters' commitment. The only textual pattern in which this can be explicitly narrated would be melodrama.

One of the few texts by Greene in which the turning point from detachment to commitment is explicitly represented is *The End of the Affair*, where the moment when a commitment is adopted – the moment of decision itself – is given great narrative prominence, with Sarah praying at the top of the stairs for Bendrix's life, "striking a bargain" with God. But even in *The End of the Affair*, one may argue, the turning point itself is left obscured from the narrative perspective of the narrator. Until he reads Sarah's diary – and it is through this device that readers have access to the information that may clarify Sarah's behavior in terms of a spiritual transformation – neither Bendrix nor the reader perceive the nature of this shift in Sarah's life except through its consequences. It is only after the device of the diary produces an effect of unveiling that we – Bendrix and ourselves – can trace our steps back and reinterpret Sarah's actions on the basis of this new information.

As in *The Power and the Glory*, the story of religious struggle is presented under the guise of a detective story (Thomson 173). Bendrix acts as the detective investigating the mysterious behavior of Sarah, and at one point he hires a professional detective to provide him with information about her. At the core of the story there is, at one end, Bendrix's incapacity to understand Sarah – the fact that he has been misreading her is constantly underlined in the novel – and, at the other end, Sarah's own resistance to explaining her actions. The fact that she keeps her religious conversion as a secret – from her husband and Bendrix at least – creates a scission in the storyworld: her behavior is perceived as irrational and censorable by those around her, subject to misinterpretation and misled feelings. Bendrix's misjudgment of Sarah derives from her refusal to give any explanation and allows for the narrative climax of his discovery of Sarah's bargain with God, when he learns that what he took for indifference was actually a sacrifice for love. Greene skillfully creates a textual gap just after the moment of revelation by placing it as the last paragraph in Book 3 (99), thus leaving a pause before Book 4 begins with Bendrix's reaction to the newly acquired knowledge: "I couldn't read anymore" (101). This "delayed decoding" (Watt 270) forces both readers and character to readjust the implicit evaluation made of Sarah's behavior and produces a (momentary) release of narrative tension.[15]

Although Sarah's is an individual act of commitment, its consequences will be suffered by others as well, starting with the bedazzled Bendrix. *The End of the Affair* offers the most melodramatic rendering of a final aspect of Greene's understanding of commitment: its irreversible nature. Individual commitment is a call for action; it sets in motion a sequence of events that cannot be stopped. Most of Greene's novels emphasize this idea, but a further qualification may be made. The inevitability of those consequences appears in some of the novels to be the product of external forces. The tragic deaths of Querry in *A Burnt-Out Case* and the Whisky Priest in *The Power and the Glory*, for example, are attributed to others acting as agents. One feels tempted to conclude that theirs is a death provoked by others in which the characters do not have a choice. In *The End of the Affair*, however, it is easy to feel that Sarah is bringing her own death upon herself. The thought is suggested by the narrator: "it was to his church that she had walked in the rain seeking a refuge and 'catching her death' instead" (145). In all three cases, however, there is a moment in the narrative in which the character is offered a different course of action, which is rejected for the sake of fidelity to the previously established commitment.

The outcome of commitment is never a "happily ever after" in Greene's novels. It involves the logic of sacrifice, and the consequences of characters' actions often lead to death; and it involves risking one's personal security, which we often see would remain intact if the commitment had not taken place, for the sake of others. In what appears to be a typically religious pattern, the logic of commitment involves martyrdom. Thus, in *The End of the Affair* Sarah risks her life to keep her vow never to see Bendrix again: walking in the rain, getting ill, and dying of pneumonia. Her apparent cruelty toward Bendrix – as perceived from *his* point of view, as the main narrator of the story – is reinscribed with the logic of sacrifice aimed at saving not herself, but Bendrix, from sin and damnation. Therefore, sacrifice appears as the ultimate expression of love. Not all sacrifices in Greene's fiction, however, are invested with such melodramatic meaningfulness. The ending of novels like *England Made Me*, *The Comedians*, and, perhaps with particular strength, *A Burnt-Out Case*, leave in the reader an impression of futility and absurd sacrifice: "When they had gone the crowd began to leave. There was nothing to wait for. There was nothing further to see" (*England* 205). In the face of such pointless deaths, affirming the relevance of commitment becomes the ultimate challenge for Greene's fiction.

6
Caritas

The final chapter of this book sets out to explore the potential fulfillment of the commitment acquired by the Greenean hero as a permanent integration into a community of destiny. The initial expression of such commitment, as analyzed in Chapter 5, is the act of compassion to others experienced as a turning point in the character's trajectory. The possibility of maintaining such commitment on a continuous basis is shaped in many of Greene's novels through the recurrent pattern of ethical action, failed integration into a community, and sacrifice. These are the narrative elements addressed in this chapter, and gathered under the category of *caritas*. This is a term that Greene never used in his novels, but it brings together two aspects which in Greene's fictional universe are combined: the ideas of love and charity. Both Frances McCormack and Cates Baldridge have used this expression in their analysis of the representation of different forms of love in Greene's fiction. In opposition to *eros*, Baldridge uses the term *caritas* to refer to "that love whose human objects are broader and whose motives are (perhaps somewhat) purer than those of eros, and that according to Greene can harness even our hatred to higher purposes" (111). Similarly, McCormack follows St. Augustine in order to distinguish between *caritas* and *cupiditas* (275). For characters in novels like *The Comedians* and *The Honorary Consul*, Baldridge argues, *caritas* appears as an alternative to human love – *eros* in his terminology – characterized by a greater tendency to "exhaustion, hypocrisy and self-delusion" (111). Although my own understanding of Greenean *caritas* is indebted to Baldridge's, I perceive two problematic aspects in his critical formulation. The first is that the companion term *eros* is used to distinguish between erotic or earthly love and another, allegedly spiritual, kind of love. However, the Whisky Priest's love for his child, which is explicitly opposed by the narrator of *The Power and the Glory* to the kind of universal love Baldridge associates with *caritas*, is far from erotic. This is why I prefer to draw a pattern of dialectical opposition between love for individuals – subject to the same faults identified by Baldridge in connection to *eros* – and universal love. The second problematic aspect is related to how his opposition implicitly assumes this same distinction between human love and charity. It seems, nevertheless, that Baldridge's articulation disengages completely one from the other, as if they belonged to two entirely separate planes of human emotion. In my perception, the key problem in Greene's articulation of love is the connection between the two, and the potential – often problematic, sometimes impossible – passage from one to the other.

Representations of love

Love appears in many of Greene's novels as the trigger that moves a character to action and commitment. The whole pattern sketched in this book may be said to find its most succinct expression in the following lines from *The Ministry of Fear*: "A sixth snare had entangled the doctor: not love of country but love of one's fellow-man, a love which had astonishingly flamed into action in the heart of respectable, hero-worshipping Johns" (181). In the narrative pattern analyzed in previous chapters, "love of one's fellow-man" is set as the ultimate step in a process frequently involving a personal transformation of the main character. However, the achievement of such transformation is rarely translated into the establishment of a new, permanent state of affairs. Love does not necessarily produce narrative closure, least of all in the form of a conventional happy ending.

Greene's characters rarely experience the fulfillment of human love, and his couples of lovers are inevitably unhappy. For most of his characters, love is suffering, and suffering is life. This is another point in common between Greene and Miguel de Unamuno, whose own understanding of love was expressed in *The Tragic Sense of Life* in these terms: "Love and suffering mutually engender one another; and love is charity and compassion, and love that is not charitable and complaisant is not love. Love, in short, is resigned despair" (Unamuno 225). According to Simone Weil, "feelings never allow thought peace" (*Lectures* 208). This might well have been contended by Greene himself, as his work amply evinces. In *The Ministry of Fear*, love is depicted as the cause of suffering. The narrator describes Rowe as he falls in love in the following terms: "like a boy he was driven relentlessly towards inevitable suffering, loss and despair, and called it happiness" (130). In *The Human*

Factor, Greene dramatizes the connection between love and danger of suffering in an explicit way: "The depth of their love was as secret as the quadruple measure of whisky. To speak of it to others would invite danger. Love was a total risk" (14). Love, understood as attachment to another human being, is linked to the risk of losing the object of love. The genre conventions of spy fiction provide Greene with the perfect narrative framework for the exploration of this understanding of love, as his spies and secret agents find themselves in the predicament of having to choose between the concrete love they may feel for individual people and the sense of duty that institutions associated to patriotism codifiy as love for one's country. In *The Ministry of Fear*, the contradictory allegiances demanded of an individual are explicitly played against one another, and the character chooses individual love over what is perceived as a snare created by power structures.

A classical *topos* of the thriller and spy fiction is repeatedly used by Greene to illustrate the central aspect of his understanding of love as suffering: that love, and human emotions in general, are incompatible with the profession of espionage. In *The Human Factor*, the point is made by Castle in conversation with fellow spy Boris: "You'd do much better to employ a man who doesn't hate, Boris. Hate's liable to make mistakes. It's as dangerous as love. I'm doubly dangerous, Boris, because I love too. Love's a fault in both our services" (113). Castle embodies a type in spy fiction: the hunted man whose emotional connections to others may threaten their lives. The novel depicts a kind of love whose mere existence constitutes a danger to its object, and often demands its sacrifice for the sake of the beloved's security. Love, in Greene's fictional universe, is necessarily linked to fear. This connection is made repeatedly by Greene's characters. In *The Human Factor*, Castle and Sarah's relationship is shadowed by this association: "he had learned during the last year in South Africa the age-old lesson that fear and love are indivisible" (89). In *The Captain and the Enemy*, again, love is continually associated to fear: "Love and fear – fear and love – I know now how inextricably they are linked" (39); "Love, it was quite clear to me now, meant fear" (51).

Along a different semantic line, love is often felt by characters to be a sort of infection. In *The Captain and the Enemy*, this is expressed by the main character, whose own experience is marked by his utter incapacity to understand the relationship between the Captain and Liza: "In my experience love was like an attack of flu and one recovered as quickly. Each love affair was like a vaccine. It helped you to get through the next attack more easily" (105). This perception, which is also shared by the protagonist of *The Confidential Agent*, is the result of characters' detachment from others (Snyder 128). Quite often, as in Brown's case (*The Comedians*), they claim to be incapable of love (291). Their attitude matches the world of Greene's fiction, which is as barren of human friendship and solidarity as what he discovered in Mexico and depicted in *The Lawless Roads*. And yet, as he wrote in that book, you can discover "the appalling mysteries of love moving through a ravaged world" (15).

Greene insistently portrayed glimpses of selfless love in the midst of a desolate world, but even those characters who are said to experience love do it in a complex and contradictory way. Bendrix's feelings for Sarah are obsessive and egotistic, and of course their perception is filtered through the character's current hate for her. The Whisky Priest's relationship with the old woman is marked by his guilt over his sins. Kate and Anthony Farrant's relationship is full of incestuous overtones, and ends with Kate's apparent betrayal of her twin brother. Scobie loves neither his wife nor his lover, but rather feels pity for both of them. The relationships between Fowler and Phuong, Brown and Marta Pineda, Plarr and Clara Fortnum are marked by instability; none of them is said to have any projected durability, in spite of the fact that the first two are said to have existed for a long time. One would feel tempted to claim that Greene's representation of love simply departs from nineteenth-century literary representations, were it not for the fact that several of his characters express their longing for exactly that kind of love involving long-term commitment, institutional sanction (through marriage), mutual support, and so on. For example, Brown keeps on making plans for Marta and himself, and Fowler's views on the practicality of Vietnamese girls regarding relationships betray his own European perspective on how young girls should perceive love.

Complications in Greene's understanding of love and friendship occur when moral codes conflict, a decision is made, and an act of betrayal is performed.[1] In many of Greene's thrillers betrayal is a recurrent element, with *The Third Man* probably standing as the epitome of Greene's exploration of the dialectics between loyalty and duty. In this novella, the main character, Rollo Martins, sees his loyalty to his friend Harry Lime radically called into question when the latter is accused by postwar Vienna police of leading a deadly penicillin racket. Martins' discovery that his friend has been responsible for the deaths of many leads him to collaborate with the police, thus placing his sense of duty before his friendship and betraying Harry. Nevertheless, it is in novels like *The Quiet American, The End of the Affair,* or *The Honorary Consul* that the question of betrayal acquires a greater narrative depth. In the latter two novels, the relationship between the two main characters is marked by one's perception of the other's behavior as an act of betrayal. Bendrix and Fortnum interpret Sarah's and Plarr's actions according to the schema of a love triangle. According to Bendrix, Sarah would have abandoned him for another man; according to Fortnum, Plarr has had him kidnapped in order to seduce his wife. In both cases, they fail to read the wider implications of the other character's behavior: in Sarah's case, her religious conversion and her attempt to attain salvation for both herself and Bendrix; in Plarr's, his involvement to negotiate Fortnum's freedom. A similar mismatched reading of a situation is enacted in the final scenes of *A Burnt-Out Case,* in which Rycker misreads Querry's relationship with his wife and starts acting like a comic type: the cuckolded husband. Rycker's incapacity to understand the situation correctly – to understand that his wife is using Querry to escape from him – triggers the tragi-comical end of the novel.

A different kind of betrayal is enacted in *The Quiet American* and *The Comedians*. Both Fowler and Brown may be said to lead others – Pyle and Jones, respectively – to their deaths. Unlike Bendrix or Fortnum, neither Pyle nor Jones is conscious of having been betrayed by their friends. In both cases, first-person narrative voice limits the reader's access to other characters' perspective.[2] For all we know, Pyle dies thinking Fowler is still a good man and a good friend: "you're the straightest guy I've ever known [...] After all you're my best friend" (75–77). Their motives, however, are ambiguous. The love triangle structure is more prominent in these texts than in other novels.[3] It is true, for example, that Fowler wants to get rid of Pyle so that Phuong will return to him, and that Brown does not like Jones to be around his lover, Marta Pineda. Nevertheless, their acts of betrayal also imply a further allegiance to one cause or community. In the standard political reading of *The Quiet American,* Fowler gives Pyle away to the communists so that Americans won't be able to install a "Third Force" in Vietnam through terrorist acts. In *The Comedians,* Brown's stratagem to lead Jones up north with the rebels gives him the opportunity to become a hero in the struggle against Duvalier's regime. The universal and personal dimensions of love are thus entangled and set in opposition through plot devices that force the hero into a course of action that remains obscure for the rest of the characters. Still, it is through those acts of misreading of characters' ethics that Greene successfully dramatizes the paradoxical nature of *caritas.*

The obligation to universal love

The ethical horizon in Greene's novels is marked by the sense of obligation to love all humanity. The idea, already sketched in previous chapters of this book, is formulated in novels like *The Power and the Glory* and
The End of the Affair, under the rubric of Christian discursive patterns.
As believers, the characters in both novels feel obliged to fulfill Christ's
commandment to love one another.

However, in *A Burnt-Out Case*, Greene deliberately disengages this
notion of *caritas* from the Christian framework. In two crucial moments
in the text, Querry depicts it as a universal ethical impulse not necessarily codified in Christian theology. First, it happens in discussion
with the Superior, who tries to make Querry's behavior fit into the pattern of Christian narrative of fall and redemption. Querry resists what
he understands to be an appropriation of human universal instincts:
"You try to draw everything into the net of your faith, father, but you
can't steal all the virtues. Gentleness isn't Christian, self-sacrifice isn't
Christian, charity isn't, remorse isn't. I expect the caveman wept to
see another's tears" (76–77). Querry's reference to the caveman, as well
as his later reference to a post-apocalyptic scenario in which human
beings would still display love for one another in the absence of organized religion, evinces a historical understanding of Christianity as an
institution and a theology. The second time this disengagement of
caritas from the Christian framework happens in the text will be in the
Superior's sermon, constructed as a response to Querry's earlier attack –
"I really believe he's answering something I said to him" (80):

> You Klistians are all big thieves – you steal this, you steal that, you
> steal all the time [...] You see a man who lives with one wife and
> doesn't beat her and looks after her when she gets a bad pain from
> medicines at the hospital and you say that's Klistian love [...] But you
> are a mighty big thief when you say that – for you steal this man's
> love and that man's mercy. (80)

The Superior's rhetorical way out of the trap set by Querry is to renounce
the theological frame of reference to Christianity as an institution, and
to re-establish the universality of *caritas*:

> Now I tell you that when a man loves, he must be Klistian. When a
> man is merciful he must be a Klistian [...] There is a doctor who lives
> near the well beyond Marie Akimbu's house and he prays to Nzambe

and he makes bad medicine [...] I tell you then he was a Klistian, a better Klistian that the man who broke Henry Okapa's bycicle. He did not believe in Yezu, but he a Klistian. I am not a thief, who steal away his charity to give to Yezu. I give back to Yezu only what Yezu made. Yezu made love, he made mercy. Everybody in the world has something that Yezu made. Everybody in the world is that much a Klistian. (81)

The Superior's re-appropriation of the notions of love and mercy can only happen, I would argue, on the basis of Pauline doctrine about the universality of Christianity. In his book on St. Paul, Alain Badiou has analyzed the universalist character of his discourse and claimed that "Paul's unprecedented gesture consists in subtracting truth from the communitarian grasp, be that of a people, a city, an empire, a territory, or a social class" (Badiou *Saint Paul* 5). Precisely because of its universal character, St. Paul's message about love (*agapē* in the original Greek) is interpreted in Badiou's terminology as an *event*, the revelation of a universal truth that stands beyond existing laws and that imposes on the subject the obligation to respond, by "deploying the power of self-love in the direction of others" (90).

In Greene's fiction, love appears to be precisely defined in the terms provided by Badiou's reading of St. Paul's doctrine, as a "nonliteral law": it is a universal call that is normally ignored by most people but that creates a sense of obligation toward others in the Greenean hero. This is expressed in *The Heart of the Matter*: "This was a responsibility he shared with all human beings, but that was no comfort, for it sometimes seemed to him that he was the only one who recognized his responsibility" (109). It is an ethical impulse, which moves the character to action, and it stands beyond – sometimes even in direct contradiction with – the human laws established by specific communities. In the teleological horizon of Greene's narratives, it is love that would provide ultimate salvation through acts of self-sacrifice, thus enacting the Pauline doctrine that assigns salvation to love alone (Badiou *Saint Paul* 91; St. Paul, Corinthians I 13:1–3). In *The Quiet American*, the Superior's speech is anticipated by Fowler, who takes it out of a Christian discursive framework, but identifies *caritas* in the same terms: "I've seen a priest, so poor he hasn't a change of trousers, working fifteen hours a day from hut to hut in a cholera epidemic, eating nothing but rice and salt fish, saying his Mass with an old cup – a wooden platter. I don't believe in God and yet I'm for that priest" (95–96). The image of such a priest may be perceived as an echo of Greene's portrayal of the Whisky Priest, or of his praise to local Mexican priests in *The Lawless Roads*.

Jean-Luc Nancy has argued that the central aspect of the idea of Christian salvation is the communal dimension that *communion* introduces into the picture: first, by proposing the idea of the "*deus communis*, brother of humankind" (Nancy *Inoperative* 10), and then through the ritual re-enactment of communion taking place "at the heart of the mystical body of Christ" (ibid.). Communal fusion with the divinity appears as the ultimate teleological image of salvation, "humanity's partaking of divine life" (ibid.), so that inevitably human beings live in the consciousness of a loss of community that should be restored. *Caritas*, in this light, may be perceived as the attempt to re-enact a communal fusion that has not taken place (11).

In this sense, the communal dimension of Greene's understanding of *caritas* should be underscored. If there were to be a utopian realization of this notion, it would be shaped in terms of individuation made possible precisely through mutual attention to the vulnerability of others, through the consideration of "the demands that are imposed upon us by living in a world of livings who are, by definition, physically dependent upon one another, mutually vulnerable to one another" (Butler *Precarious* 27). However, as Butler states, there is no guarantee that in an ethical encounter the vulnerability of the other will be recognized (43). In other words, such vulnerability is not self-evident, but rather the outcome of a continuous work of attention.

This universalist conception of ethical obligation toward others, as has already been hinted at in previous chapters, is shared by authors like Simone Weil and Iris Murdoch, with whose thought Greene's work seems to have many points in common. Simone Weil expresses the idea of obligation in *The Need for Roots*: "There exists an obligation towards every human being for the sole reason that he or she is a human being, without any other condition requiring to be fulfilled, and even without any recognition of such obligation on the part of the individual concerned" (5). Weil understands ethics in terms of "attention" to that which is not the self: "Attention alone, that attention which is so full that the 'I' disappears, is required of me" (Weil *Gravity* 171). In her understanding, all ethical action ensues from this initial moment of attention which triggers an automatic response of love: "To know that this man who is hungry and thirsty really exists as much as I do – that is enough, the rest follows of itself" (173). Hence, according to her, "belief in the existence of other human beings as such is love" (113).

Considering the connections between Weil and Greene, it is interesting to note how frequently Greene's novels depict the acts of love and charity on the part of his characters as springing from moments of contemplation of the pain of others. The paradigmatic scene of "attention" reappears in many of his novels: in the Whisky Priest observing his cell mates during his night in prison, in Fowler's horrified gaze upon the dead and injured after the explosion in Place Garnier, in Brown's discovery of Dr Philipot's suicide, in Querry accompanying the impaired Deo Gratias in the woods, and so on.

In *Existentialists and Mystics,* Iris Murdoch articulates a critique of what she calls the "solitary moral agent" (268) of much contemporary fiction. Against a fictional pattern that tends to linger on the moment of choice (ibid.) and underscores individual freedom to decide upon different courses of action, she calls for a different model of fictional representation of ethics in which "the most important thing to be revealed is that other people exist" (282). The same opposition between two models of representation is articulated by her in *The Sovereignty of Good.* Here, she explores in further detail the concept of "attention" borrowed from Weil, and claims that the main characteristic of the active ethical agent is "the idea of a just and loving gaze directed upon an individual reality" (33). As for Greene, the expression of ethical action is always directed to others, and it may be said to spring from the realization of someone else's suffering. In *The Quiet American,* this is dramatized in the argument between Pyle and Fowler while hiding in a watchtower guarded by two Vietnamese soldiers. While Pyle seems unable to think beyond his abstract political convictions, Fowler's ethical stance is underscored through his attention to the existence of the Vietnamese: "I've no particular desire to see you win. I'd like those two poor buggers there to be happy – that's all. I wish they didn't have to sit in the dark at night scared" (97).

Murdoch's most determinant contribution to this understanding of ethics as obligation toward others is the conviction that the moment of decision or choice on the part of the individual, when guided by true attention to others, is actually nonexistent: "if we understand the work of attention, how structures of value build up in time, we realize how at crucial moments of choice most of the business of choosing is already over" (36). Her argument points to a central element in the narrative pattern drawn in Greene's fiction: that the moment of decision is never presented to the characters – and hence nor to the reader – as a conscious one, explicitly stated and isolated in time. Obligation seems to pre-exist the consciousness of it, and the Greenean hero is often forced to act on a conviction that sometimes he did not even know he had.[4]

The singular moments of compassion analyzed in Chapter 4 may be said to correspond to what Murdoch called "an occasion for unselfing" (*Sovereignty* 82): "we cease to be in order to attend to the existence of something else, a natural object, a person in need" (58). The problem, as it will be explored in the next section, is to "keep the attention fixed" (89) on "that which is not ourselves" (100).

The tensions between kinds of love, kinds of community

The ethical framework sketched in the preceding section sets the basis for the narrative tensions articulated in Greene's fiction around the idea of *caritas*. On the one hand, the incommensurable gap between the particular and universal expressions of love is often rendered as the central ethical conflict in his novels. The Greenean hero is conscious of his obligation to love all humanity, but he feels unable to transcend the limitations of selfish love oriented toward particular individuals. This idea is expressed as a maxim in *The Heart of the Matter*: "In our hearts there is a ruthless dictator, ready to contemplate the misery of a thousand strangers if it will ensure the happiness of the few we love" (175). On the other hand, narrative tension emerges in his novels from the conflict established between the socially sanctioned limited exertion of charity and love for one's neighbor that Weil would identify as pharisaic, and the need to transcend the existing law in order to fulfill what is understood as a deeper and more primary obligation.

The tension between particular human love and the sense of obligation toward all humanity is dramatized most explicitly in *The Power and the Glory*. Upon meeting his natural daughter Brigitta, the Whisky Priest focuses all his love on her, and on the idea of her salvation. His love for the child, however, is immediately contrasted to the love for all human beings, the kind of love he was supposed to have felt: "This was the love he should have felt for every soul in the world: all the fear and the wish to save concentrated unjustly on the one child" (206). In this passage, Greene insists on pointing out that this kind of attention to others' souls should be extended to the rest of humankind. For the Priest, being unable not to think only of his child is perceived as a final failure:

> He thought: this is what I should feel all the time for everyone, and he tried to turn his brain away toward the half-caste, the lieutenant, even a dentist he had once sat with for a few minutes [...] He prayed "God help them," but in the moment of prayer he switched back to his child beside the rubbish-dump, and he knew it was for her only that he prayed. Another failure. (206)

The Priest will set the pattern to be followed by other Greenean heroes, but none of them seems equally conscious of the notion here sketched: that true ethical commitment should be an obligation toward humanity as a whole, and not only to those who are close. The end of the novel suggests that, in spite of his perceived failure, the Priest has managed to give his life for others, thus replicating a Christological pattern that the novel had been anticipating since the beginning (Baldridge 49; Bosco 92).

In an earlier moment of the novel, during his stay in prison, the Priest had in fact come close to the act of love which, in the terms articulated by Weil and Murdoch, comes from the work of attention:

> When you visualized a man or a woman carefully, you could always begin to feel pity – that was a quality God's image carried with it. When you saw the lines at the corners of the eyes, the shape of the mouth, how the hair grew, it was impossible to hate. Hate was just a failure of the imagination. He began to feel an overwhelming responsibility for this pious woman. (129)[5]

Throughout this passage, the Priest's attitude toward the prison cell inmates is transformed in a way that suggests the communal fusion evoked in the Christological pattern. At first, he is said to start feeling love for those around him in a sense that denotes distance from them, a certain sense of superiority or otherness: "Everybody, when he spoke, listened attentively to him as if he were addressing them in church. He wondered where the inevitable Judas was sitting now, but he wasn't aware of Judas as he had been in the forest hut. He was moved by an irrational affection for the inhabitants of this prison" (125). The prisoners see him still as a priest, someone different and allegedly superior to them in a moral sense. It is only when he admits being a criminal himself, when he eliminates the social differences created by his institutional status, that he experiences *caritas*: "Again he was touched by *an extraordinary affection*. He was just one criminal among a herd of criminals [...] He had *a sense of companionship* which he had never experienced in the old days when pious people came kissing his black cotton glove" (126; emphasis added). Love for others is here again expressed as communal fusion. The establishment of such communities, however, tends to be temporary, as if the dissolution of differences into this sort of universal commonality could not last on a permanent basis. In the prison cell, when the morning comes, the Priest will be a priest, and the prisoners will remain "a herd of criminals."

In spite of this moment of communion, the Priest will die thinking himself a failure for having been unable to keep his attention fixed on love for humanity. The predicament in which individuals find them-selves regarding such obligation was noted by Simone Weil in her work, but not resolved in a way that Greene's characters may find satisfactory as alleviation of their guilty consciousness. In *Gravity and Grace*, she addresses the issue of the need to fulfill a duty that seems impossible, that of loving all humanity: "We should do only those righteous actions which we cannot stop ourselves from doing, which we are unable not to do, but, through well-directed attention, we should always keep on increasing the number of those which we are unable not to do" (91).

In *the Need for Roots*, Weil acknowledges the ethical *aporia* of poten-tially contradictory obligations: "No human being, whoever he may be, under whatever circumstances, can escape them [obligations] without being guilty of crime; save where there are two genuine obligations which are in fact incompatible, and a man is forced to sacrifice one of them" (4). Greene explores such incompatibility in *The Heart of the Matter*, but the use of such ethical dilemmas is a classic narrative device is to be found in novels like Victor Hugo's *Les Miserables* (1862), Fyodor Dostoyevsky's *Crime and Punishment* (1866), and Joseph Conrad's *Under Western Eyes* (1911). Scobie's dilemma springs from the incom-mensurability between his ordinary responsibilities toward his wife and his job, on the one hand, and the excess of responsibility he feels toward everyone else. While the first are created within the institutional framework and make him part of socially sanctioned communities of a familial and professional kind, the second exceeds the normative plane of what is to be expected of any citizen. They stand beyond what Murdoch called "ordinary mediocre conduct" (*Sovereignty* 76) and derive from what Scobie perceives as a constant demand for help on the part of those in need. Scobie's predicament, then, may be understood in the light of Simone Weil's radical view of universal duty toward the other, "for the sole reason that he or she is a human being" (*Need* 5). In the novel, this is expressed in nearly Lévinasian terms, as the need to respond to a command made by another: "he could tell the command was going to be given again – the command to stay, to love, to accept responsibility, to lie" (171).[6] Scobie feels this responsibility as a burden he must bear alone: "I've got nothing to give them that they can't get elsewhere: why can't they leave me in peace?" (173).

Scobie's relationship with Helen Rolt may be understood in this light. Scobie feels responsible for her after she survives a shipwreck, and he becomes her lover, as Evelyn Waugh argued, in order to protect her from other potential suitors: "Scobie arrogates to himself the preroga-tions of providence. He presumes that an illicit relation with himself is better than an illicit relation with Bagster" (100). In doing this, of course, he sets himself a trap, by establishing two contradictory commitments: to his wife, and to his lover. Those are "two genuine obligations which are in fact incompatible," as Weil argued, and Scobie is well aware of his situation: "how can one love God at the expense of one of his creatures? Would a woman accept the love for which a child had to be sacrificed?" (171). When faced with the need to sacrifice one of them, however, he makes an unexpected turn, and decides to eliminate himself from the equation: "He wanted happiness for others and solitude and peace for himself [...] O God, give me death before I give them unhappiness" (174).

The second source of narrative tension related to the notion of *caritas* is explicitly articulated in communitarian terms. As was noted in Chapter 5, the Greenean hero's commitment tends to be articulated as the shift from belonging to a community of origin from which he feels alienated into the embrace of a cause that will allow the character a renewed sense of belonging, and often a sense of home. Repeatedly, Greene's characters embrace communities of dispossessed, oppressed, and vulnerable people, who find themselves in the midst of power games played by other forces: the Mexican Catholics, the Haitians, the Vietnamese, the lepers, the poor in Paraguay.

This kind of situation may be read in communitarian terms, whenever Greene explores a situation in which the codes of a specific community demand a particular line of action, which the characters feel the need to trespass in order to respond to a summons coming from a different source – usually from an oppressed, suffering community – and, ultimately, as a summons to *caritas*. Colonial communities of the kind portrayed in novels like *The Heart of the Matter*, *A Burnt-Out Case*, *The Quiet American*, *The Comedians*, or even *The Honorary Consul* (where the community of British expatriates in Corrientes, Argentina, is not colonial as such, but fulfills the conditions Anderson attributed to creole communities)[7] allow Greene to represent a microcosm of British society at large, as Anthony Burgess has argued: "the petty minds of men and women who have brought lending-library gossipy suburban England with them into the African darkness" (Burgess 99). They are relatively closed communities, ruled by social and ethical codes against which the character's predicament stands out as an unnecessary one. Readers perceive the futility of Querry's rescue of Deo Gratias through the eyes of the community in *A Burnt-Out Case* in the passage when some of the colony's notables ironically comment on his "saintliness" during a party: "So we have a saint among us" (64). A similar effect, when the character's line of action is contrasted with this sort of collective comment on it, is achieved in *The Honorary Consul* through the useless procedures adopted by the other characters to help in Charles Fortnum's liberation.

A different narrative device producing the same mechanism is the contrast between the hero's behavior and that of other characters, stressing how the former goes beyond what would be expected of him according to social custom. The unnecessary nature of the hero's acts is stressed in these situations, often leading reviewers to frustrated reactions against the illogical behavior of characters. A case in point would be Scobie's behavior in *The Heart of the Matter*, and George Orwell's famous irate reaction to it.[8] One may wonder, from this perspective, about Scobie's need to care so much for Helen Rolt, or about the reasons why Brown and Jones go as far as joining the rebels against Duvalier's regime in *The Comedians*, when all the other foreigners in the country – epitomized in the Americans Mr and Mrs Smith – have run away to safer locations.

In all these cases, the passage from detachment to commitment on the ethical plane slides over the dialectical pattern established through the opposition between two kinds of communities: the institutional one, aligned with power structures – the Church, the colonial rule, the creole community, the intelligence agency – and the oppositional community of the marginalized, which often finds its most openly political expression in the idea of "the people." Therefore, the practice of *caritas* is frequently dramatized as the work of attention to those who suffer as a consequence of the social asymmetries created in specific historical circumstances.

In this respect, many critics have noted the intersections between Greene's narrative patterns and the ideas of liberation theology expressed by Gustavo Gutierrez and others (Baldridge 192; Bosco 100–5; Brennan 129; Friedman *Fictional* 230). In Greene's work, it is precisely the poor and dispossessed who truly become the object of *caritas*. In the strictly Catholic context, the institutional Church tends to be regarded, in Greene's work, as corrupted and pharisaic. In opposition to it, the spontaneous expressions of belief, often depicted as primitive and infantile, are depicted in a more favorable light.[9] Greene's view of the institutional Church as being responsible for the situation of the vulnerable communities may be said to coincide with the one expressed in liberation theology, in which the theological pattern is ingrained in political struggle (Bosco 101). According to William Thomas Hill, the portrayal of the Church in *The Power and the Glory* shifts from the institutional view to that of a community of believers (Hill *Perceptions*, 155). In Greene's articulation, however, the shift is also a sociological one. The Church evoked through glimpses of the Priest's past is one patronized by the bourgeoisie – part of ideological state apparatuses, to use Althusser's terminology. The Church foregrounded in the main narration is one sustained by the lower classes against newly established power structures, embodied in the Lieutenant's application of Garrido Canabal's law (referred to in the novel as "the Governor"). Novels like *Monsignor Quixote*, *A Burnt-Out Case*, *The Honorary Consul*, and *The Power and the Glory* dramatize this opposition between two models of religious expression through the "rebel priest" figures set against the background of a Church complicit with those in power. It is easy to see that the political and religious powers are equally damaging for the poor in Greene's novels, and the Church is frequently aligned with the political structures.

Thus, as Bosco has argued, Greene's novels sketch a dialectical pattern of opposition between two kinds communities, in the midst of which his heroes are set: "His exiles live in a space between two worlds that is often portrayed in stereotypical fashion: on the one hand, the world of coercive power and empty affluence presented by European-American modernity and, on the other hand, the world of the familial, religious, premodern 'third world'" (105). These two opposed kinds of communities may be said to correspond to the opposition established by Ferdinand Tönnies between "society" (*Gesellschaft*) and "community" (*Gemeinschaft*) (17). The first is characterized by Tönnies as corresponding to the complex institutionalized forms of social organization, whereas the second, depicted as more "organic" and authentic, corresponds in his articulation to the basic forms of communal life, all of them springing from family structure in the first place.

Greene's characters find themselves unable to fit into any of the pre-established models of community thus articulated, and are recurrently depicted as being beyond traditional criteria for the delimitation of community: "Greene continues to set his late novels on geographical borders between nations and ideologies, where characters are involved in physical and personal claims that transgress the lines of a single race, nation, religion, or political affiliation" (Bosco 105). They have been frequently depicted by critics as "wanderers, incomplete and disconnected from any community of dwellers" (Hill *Wanderers* 2), precisely because of their lack of attachment to a specific community in which its members are mutually identified by what they have in common. In all these models of communal organization, the bond is established on the basis of all its members having something in common, and it is reinforced by reciprocal affirmation of identity on the basis of what is "proper" to several individuals (Esposito *Communitas* 3; see also Blanchot *Unavowable* 8). This is what Jean-Luc Nancy describes as an operative or organic community, in which each member is recognized as a functioning element within a structure meant to provide itself – and all its members – with such a sense of belonging (Nancy *Inoperative* 13).

This process of assigning identities is most clearly identified in the discursive practices of institutional communities.[10] A crucial aspect of the pattern sketched above is the fact that acts of selfless love, compassion, and sacrifice are generally misread by the communities of origin of the Greenean heroes. Thus, those communities play the part of an ironic chorus, enhancing the loneliness and futility of the hero's actions against the backdrop of an uncomprehending collectivity. This is very explicit in novels like *The Heart of the Matter*, *A Burnt-Out Case*, and *The Honorary Consul*, in which "the gossipers of a small colony" (*Heart* 176) constantly misinterpret the hero's actions and try to incorporate them into their own patterns of interpretation. Thus, Scobie's suicide is never understood as the act of sacrifice he intended, but rather as an act of despair; and Querry's death is the accidental outcome of a misunderstanding provoked by Marie Rycker which triggers her husband's jealousy.

In the context of Greene's fiction, his understanding of love always exceeds the forms of institutionalized communities where love seems to be the rationale – love for one's family, for a lover, for one's country or people. The acts of commitment on the part of Greene's heroes, which lead them to the experience of *caritas* sketched in this chapter, may be said to embody what, according to Nancy, is the ultimate model of the operative community, the Christian pattern (Nancy *Inoperative* 10). Thus, when characters are said to awaken to feelings they no longer thought they had, the pattern is one of recuperation of a community that was thought to be lost.

In this sense, characters like Querry, Fowler, or the Whisky Priest aspire to a permanent expression of commitment to an organic community, a meaningful bond based on solidarity and compassion. However, the Greenean hero never truly achieves that complete fusion with the community of the oppressed. Therefore, his glimpses of *caritas* turn out to be momentary encounters with an otherness that can never be fully eradicated. As Nancy has argued, it is precisely in the impossibility of total communal fusion that community takes place, precisely as an irreducible resistance to ecstatic fusion into "a unique and total being"

(*Inoperative* 20). What we repeatedly witness in Greene's fiction, therefore, is the expression of an inoperative community, finite and transient and never meant to lead to organic articulations based on commonality: "Inert, immobile, less a gathering than the always imminent dispersal of a presence momentarily occupying the whole space and nevertheless without a place" (Blanchot *Unavowable* 33). As long as the hero tries to turn his passing communal encounters into a permanent articulation of community he is bound to fail.

It could be claimed, from his perspective, that the aspiration to become permanent members of a community is rendered in Greene's fiction as catastrophic involvement leading to sacrifice and destruction. Only through the enactment of a sacrifice for the sake of the community's wellbeing can the Greenean hero be incorporated into an organic community. His or her death will serve a double narrative purpose: on the one hand, it evinces full commitment, the complete surrendering of the self for the sake of others, the definitive enactment of *caritas*. In Nancy's terminology, the community reabsorbs that death, initially perceived as an unmasterable excess of finitude, and transforms it into a meaningful fulfillment of the individual (Nancy *Inoperative* 13). The act of self-sacrifice that frequently closes Greene's novels is the expression of how death may be "reabsorbed or sublated in a community" (ibid.). On the other hand, it is precisely by accepting the hero's sacrifice and identifying it as such that the community itself attains visibility: "Death is indissociable from community, for it is through death that the community reveals itself – and reciprocally" (14). Thus, Nancy identifies "the motif of the revelation, through death, of being-together or being-with, and of the crystallization of the community around the death of its members" (ibid.).

The end of *The Power and the Glory* reveals that double function of the hero's sacrifice: the Whisky Priest's death is incorporated into the communal narrative about Christian martyrology as "one of the heroes of the faith" (218). Hence, what appeared as the arbitrary, meaningless death of an obscure priest is aggrandized by incorporation into a communal discourse, while simultaneously serving the purpose of inspiring the community of persecuted believers. At the beginning of the novel, the Priest is identified as one of the frequent border figures in Greene's work; he is simultaneously internal and external to the community. He is Mexican, but he has been educated in America: "He can pass as a gringo. He spent six years at some American seminary" (16). The first time he appears in the novel he speaks in English with Mr Tench, who takes him for an Englishman (3). Further evidence of his initial distance from the native community is the picture hanging from the wall of the prison house, featuring him among wealthy ladies. Education and class seem to position him apart from them. The Lieutenant, on the other hand, is one of the people, and part of his resentment regarding the Priest emerges precisely from direct experience of the class separation between clerics and laymen during his childhood. Like Plarr in *The Honorary Consul* or Brown in *The Comedians*, his process of ideological and spiritual transformation may be read in terms of his approximation to native life, of coming closer to the community in which he was, at the beginning of the story, only half integrated. The Priest's position regarding the community, moreover, is an instrumental one, as he is one of the few priests left in the region, and he is required to perform the religious rituals only he has the power to perform. The villagers hide him not because he is, using the Conradian idiom, "one of them." They do it because they need him to hear their confessions and give them communion.

Because he administers the sacraments in a clandestine way, thus risking his own life, the Priest provides the ritual that glues the community together; he is in this sense a sacrificial victim of the community, through whom they can state their resistance to power and authority. The practice of religious ritual is reinscribed with a subversive potential it only acquires under oppressive conditions. Hence, Greene evokes primitive Christianity when he expresses his admiration at "how courage and the sense of responsibility had revived with persecution" (*Ways* 85). At the end of the novel, when the boy Luis symbolically revolts against the Lieutenant by spitting on his weapon (219), the Priest has already been placed on the side of those who fight oppression: "There were no more priests and no more heroes [...] Zapata, Villa, Madero, and the rest, they were all dead, and it was people like the man out there who killed them" (219). Faith and ritual become, through the mother's narrative, the emblems of rebellion and political resistance: "He was one of the martyrs of the Church [...] He was one of the heroes of the faith" (218). The logic of this passage resonates with Frantz Fanon's explanation in *The Wretched of the Earth* (1961) about how oppressed communities create their own myths:

> In order to maintain their stamina and their revolutionary capabilities, the people also resort to retelling certain episodes in the life of the community. The outlaw, for example, who holds the countryside for days against the police, hot on his trail, or who succumbs after killing four or five police officers [...] constitute for the people role models, action schemas, and "heroes." (30)

Scapegoats

The narrative logic of sacrifice for the sake of a community needs to be addressed as the final element in the narrative pattern explored in this book. Many critics have mentioned, often in passing, that several of Greene's heroes are "scapegoats being hunted by society" (Prasad 173). Norman Sherry has identified several of Greene's characters as "scape-goat heroes" (*Life* 2, xiii, 118; 3, xix, 154). Mostly, however, critics don't analyze this motif in depth, and use it simply as identification for the persecuted hero. Francis L. Kunkel has written one of the few essays that explicitly address the figure of the scapegoat in Greene's fiction.[11] He focuses specifically on *The Power and the Glory*, in order to argue that the Priest is an outcast both in the eyes of the Lieutenant, who "blames the Priest, the sole visible sign of Catholicism in the whole country-side, for misery, poverty and superstition" ("Priest" 74), and of the people, who "need his sacramental powers to loose their sins" (ibid.) and thus use him, even at the risk of his life and damnation. Kunkel's reading of the novel underscores the idea that "the priest as scapegoat images Christ" ("Priest" 75), as he endures sacrificial suffering for others.[12]

Kunkel points to a central element in the scapegoating mechanism, as analyzed in depth by René Girard in *Violence and the Sacred* and *The Scapegoat*: the unanimous identification of the scapegoat whose death will purge the community of its ills (Girard *Violence* 251). The scapegoat resolves a crisis by eliminating the discordance between members of society, who are united in their identification of the scapegoat figure as the one to be blamed and expelled from society. In the case of the Priest in *The Power and the Glory*, "he is hated almost as much by those for whom he risks his life as by those who risk their lives to take him" (Kunkel "Priest" 75).

Several of Greene's heroes find themselves in the same position: for example, Querry in *A Burnt-Out Case*, Jones in *The Comedians*, Plarr in *The Honorary Consul*. They end up playing a major role in a conflict between two collectivities that eventually identify them as scapegoats. For the institutional communities they are trouble-makers, former members gone astray who resist being re-incorporated into their "proper" places within the community. For the collectivities we could call their com-munities of destiny, they are never fully integrated as "one of them." Therefore, these characters are stuck halfway between two communal adscriptions. The communities of origin (institutions to which the hero was affiliated in the past) claim him back, thus making a permanent integration into a new community impossible. The communities of destiny do not identify him as a member, but rather make instrumental use of him, often related to his professional skills. Thus, Plarr is called to cure the injured as he is the only doctor at hand; Querry is asked to do construction work, as he is an architect; and Jones is turned into a rebel leader by virtue of his alleged status as soldier of fortune. Eventually, the hero realizes that the best thing he can offer to them is his own death, rather than his skills, as a way of protecting this community from the threat of the powerful authorities. A sacrifice is called for, and the hero, whose position within the community is only marginal, is appointed as scapegoat.

Girard's work on sacrifice as a mechanism meant to restore communitarian stability provides an apposite explanation for this pattern. According to him, the scapegoat mechanism is triggered as a consequence of a social crisis that upsets the pre-established balance and unleashes mutual violence amongst members of a community. Identifying an individual who can play the role of surrogate victim for all community members serves a crucial function: "The sacrifice serves to protect the entire community from its own violence; it prompts the entire community to choose victims outside itself. The elements of dissension scattered throughout the community are drawn to the person of the sacrificial victim and eliminated, at least temporarily, by its sacrifice" (Girard *Violence* 8).

In Girard's understanding, the fact that the victim is not a full member of the community is a fundamental element, and so it is in Greene's fiction: "between these victims and the community a crucial social link is missing, so they can be exposed to violence without fear of reprisal" (*Violence* 13). The Greenean hero is simultaneously in and out of two communities, neither of which claims him fully as one of their own. In this sense he is the perfect scapegoat. His death, however, will not so much serve the purpose of restoring order in a definitive way as return the balance of forces that had existed before his intromission in an otherwise stable balance of oppression and power. In this sense, Greene's understanding of the role played by his characters in the political dynamics portrayed in his novels may be said to respond to the logics of what Jacques Derrida calls "auto-immunity": "A principle of sacrificial self-destruction ruining the principle of self-protection (that of maintaining its self-integrity intact), and this in view of some sort of invisible and spectral sur-vival" (Derrida *Gift* 51). Nowhere in Greene's fiction is this idea so clearly expressed as in the final pages of *The Power and the Glory*, where the repetition of the story undergone by the Priest is perceived as a loop mechanism feeding the community's faith: martyrs are necessary so that people will keep on believing, and thus every new priest will be identified by the community as a potential "hero of the faith." The final act of *caritas* on the part of these characters is their acceptance of that role as scapegoat.

In *The Comedians*, Jones fulfills the role of scapegoat hero. His involvement in the revolt against the Tontons Macoute in Haiti turns him into a dangerous presence for everyone around him. He is no longer accepted as a member of the foreign community to which he may be said to have belonged at the beginning of the story. His conversation with the Captain of the *Medea*, where he tries to hide, reveals his status as a scapegoat: "You were never a welcome guest, Mr. Jones. I had too many enquiries about you" (213). Making up his mind about the impossibility of accepting him on board, the captain forces him to identify himself as an outcast from any community: "'I do not know whether you have a family, Mr. Jones. But I have one'. 'No, I have no one [...] You're right, captain, *I'm expendable*'" (ibid.; emphasis added).

In a novel in which narrator and characters make continuous claims to anti-heroism – "I am no hero" (124), claims Brown after a tense encounter with the Tontons Macoute – Jones will finally emerge as a heroic figure who chooses his love of community and the sense of home discovered in Haiti over his own security. In a scene that echoes the funeral scenes at the end of many of Greene's novels, Philipot and Brown assess Jones's death: "'He told me once that there was no room for him outside of Haiti.' 'I wonder what he meant.' 'He meant his heart was there'" (287). As a homeless individual, Brown identifies in Jones the imprint of the Greenean hero: "*we find ourselves the only ones truly committed – committed to the whole world* of evil and good, to the wise and to the foolish, to the indifferent and to the mistaken." (283–84; emphasis added).

The final pages of the novel constitute Greene's most open defense of the transformative power of *caritas* understood as a commitment "to the whole world." In the funeral offered to honor the victims of the revolt, including Jones, the priest states what could be taken as a condensed version of Greene's conviction:

> Our hearts go out in sympathy to all who are moved to violence by the suffering of others. The Church condemns violence, but it condemns indifference more harshly. Violence can be the expression of love, indifference never. One is an imperfection of charity, the other the perfection of egoism. In the days of fear, doubt and confusion, the simplicity and loyalty of one apostle advocated a

political solution. He was wrong, but I would rather be wrong with St. Thomas than right with the cold and the craven. Let us go up to Jerusalem and die with him. (288)[13]

Images of sacrifice for others accumulate, like that of Dr Magiot, killed when going to help a sick child: "The true story is that they sent a peasant to his door asking him to come and help a sick child. He came out on to the path and the Tontons Macoute shot him down from a car. There were witnesses. The peasant was killed too, but that was probably not intended" (289). Before dying, Dr Magiot writes a letter to Brown, in which he asks him: "if you have abandoned one faith, do not abandon all faith. There is always an alternative to the faith we lose" (291).

Brown remains until the very end the last "comedian" of the story, detached from the situation around, refusing to become engaged: "I had left involvement behind me [...] I had felt myself not merely incapable of love – many are incapable of that, but even of guilt" (ibid.). The use of the past perfect throughout this passage indicates that Brown may be at the turning point toward ethical commitment. It is the same narrative situation found with Bendrix at the end of *The End of the Affair* and the second priest in *The Power and the Glory*. It suggests that the sacrifice of the Greenean hero – Jones, Sarah, the Priest – may have a contagious effect, that of turning those around to commitment and action. This, I would suggest, is the ultimate meaning of Greene's pattern of commitment, love, and sacrifice: "In the last cooling of the world, when the emptiness of your belief is finally exposed, there'll always be some bemused fool who'll cover another's body with his own to give it warmth for an hour more of life" (*Burnt-Out* 77).

Conclusion: The Ethics of Reading (Graham Greene)

In his foreword to the collection of essays entitled *Dangerous Edges of Graham Greene* (Gilvary and Middleton), David Lodge tries to give an answer to the question of Greene's popularity: Why should we continue to read his work today? His own answer to this question speaks of Greene's ability to combine a wide range of political, philosophical, and religious interests with a mastery of popular genres of fiction. A similar point is made by Jon Wise and Mike Hill in their introduction to *The Works of Graham Greene: A Reader's Bibliography and Guide* (6). In both cases, the authors point out how Greene's popularity seems not to have declined with time. In what follows, I intend to provide a different kind of answer to the question of why we still read Greene, and why we should continue to do so. As the title of this section announces, my own conclusion emerges from the conviction that Greene's work exemplifies, precisely in its refusal to be exemplary, the ethics of reading.

The lexico-conceptual analysis developed in the preceding pages has resulted in a sort of master narrative, a metadiscursive account of Graham Greene's fiction that emphasizes the ethical dimension in his work. Writing about Henry James, whom he so admired, Greene stated the following: "In all writers there occurs a moment of crystallization when the dominant theme is plainly expressed, when the private universe becomes visible even to the least sensitive reader" ("Henry James: Private" 21). In this book, I have claimed that such crystallization takes place, in Greene's fiction, around the notion of ethical commitment. Borrowing Fredric Jameson's terms, it is from this perspective that I have read Greene's novels "as vital episodes in a single vast unfinished plot" (*Political* 19).

A question for further exploration remains open, however, as to the character of such ethical dimension. Does it emerge from the expression of ethical themes in the texts? Or does it relate to what J. Hillis Miller has called in his writings "the ethics of reading"? According to Miller, there is "an ethical dimension to the act of reading as such" (*Versions* 13), something which does not originate in the thematic rendering of ethical problems, but with the act of reading on a general basis. The question, in other words, has to do with whether Greene's texts would be a thematic rendering of the author's ethical concerns, or whether they may be said to activate the reader's capacity for ethical judgment through a series of ethical conflicts and/or aporias presented in them.

The hypothesis that I would like to defend in this conclusion is that Greene's novels may be perceived not just as thematic dramatizations, but as enactments of an ethical process which involves each reader, each time we read one of his texts. In this, I follow J. Hillis Miller's argument in *Versions of Pygmalion* (1990), where he writes the following:

> Narrative examples are especially appropriate for an investigation of the ethics of reading. But it is not because stories contain the thematic dramatization of ethical situations, choices, and judgments that makes them especially appropriate for my topic; it is, on the contrary, because ethics itself has a peculiar relation to that form of language we call narrative. The thematic dramatizations of ethical topics in narratives are the oblique allegorization of this linguistic peculiarity. (*Versions* 16–17; see also *Ethics* 3)

The linguistic peculiarity mentioned by Miller is the inextricable narrative quality of ethical thought. One cannot think of the ethical in abstract, universal terms, but only through reference to specific examples. In *The Ethics of Reading* (1987), Miller states: "ethics involves narrative, as its subversive accomplice. Storytelling is the impurity which is necessary in any discourse about the moral law as such, in spite of the law's austere indifference to persons, stories, and history" (23). Jacques Derrida also refers to the narrative as a parasite of the law in the essay "Before the Law" (1992), his reading of Kafka's story of the same title (190). According to him, "the law is neither manifold nor, as some believe, a universal generality. It is always an idiom" (210). This idiomatic nature, the particularity of the law, which is effaced in the notion of the categorical imperative presented as a universal, eternal principle detached from specific circumstances, is precisely what re-emerges in narrative in a most explicit fashion. In connection to Kant's illustrations of the categorical imperative, Miller claims that "narrative as a fundamental activity of the human mind, the power to make fictions, to tell stories to oneself or to others, serves for Kant as the absolutely necessary bridge without which there would be no connection between the law as such and any particular ethical rule of behavior" (*Ethics* 28).

The question asked at the beginning of this section stands on the basis of a problem often detected by Greene himself regarding the reception of his work, namely, the insistence with which readers approached him for answers to the problems that his novels often posited in terms of fictional conflict. In *Ways of Escape*, he reflects on this with bitterness upon the publication of *The Heart of the Matter*: "Never had I received so many letters from strangers [...] a better man could have found a life's work on the margin of that cruel sea, but my own course of life gave me no confidence in any aid I might proffer. I had no apostolic mission, and the cries for spiritual assistance maddened me because of my impotence" (252–53). Greene resented how readers often demanded from his works a sort of universal philosophical or religious validity, and frequently expressed his conviction that the writer's realm was that of the particular, not the universal. In an interview with Robert Osterman in 1950, he claimed that "ethics, and other subjects like it, are concerned with what ought to be, and the only material the novelist has is what is, human material" (Osterman, rpt. in Donaghy *Conversations* 23). Again, in *Ways of Escape*, he reproduces his argument with Evelyn Waugh about the nature of fiction, and criticizes "the confusion between the functions of a novelist and the functions of a moral teacher or theologian" (256).[1] In Greene's resistance to acknowledging a universal dimension to his work, however, may lie the key to understanding its success: it is successful precisely because it offered no moral solutions – the untroubled sea he compares self-complacent faith to (*Ways* 253) – but simply threw its readers into the tempest of doubt and faith (ibid.).

In the Preface to *The Golden Bowl* (1904), Henry James writes that "the whole conduct of life consists of things done, which do other things in their turn" (1971, xxiv; qtd. Miller *Versions* 15). Greene himself might have endorsed such a statement as a succinct description of his own work. After all, his stories are always about characters who take on action, and about the consequences of such actions. But James's statement may be extended as well to the tasks of writing and reading, for if a novel is one "thing done," the reading of that same novel should be regarded as the moment in which "other things" start to happen. So, what happens when we read? According to J. Hillis Miller, we receive a summons to ethical responsibility:

> The ethics of reading is not some act of the human will to interpretation which extracts moral themes from a work, or uses it to reaffirm

what the reader already knows, or imposes a meaning freely in some process of reader response of perspectivist criticism, seeing the text in a certain way. *The ethics of reading is the power of the words of the text over the mind and words of the reader.* (Miller *Ethics* 41; emphasis added)

On a similar note, Derek Attridge claims in *The Singularity of Literature* that reading consists basically in accepting the otherness of the literary work and of the fictional universe presented to us in it: "respect for the singularity of the other involves a willingness to have the grounds of one's thinking recast and renewed" (128). He describes the ethics of reading as "a preparedness to be challenged by the work, an alertness to its singular otherness" (130). Greene saw his own work essentially as a depiction of the real world, or of his view of the real world. What he failed to admit, I would claim, was the ethical, the performative effect of his work upon readers.

In order to illustrate how Greene's works may be said to challenge his readers, who are performatively "summoned to take responsibility" (Miller *Others* 166), I would like to focus once more on the typical ending of many of his stories: the main character has died, his/her commitment fulfilled, a sacrifice made, and the survivor members of the communities that have claimed this character as one of their own discuss the nature of what has happened. Many of these ending scenes are set in cemeteries or churches, during funeral rites. The dialogues that often close his novels, therefore, have the function of eulogies for the deceased character. Interestingly, and apart from exceptions like Brown's words about Jones at the end of *The Comedians* (which are delivered as a monologue), these eulogies tend to be shaped as *dialogues*, enacting a final assessment on the meaning and purpose of the character's life and death. In this kind of scene, one of the characters is typically a priest. It should be noted, for the sake of religious accuracy, that Catholic priests are not allowed to do eulogies during a funeral mass, according to the General Instruction for the Roman Missal. Therefore, the dialogue usually takes place after the service is over, as in *A Burnt-Out Case* or *Monsignor Quixote*. These dialogues have a clear dialectical character, in which each of the speakers represents a different view of what has happened and how to interpret the meaning of the character's death or sacrifice. They are, however, inconclusive dialogues. Unlike the kind of dialectics governing literary forms like the morality play, there is no explicit resolution regarding the opposing views expressed in these dialogues. As A. A. De Vitis noted, Greene's novels work by "exciting the pity and the curiosity of the reader as they move within the boundaries of a problem that often seems to admit no earthly solution" ("Catholic" 116). They are left unresolved, often ending on an inter-rogative note, and in this sense they open a sort of metaleptic gap at the end of the narration: Who is to answer the questions posited by these endings? Who is to decide whether Scobie is to be saved or condemned, whether Bendrix has started to believe, whether Querry has recovered his will to live, or whether Mayor Sancho will bear witness to Monsignor Quixote's love? The reader. Miller has claimed that "reading always has a performative as well as a cognitive dimension" (*Versions* 22). The undecidability of the final judgment passed on characters in the closing scenes of many of his novels speaks not only of the lack of narrative closure per se, but also of the lines of continuity established between Greene's fictional universe and the reader's. The endings of his novels constitute invitations to the reader to take responsibility for what she has just read; they are enactments of such a performative dimension.

The uncertainty as to how to interpret such endings, moreover, speaks of the difficulty of such a call to ethical responsibility. What Greene's novels prove repeatedly is that the particular circumstances of each story, of each character, often contradict normative behavior, universal moral codes. The problem faced by the critics of Greene's fic-tion, the problem of what Greene again and again rejected about critical readings of it, is the one of the particularity versus universality of the ethical law it incarnates and enacts.

The problem of ethical universality, moreover, overlaps with the problem of community explored in this book. The narrative pattern analyzed in the preceding chapters has a clearly teleological character, one articulated around the notions of individual and community. The sequence of events through which a conspicuous number of Greene's heroes abandon their initial ennui for the sake of some form of commit-ment takes the shape of a search for community. This search, however, as was pointed out in the last chapter, rarely ends in a successful inte-gration on the part of the character into any form of stable community. None of Greene's characters gets to live happily ever after, not even live unhappily with others. From the perspective of the models of commu-nity we may extract from Greene's work, his novels illustrate once again the failure of community, or rather the failure of the individual in his attempt to "commune" with others. At best, we get to see glimpses of unstable, fragile, momentary communal life. These are the precarious communal encounters between Scobie and Deo Gratias, the Priest and the bandit, Father Quixote and Mayor Sancho ... encounters traversed by the proximity of death, in most cases.

I have claimed, throughout this book, that Greene's fiction enacts a communal dynamics that has come to be articulated, on a theoretical plane, by Maurice Blanchot and Jean-Luc Nancy, among others. For six decades, his fiction set out to unmask the pretense of transcendence on the part of the different communities claiming the subject's allegiance on political, religious, social grounds. In this sense, it may be worthwhile to remember once more that Greene is the direct heir of Joseph Conrad, whose work exposed the inhuman workings of the structures that rule human life, with a special focus on the economic and political interests often masked by communal alibis. Greene's unveiling of the "seediness" of life echoes to a large extent Joseph Conrad's conviction that "things did not stand being looked into" (*Secret* 178).[2] If one does look into things, one is sure to discover that most of the forms of relationship to others sanctioned as "communities" are forms of manipulation and control over individual life. Thus, like Greene's, Conrad's characters are continually trying to run away from such communities. It was precisely from Conrad that Greene borrowed his epigraph for *The Human Factor*, one of his most pessimistic novels, about the instrumentalization of the individual at the hands of the political: "I only know that he who forms a tie is lost."[3]

However, there seems to be an essential difference between both authors regarding the possibility of a "true" community. Conrad was a nihilist in his conviction that man is fundamentally alone, and in his realization of the impossibility of continuing to live after one has come to acknowledge such a fact. Greene, on the other hand, was ultimately a humanist. In the passage from *A Burnt-Out Case* quoted at the end of the preceding chapter, he expresses the conviction that even in the absence of any form of civilization, human beings will still be moved to care for one another. "Caring" is, therefore, man's natural state. Many of his novels, from *The Power and the Glory* to *The Comedians*, from *The End of the Affair* to *Monsignor Quixote*, end on the verge of a further take on community and compassion. Love for one's neighbor, so to speak, takes the shape of a promising interrogation: "for how long, he wondered with a kind of fear, was it possible for that love of his to continue? And to what end?" (*Monsignor* 247). This may be what John le Carré, called, in a blurb for the back cover of *The Third Man*, Greene's "transcendent universal compassion," or what John Updike, in his introduction to the Vintage edition of *The Power and the Glory*, referred to as his "will toward compassion" (xii).

The momentary glimpses of human community which punctuate Greene's fiction may be regarded as occurrences of what Jean-Luc

Nancy and Maurice Blanchot have called, in their theoretical work, the inoperative community: "Inert, immobile, less a gathering than the always imminent dispersal of a presence occupying the whole space and nevertheless without a place (utopia), a kind of messianism announcing nothing but its autonomy and its unworking" (Blanchot *Unavowable* 33). Borrowing Nancy's words, I'd like to claim that in Greene's fiction, community is what happens in the wake of society (Nancy *Inoperative* 11). The problem remains, however, as to the lack of constructive value in Greene's communal exploration.[4] Can one extract a model of community from Greene's fiction? I would say no, because community for him is just a passing, momentary interruption of what is perceived as a constant state of doubt and communal drifting. "The singular crosses the universal" (Derrida "Before" 213): community is what happens in the wake of society, of any form of communal organization that claims universal, eternal, teleological status. You cannot deduce a model of communal life from Greene's fiction, in the same way as you cannot read his novels as codes for ethical behavior with a universal validity. His interest, as a writer, is in the particular. And only in the particular can ethics and community find their authentic expression.

I resume, then, the question posited at the beginning of this section: why do we read Graham Greene? Not for answers to existential questions, or for a life guide to be followed as a rule book. Not to become better people, to learn about human compassion or courage. His novels do not really teach anything. And yet, by reading them, I'd claim, we are frustrated, challenged, and transformed by the particularities of the situations presented in them. Derek Attridge has stated: "Respect for otherness does not inhibit intervention in the affairs of others, but it does away with any thought that there might be an algorithmic solution to such problems. They can only be addressed as specific and singular cases" (129). Attridge's words resonate with Greene's emphasis on "what is, human material," that is to say, on the particular: "to the novelist, of course, his novel is the best he can do with a particular subject" (*Ways* 123). Graham Greene refused to perceive his work as an algorithmic solution to moral problems, to claim any kind of universal validity for his depiction of the world. This insistence on the particular, the lack of exemplary character of his fiction, the persistence of doubt and uncertainty, the ethical aporias dramatized in his novels, makes it the perfect example of the singularity of literature, of the performative power of narrative on ethical grounds.

Notes

Introduction: Occasions for Unselfing

1. The absence of female protagonists in Greene's fiction has been noted by Adamson ("Long" 210), Brennan (2–3, 30), and Malik. Against current usage, and attending to this peculiarity, throughout this book I refer to Greene's "hero," using the masculine form. As Malik observed, in the only feminist study of Greene's work published to date, "from the feminist point of view, it is significant that out of all the twenty-five novels, from *The Man Within* (1929) to *The Captain and the Enemy* (1988) written by Graham Greene, none is endowed with a memorable female protagonist [...] his concept of the autonomous individual seems to exclude the autonomous female". A similar point is made by Judith Adamson when she claims that Aunt Augusta, from *Travels with my Aunt*, is "Greene's only fictional woman to approximate the narrative power of men" ("Long" 210).

2. Brian L. Thomson has referred to such biographical patterns of explanation as "auteurism" (156), criticizing the tendency to reproduce the author's intellectual biography as a rationale for interpretation (5), according to which the identification of the author's "distinctive qualities of the voice, unraveling the pattern of the mind" may provide access to the meaning of his works (6). An early example of this kind of interpretive pattern may be John Atkins' *Graham Greene* (1957), which literally defines Greene's work as an "onion" to be peeled by the critics trying to reach at a core truth of a psycho-biographical kind: "one peels off layer after layer to get to the true, basic onion" (Atkins 11).

3. Along a diachronic axis, this division corresponds roughly to what critics have called the Catholic cycle – from *Brighton Rock* to *The End of the Affair* – and the post-Catholic period – allegedly inaugurated with *The Quiet American* (1955) (see Bosco 10–11). This classification seems to spring from Greene's own statements about his novels' subjects: "For one period I did write on Catholic subjects [...] My period of Catholic novels was preceded and followed by political novels" (Philips 173, qtd. Land 6).

4. For a practical illustration of such critical positions, one may compare the argumentative strategies of monographs like Bosco's and Adamson's (*Graham Greene*) – the first offering a religious interpretation, the second a political one. For an attempt to provide a synthesis of the religious versus political interpretations of Greene's work, see Sharma's *Graham Greene, the Search for Belief*, where she claims that "the quest for belief is not confined to the religious experience alone, for Greene is concerned with the total experience of man" (27).

5. This is the second of the three questions formulated by Kant in his *Critique of Pure Reason* (1781) as the ones on which "all the interest of my reason" should be focused: "1. What can I know? 2. What should I do? 3. What may I hope?" (677).

6. This statement was originally made in the 1953 interview conducted by Martin Shuttleworth and Simon Raven for *The Paris Review*'s series "The Art

of Fiction" (1953; 25–41). References to it can be found in Hoskins (ix–xi) and Sharma (163).

7. I am referring here to the kind of methodology famously used by Vladimir Propp in his *Morphology of the Folktale* (1928). Other monographs which have focused on patterns of characterization in Greene's work, looking for types and for recurrent relationships between them, include Sharrock's *Saints, Sinners and Comedians* (1984), Erdinast-Vulcan's *Graham Greene's Childless Fathers* (1988), or Gordon's *Fighting Evil: Unsung Heroes in the Novels of Graham Greene* (1997), among others.

8. Land's "three-phase classification of Greene's novels" distinguishes between 'early (or experimental)', 'middle' and 'late'" (Land 6).

9. Greene is making reference to Henry James's "The Figure in the Carpet" (1896), but he misquotes the title as "the pattern in the carpet" both in *Ways of Escape* (134) and in the aforementioned interview with Allain (23). Greene's use of the Jamesian metaphor has become a critical *topos* (see Bosco 3). Robert Hoskins, for example, anchors his study in the belief "that a revealing and important pattern in Greene's work has gone unnoticed" (xv). The titles of works such as Bedard's *The Thriller Pattern in Graham Greene's Major Novels* (1959) or Gamer's *Breaking the Carpet's Pattern: The Border Novels of Graham Greene* (1989) also illustrate this point. For an exploration of "the figure in the carpet" metaphor in connection to narrative, see J. Hillis Miller (*Ariadne's Thread* 18–21).

10. "Some critics have referred to a strange 'seedy' region of the mind (why did I ever popularize that last adjective?) which they call Greeneland" (*Ways* 77).

11. Definitions quoted from the *Merriam-Webster Dictionary*.

12. See Emmanuel Lévinas, *Totality and Infinity* (1969), where he defines ethics as the realm "where the same takes the irreducible Other into account" (47).

13. On the interaction between notions of community, nativism, and colonialism, see Fanon's *The Wretched of the Earth* and Parry's *Postcolonial Studies*.

14. See Kunkel (*Labyrinthine* 123), Burgess (99), Baldridge (154), Hoskins (264–65), Donaghy (*Graham Greene* 60), Brennan (4, 153); for a discussion of paradox as a feature of Catholic doctrine, see Bosco (14).

15. Baldridge also talks about "the paradox of commitment" (154).

16. Problems of definition are frequently noted by Greene's critics (Baldridge 58). Greene himself has often been concerned with the appropriate definition of the terms he uses and the way in which they affect the interpretation of his novels. Being asked by an interviewer whether characters like Pinkie, Scobie, or Rose in *The Living Room* (1953) are redeemed through suicide, Greene's answer was: "Yes, though redemption is not the exact word. We must be careful of our language. They have all understood in the end. This is perhaps the religious sense" (Donaghy *Conversations* 30; from *Paris Review* interview, 1953).

17. The Greenean hero may be described as an extreme version of what Richard Rorty would call a "liberal ironist," characterized by "a sense of the contingency of their language of moral deliberation" (60).

18. The motive is a classic device in film noir as well, and is one of the cornerstones of Alfred Hitchcock's filmography (in films like *North by Northwest* (1959), *Spellbound* (1945) and, of special Greenean resonances, *I Confess* (1953)). Its origin, however, can be traced back as far as William Godwin's

Caleb Williams, which according to some critics was actually the first detective story in the British tradition. In Godwin's Jacobin novel, the detectivesque plot revolves around the false accusation thrown by Lord Falkland on his servant Caleb Williams. The repeated misidentification of the roles of hero and villain (in the trial scenes which abound in the novel) triggers Williams' escape and later hunt. Indeed, the idea that society can destroy a perfectly innocent man when manipulated in the interest of powerful individuals like Falkland served as the fictional illustration of Godwin's political theories.

19. For an explanation of the origin and critical usage of the term "Greeneland," see Watts (142–48).
20. On narrative functions and sequentiality, see Propp (21–23), Chatman (45–48).
21. The parallels between Murdoch's moral philosophy and Weil's universal ethics, on the one hand, and Lévinasian ethics of otherness, on the other, may come to mind on this point. They fall beyond the scope of this research project, although it should be mentioned that both Murdoch and Weil share Greene's religious perspective on morality, and therefore their understanding of the matter of love comes closer to Greene's own vocabulary.

1 Peace

1. Most thrillers written in the 1930s share a storyline based on the idea of the persecuted hero, including *The Man Within, The Name for Action, Rumour at Nightfall, A Gun for Sale,* and *The Confidential Agent,* among others. The conflation of physical safety and spiritual redemption is expressed with particular insistence in *The Man Within* and *Rumour at Nightfall.*
2. It should be noted that these two characters would be saved if their situation was to be regarded from the perspective of Catholic dogma, in which confession may actually bring peace and redemption, even in the face of such sins. It is interesting to observe the narrative role played by this religious idea. *The Quiet American* does not entertain this possibility at all, letting the novel end with the main character left to live with his guilt. *The End of the Affair,* on the other hand, pivots precisely around this idea, suggesting the possibility of a conversion to faith that would grant Bendrix redemption. The same idea is used at the end of *The Power and the Glory,* in which the Catholic belief in deathbed confession is used as a narrative device to grant redemption in a last-minute act of contrition.
3. It is interesting to note how Greene's ethnocentric view of human beings often ascribes the possibility of a permanent peace of mind to those who belong to other ethnic groups, thus contributing to a kind of mystification codified as the Rousseaunian figure of *le bon sauvage.* Whereas his protagonists seem unable to find peace – that is, unable to detach themselves from the suffering of others – the Muslim Yusef or the sleeping Indian in *The Honorary Consul* find perfect rest. In this last novel, this is attributed to the imperfect humanity of the Indian, to his primitive nature: "Look at him, lying quietly there while we talk. I envy him. That is real peace. Sleep is meant to be like that for all of us, but we have lost the animal touch" (178). On the ethnocentric view that attributes animal qualities to native peoples,

see Fanon (7): "The colonist refers constantly to the bestiary [...] this explosive population growth, those hysterical masses, those blank faces, those shapeless, obese bodies, this headless, tailless cohort, these children who seem not to belong to anyone, this indolence sprawling under the sun, this vegetating existence [...]."

4. Rowe's guilt, it should be noted, springs from what may be interpreted as an earlier "excess" of action: he killed his sick wife to prevent her suffering (27, 31). From the moral perspective, it could be claimed that his decision to act implies trespassing the normative limits for human intervention. In the novel, Greene stresses how the social treatment of this "mercy killing" (27) reinforces Rowe's guilt and results in his subsequent moral paralysis (34).

5. On suicide as relief from pain, see Bergonzi (120) or Miller ("Saddest" 140).

6. Even in real life, Greene associated peace with romantic love, as noted by Norman Sherry in his biography of the author. He associated the word "peace" with his lover, Vivien, as expressed in phrases such as "the peace we have so often got together" (Sherry *Life* 2, 329).

7. The parallelism between *The Heart of the Matter* and *A Burnt-Out Case* has been a recurrent focus of critical attention (Dobozy, Kelly, Nordlof). The African setting has obviously helped critics to couple both novels, but the structural symmetry is worthy of attention: the main characters in both novels undergo processes of spiritual transformation and find a tragic end. For both of them, involvement with others proves to be fatal. Both texts offer an epilogue in which other characters – like a chorus in classical tragedy – pass judgment on the hero after his death. However, whereas *The Heart of the Matter* has been recurrently read as a tragedy, *A Burnt-Out Case* – specially its self-conscious ending, full of "the clichés from the *Marie-Chantal* serials" (*Burnt-Out* 168) – is said to belong to the realm of farce.

8. This rhetoric of bareness connects, in *A Burnt-Out Case*, the desire for peace with the description of the African "blankness," and with the colonialist implications of the concept of Africa as *terra nullius*. On the *topos* of Africa as "blankness," see Boehmer (155–56), or Darian-Smith et al., both discussing Western representation of the African bush "as impenetrable and empty" (Darian-Smith et al. 136).

9. The parallel has been observed by many critics (Hoskins 167; Watts 125). Pendleton claims that this novel is actually a re-enactment of a "Conradian masterplot": "*A Burnt-Out Case* begins where *Heart of Darkness* leaves off" (Pendleton 113). See also Edmonton, who claims that "the foundation text of Greene's leprosy writing is Conrad's *Heart of Darkness*" (233).

10. Leprosy has, of course, strong symbolic connotations in Christian discourse, particularly in the New Testament. In the Old Testament it is a mark of social rejection and implies expulsion from the community (see Numbers 5, 2: "Command the children of Israel, that they put out of the camp every leper, and every one that hath an issue, and whosoever is defiled by the dead"). The physical condition was said to be a reflection of the spiritual state, that is, a visible mark of sin (Douglas *Purity* 49). Querry's initial condition as a wanderer may touch upon this symbolic codification. In the New Testament, however, leprosy plays a different role, for its healing is a sign of Jesus' divinity and of the faith of the sick. Dwelling among lepers becomes

an act of faith and charity, thus denying the contagious potential of the disease and giving it a socially subversive quality. Greene's story partakes of this logic. The story of Jesus and the leper is told, in different versions, in the Gospels of Mathew, Mark, and Luke. For a contemporary revision of this social-symbolic use of leprosy, one could think of Ernesto Guevara's *The Motorcycle Diaries* (1993). Guevara's stay in the *léproserie* of San Pablo is more or less contemporary with Greene's visit to a similar one in Congo (early 1950s). On the cultural significance of leprosy for modern Western cultures, see Edmonton's *Leprosy and Empire: A Medical and Cultural History* (2006).

11. This idea is suggested in the Pascalian maxim quoted by the Superior: "a man who starts looking for God has already found him. The same may be true of love – when we look for it, perhaps we've already found it" (*Burnt-Out* 198).

2   Bargain

1. The episode was inspired by the death of Greene's own father, as he relates in *A Sort of Life* (Sherry *Life* 2, 150–51).

2. For a psychoanalytical reading of this novel, see Pierloot's chapter in the book *Psychoanalytic Patterns in the Work of Graham Greene* (1994). According to Pierloot, the dying child would be an "object of reparation" in Scobie's flawed mourning process for his dead child (108).

3. Lewis coincides with De Vitis in claiming that "Scobie's Catholicism is something akin to the fatality of Greek drama" (De Vitis *Graham Greene* 87). See also Dobozy (444).

4. Philippe Lejeune, who has researched the origins of the forms of self-address in the diary tradition from the eighteenth century onward (2009), claims that the diary lies at the crossroads of two opposite systems of expression: "the monologic system of the chronicle" and "the dialogic system of the letter or the prayer" (93). Addressing your diary, Lejeune concludes, implies that "someone is being 'spoken to'" (94). Sarah's diary is full of expressions indicating this, passages in which the presence of a "You" is constant, as in the entry dated February 10, 1946 (90).

5. The question of to whom – God or the Greenean hero – these dealings are more advantageous is an aspect that should not be overlooked, as it is directly related to the theological framework within which this narrative motif is articulated. It will be dealt with in the third section of this chapter.

6. In Camus's essay *The Rebel* (1951), the image of the suffering child is also put at the center of human revolt against the order of things dictated by religious thought: "The protest against evil which is at the very core of metaphysical revolt is significant in this regard. It is not the suffering child, which is repugnant in itself, but the fact that the suffering is not justified" (99). Unlike Camus's rebel, however, the characters in Greene's fiction react not by killing God, but bargaining with Him.

7. The connection between Greene's work and theodicy has been pointed out in two scholarly edited volumes: Erlebach and Stein's *Graham Greene in Perspective: A Critical Symposium* (1991; 108); Freiburg and Gruss's *But Vindicate the Ways of God to Man: Literature and Theodicy* (2004).

3   Despair

1. According to Catholic doctrine, suicide is the only sin which does not allow for an aftermath in which repentance may happen. Hence, it is unforgivable because it leaves no time margin for repentance and forgiveness.
2. The connection between hope and despair as existential categories may be traced back to Gabriel Marcel's understanding of those terms as dialectically engaged. See Marcel's *The Philosophy of Existentialism* (26). The connection between Marcel's ideas and Greene's writings was identified by Robert Evans in his 1957 essay "Existentialism in *The Quiet American*" (241).
3. On Greene's use of this expression, see Brennan (94). Greene explicitly used the mystical concept of the "dark night" in *The End of the Affair* (36) in order to draw a parallelism between human love and mystical experience. On this secular version of the dark night, see Bosco (61).
4. Friedman includes in his list characters who "desperately seek death" like the Whisky Priest or Sarah (*Fictional* 232). He does not mention Querry, although in his own logic he should be included. However, in those three cases, as I will argue in subsequent chapters, the character's death is brought about as an act of sacrifice, after a strong ethical commitment has created in them a sense of obligation that not even the thought of death can ameliorate.
5. Unamuno wrote about the characters created by Miguel de Cervantes in *Our Lord Don Quixote* (1905).
6. Unamuno describes the end of human existence as the sacrifice of individual consciousness for the sake of "one collective being with a true consciousness" (277) – that is, he depicts heaven in terms of communal fusion. As will be analyzed in the last chapter of this book, such a "grand dream of the final solidarity of mankind" (ibid.) remains for Greene in the realm of utopia, and is never realized by his characters.
7. Sunita Sinha, in her existentialist reading of Greene's early novels, has noted the connection between the ethical predicament in which characters often find themselves and the sense of uncertainty: "In these novels he gives a searching analysis of the individual as the agent who has to choose between right and wrong in a world of despair and uncertainty" (153).
8. The passage quoted by Greene is from Unamuno's *The Tragic Sense of Life* (212).
9. On the issue of hatred of God, the inevitable reference is Camus' *The Rebel*, in which rebellion is said to start from a simultaneous and paradoxical feeling of revulsion and loyalty to an idea (14). In this sense, it may be observed that hatred is the primary expression of active engagement, a symptom of how despair – "in which a condition is accepted even though it is considered unjust" (14) – has been abandoned.
10. Brendan Sweetman reads *The End of the Affair* as an illustration of Gabriel Marcel's Catholic existentialism, and particularly his idea "of the possibility of religious faith in a hostile world" (77): "The question of the transcendent forces itself upon the characters despite their best attempts to resist it" (Sweetman 76). This kind of existentialist reading tries to counteract the Jansenist view about notions of determinism and denial of

individual free will (Sweetman 77; Friedman "Dangerous" 133; Friedman *Fictional* 248–49).

11. On the role of delay as a narrative tool, see Malamet, "The Uses of Delay in *The Power and the Glory*."

4   Pity and Compassion

1. Definitions quoted from the *Merriam-Webster Dictionary*.

2. I am indebted, in the discussion of Aristotle's understanding of "pity," to Marjolein Oele's "Suffering, Pity and Friendship: An Aristotelian Reading of Book 24 of Homer's *Iliad*."

3. The notion of suffering together is further explored in the *Nichomachean Ethics* when Aristotle wonders about the effects of sharing one's sorrows with friends (IX, 11, 117a30–32).

4. Shaftesbury's understanding of moral virtue was also universalist, but it was grounded on affection for one's species. See *An Inquiry Concerning Virtue or Merit (Characteristics* I.ii.2, 171). Specifically, he refers to compassion as a "natural affection" (ibid., 192).

5. I'm not thinking about the consideration of God's mercy that stands at the basis of Christian thought – inherited from the Hebrew term *chesed*, referring to God's attitude to mankind – but about the strictly human dimension of compassion toward other human beings.

6. David Hume explored the contradictory nature of the apparent good will implicit in pity in his *Treatise of Human Nature* (book II, 2. ix), but the critique of pity probably found its most virulent expression in Nietzsche's railing against it in *AntiChrist*. Stephen Leighton argues, nevertheless, that the critique of pity is already present in earlier philosophers, beginning with the Stoics and Plato, and continuing in Descartes and Spinoza (Leighton 100).

7. On the philosophical use of the dialectics between pity and compassion in the classical and early Christian world, see Konstan's *Pity Transformed*, particularly chapter 2: "Pity versus Compassion."

8. It is worth noting here that this opposition between the particular and the universal is repeatedly brought into the political realm in Greene. The constant debates between Pyle and Fowler in *The Quiet American*, and the ending passage from *Our Man in Havana* may serve as instances of this: "I can't believe in anything bigger than a home, or anything vaguer than a human being," claims Wormold at the end of *Our Man in Havana* (226).

9. See for instance Brennan (70) and Bergonzi (111) on *The Power and the Glory*; or Thomson (189) and Christopher (158) on *The Quiet American*.

10. See also Dobozy (429), who talks about "Greene's conflation of Christian ideology with the colonial setting, in all its political and spiritual complexity."

11. The terms "kernel event" and "narrative crux" come from Seymour Chatman's *Story and Discourse* (53), which remains one of the most illuminating tools for the analysis of narrative plot from a structuralist perspective.

12. The same image is used in *The Confidential Agent*: "It was like sensation painfully returning to a frozen land. He didn't love, he was incapable of loving anyone alive, but nevertheless the prick was there" (154).

5   Commitment

1. Rowland Smith is one of the few authors who has explored the persistence of this pattern of communal affiliation in Greene's works set during World War II, pointing to the rhetorical articulation of a British community in texts like *The Ministry of Fear* (104–17).

2. In *Giving an Account of Oneself* (2005), Judith Butler relates the notion of responsibility to the emergence of the subject in Nietzschean terms. For Nietzsche, the subject emerges through a retrospective understanding of itself as the cause of an injury (Butler 85). One becomes a subject when realizing that one is responsible for the pain caused to others.

3. The problem of national allegiance is particularly relevant in this novel, where the protagonist, Anthony Farrant, is said to live "the life of a generation before him" (166) precisely because of his attachment to a British identity perceived by his sister to be disappearing in the context of globalized economic forces, embodied in the tycoon Krogh: "'After all, here we are foreigners'. 'We're national. We're national', Kate said, 'from the soles of our feet. But nationality's finished. Krogh doesn't think in frontiers. He's beaten unless he has the world'" (135).

4. The possibility of making of this integration a permanent affair, however, is a different question. The logic of sacrifice is often involved in the act of commitment, and the Greenean hero is prone to become a martyr of the people, as the cases of D., the Whisky Priest, or Jones exemplify. This problematic integration into a community will be analyzed in detail in the next chapter.

5. The passage reminds one of Modernist expressions of skepticism about patriotic political discourse, from Ford Maddox Ford's *The Good Soldier* (1915) – "full of the big words, courage, loyalty, honour, constancy" (31), to Hemingway's *A Farewell to Arms* (1929) – "I was always embarrassed by the words sacred, glorious, and sacrifice and the expression in vain [...] I had seen nothing sacred, and the things that were glorious had no glory and the sacrifices were like the stockyards at Chicago" (165) – or, with some variation, D. H. Lawrence's *Lady Chatterley's Lover* (1928): "Home! ... it was a word that had had its day. It was somehow canceled. All the great words, it seemed to Connie, were canceled for her generation" (65).

6. The rhetoric of familial imagery, however, can traced much further back in time than Romanticism. It is constant, for example, in enlightened political discourse, exemplified in texts like Kant's "What Is the Enlightenment?" (1784) or Paine's *Common Sense* (1776). For an analysis of this issue, see Olson; Brown.

7. As Roger Sharrock noted in *Saints, Sinners and Comedians*, "Greene's alienated man is essentially a traveller wandering or escaping even if is only an escape from himself" (18).

8. Hill's terminology, in turn, draws on Martin Heidegger and Bernd Jager. It should be noted that Hill's book does not focus on *The Comedians*, which I'd argue is the novel where Greene discusses most explicitly the issues of heritage, home, roots, and nation. He does, however, devote separate chapters to *The Honorary Consul* and *The Human Factor*, where these issues are also crucial.

9. See, for instance, Fichte's *Addresses to the German Nation* (1808). In the concluding remarks of the Fourteenth Address, the notions of "people" (*Volk*) and "soil" (*Bodens*) are brought together: "I want to gather to them from over

the soil of our common land men of similar sentiments and resolutions, and to link them together, so that at this central point a single, continuous, and unceasing flame of patriotic disposition may be kindled, which will spread over the whole soil of the fatherland to its utmost boundaries" (248).

10. Weil's understanding of "roots," in any case, shares to a great extent the romantic outlook of nationalistic discourse: "a collectivity has its roots in the past. It constitutes the sole agency for preserving the spiritual treasures accumulated by the dead, the sole transmitting agency by means of which the dead can speak to the living" (*Roots* 8).

11. The parallelisms in the portrayal of American characters in both novels contribute to the critical perception of Greene's anti-Americanism. On Greene's alleged anti-Americanism, particularly in connection to the reception of *The Quiet American*, see Nashel (154–55).

12. On Guevara's pan-American revolution, see for instance his 1967 "Message to the Tricontinental": "In this continent practically only one tongue is spoken (with the exception of Brazil, with whose people, those who speak Spanish can easily make themselves understood, owing to the great similarity of both languages). There is also such a great similarity between the classes in these countries, that they have attained identification among themselves of an international *americano* type, much more complete than in the other continents. Language, habits, religion, a common foreign master, unite them. The degree and the form of exploitation are similar for both the exploiters and the men they exploit in the majority of the countries of Our America. And rebellion is ripening swiftly in it" (*Guerrilla* 171).

13. This is a common device in Greene's fiction, through which the surviving characters often comment on the protagonist's life and death. It appears in *England Made Me*, *Brighton Rock*, *The Third Man*, *The Heart of the Matter*, *A Burnt-Out Case*, and *The Comedians*, among others. With slight variation, individual elegies for the departed also close the narratives of *The Quiet American* and *The End of the Affair*.

14. For a discussion of this kind of narrative retroactivity in connection with the impossibility of representing certain things in narrative form, see J. Hillis Miller's "The Grounds of Love: Anthony Trollope's *Ayala's Angel*." Miller discusses this idea also in an interview with Julian Wolfreys included in *The J. Hillis Miller Reader*, talking about this same kind of "catachrestic" moment in Anthony Trollope's novel *Ayala's Angel* (1882): "He asks an obvious question: 'When did you begin loving me?' Ayala says, 'I think I was in love with you the first time I met you'. You say to yourself, or I did anyway, I must have missed something. So you go back to the scene when they first meet, and look again at all of the scenes of their meetings in-between. In no one of these does Trollope represent a transition from harsh rejection of Stubbs to being in love with him. It must have happened without happening, so to speak, *or it must not be possible to represent it*" ("Why" 419; emphasis added).

15. Greene's use of this device – keeping a secret that may destroy a relationship – may be related to 1930s and 1940s melodrama. For instance, Leo McCarey's two versions of *Love Affair* (the first in 1939 and the second, as *An Affair to Remember*, in 1957) make use of a very similar device leading to an intensified climax, when the male protagonist belatedly discovers the reason why his beloved (apparently) betrayed him in the past.

6   *Caritas*

1. Betrayal, Greene claimed, was the major topic of Henry James's fiction, and the substance of melodrama. See Greene's "The Portrait of a Lady" (1947): "what deeply interested him, what was indeed his ruling passion, was the idea of treachery, the 'Judas complex'" (49). To some extent, the same could be said of Greene's own work.

2. The same problem would have existed in *The End of the Affair*, were it not for the device of Sarah's diary, which allows direct access to her version of the story.

3. On the issue of the love triangle, particularly in the colonial context, see Kramer's "Postcolonial Triangles." Kramer's analysis follows Eve Sedgwick's exploration of the "triangle" (21) in her seminal work *Between Men: English Literature and Male Homosocial Desire* (1985).

4. This point was made by Greene in *The Ministry of Fear*: "words however emptily repeated can in time form a habit, a kind of unnoticed sediment at the bottom of the mind, until one day to your own surprise you find yourself acting on the belief you thought you didn't believe in" (73).

5. Throughout this passage, Greene used the term "pity" to refer to the Priest's relation to his cellmates. It should be noted that this usage is anomalous in the context of Greene's frequent articulation of pity as opposed to compassion. Here, pity actually denotes authentic responsibility for others, and not the asymmetrical kind of relationship based on pride that Greene normally labeled with that term. In this sense, the passage constitutes an exception within the pattern analyzed in Chapter 4.

6. In *Totality and Infinity*, Lévinas articulates an ethics that articulates the subject as being addressed by an Other who demands a response: "The existence of this being [...] is effectuated in the non-postponable urgency with which he requires a response" (212).

7. In *Imagined Communities* (1991) Benedict Anderson defines creole communities in terms of their establishing a differentiated group separated both from natives and from foreigners (47–58), regarded at the same time as "a colonial community and an upper class" (58).

8. In a review of *The Heart of the Matter* entitled "The Sanctified Sinner" and published in the *New Yorker* (July 17, 1948).

9. Maria Couto has studied how Greene tends to incarnate this opposition through the mirrored characterization in novels like *The Power and the Glory* or *The Honorary Consul*, where priests are shown to be part of a bourgeois social order, confronted by a demand for political and social justice advocating an order in which they have no place. In these novels, the Whisky Priest and León Rivas are confronted with reverse images of themselves, those of other priests who have remained indifferent to this demand (Couto 71).

10. On the role of institutionalized communities in defining individual identity in the context of Greene's fiction, see Martín Salván ("Community" 303–8).

11. Kunkel identifies that "the recurrence of the archetype" of "the priest as a Christ-like scapegoat" is found in the work of a group of authors including not only Greene, but also Georges Bernanos, François Mauriac, and Maurice West (Kunkel "Priest" 72).

12. It should be noted that, although Kunkel's reading is strictly Christological, the priest appears to be connected to the apotropaic figure of the sin-eater (Douglas *Scapegoats* 9), as he takes the burden of people's sins while remaining in a state of mortal sin himself, which suggests the idea of the transferability of evil, rather than the sacramental function of cleansing it away.

13. The inspiration for Greene's preference of evil over indifference may be found in T. S. Eliot's essay on Baudelaire, which Greene read and admired: "So far as we are human, what we do must be either evil or good; so far as we do evil or good, we are human; and *it is better, in a paradoxical way, to do evil than to do nothing*: at least, we exist" (Eliot 380; emphasis added). Greene quoted from this essay in his own text "Henry James: The Religious Aspect" (1936), precisely from the passage that the ending sermon from *The Comedians* seems to echo (41).

Conclusion: The Ethics of Reading (Graham Greene)

1. It should be noted, however, that critics like Arnold Kettle accused Greene of putting his literary talent at the service of his religious ideas: "In *The Heart of The Matter* one has, moreover, constantly the sense of the screw being turned, not in order to satisfy the developing needs of the novel as a work of art but in order *to satisfy Graham Greene's abstract convictions*" (174; emphasis added).

2. An idea expressed by Winnie Verloc in *The Secret Agent* (1907) and by Axel Heyst in *Victory* (1914): "Man on this earth is an unforeseen accident which does not stand close investigation" (167).

3. The reference is to a statement made by Axel Heyst in *Victory* (169).

4. On a theoretical plane, the discussion regarding the validity of Nancy's and Blanchot's models of community has been articulated on the basis of two key problems: their emphasis on the *cum* of "community," that is to say, of the being in common at the expense of any stable notion of individual subjectivity, and the impolitical (Esposito *Bios* 152) character of their proposal, which underscores the precariousness and temporality of any inoperative community to the extent of precluding any potential application to any long-term situation. For a critique of their thought on the grounds of these two ideas, see Esposito's "Community, Immunity, Biopolitics" (84).

Bibliography

Ackroyd, Peter. "'Of Gods and Men.' Review of *The Honorary Consul*." *The Spectator*, September 15, 1973: 344–45.

Adamson, Judith. *Graham Greene, the Dangerous Edge: Where Art and Politics Meet*. New York: St. Martin's Press, 1990.

Adamson, Judith. "The Long Wait for Aunt Augusta: Reflections on Graham Greene's Fictional Women." In Gilvary and Middleton, eds. 210–21.

Adorno, Theodor W. *Problems of Moral Philosophy*. Ed. Thomas Schröder. Trans. Rodney Livingstone. Stanford, CA: Stanford University Press, 2000 [1996].

Ali, Monica. "Introduction" lto Graham Greene, *The End of the Affair*. London: Vintage, 2004 [1951]. vii–xvi.

Allain, Marie Françoise. *The Other Man: Conversations with Graham Greene*. New York: Simon & Schuster, 1983.

Allott, Kenneth, and Miriam Faris. *The Art of Graham Greene*. New York: Russell & Russell, 1963 [1951].

Anderson, Benedict. *Imagined Communities: Reflections on the Origin and Spread of Nationalism*. London: Verso, 1991.

Aquinas, Thomas. *Summa Theologica*. Raleigh, NC: Hayes Barton Press, 1952 [1273].

Aristotle. *The Rhetoric and the Poetics of Aristotle*. Ed. W. Rhys Roberts. New York: The Modern Library, 1984.

Armstrong, Nancy. *How Novels Think: The Limits of British Individualism from 1719–1900*. New York: Columbia University Press, 2005.

Atkins, John. *Graham Greene*. London: Calder & Boyars, 1966 [1957].

Attridge, Derek. *The Singularity of Literature*. London: Routledge, 2004.

Auden, W. H. "The Heresy of Our Time." In Hynes, ed. 93–94.

Augustine, Saint Bishop of Hippo. *The Trinity*. Ed. Edmund Hill. New York: New City Press, Augustinian Heritage Institute, 1991.

Badiou, Alain. *Ethics*. London: Verso, 2001 [1993].

Badiou, Alain. *Saint Paul: The Foundation of Universalism*. Stanford, CA: Stanford University Press, 2003.

Baldridge, Cates. *Graham Greene's Fictions: The Virtues of Extremity*. Columbia: University of Missouri Press, 2000.

Barthes, Roland. *S/Z*. Trans. Richard Miller. New York: Hill & Want, 1974 [1970].

Bataille, Georges. *Inner Experience*. Trans. Leslie Anne Boldt. Albany, NY: State University of New York Press, 1988 [1954].

Bedard, Bernard John. "The Thriller Pattern in Graham Greene's Major Novels." Doctoral dissertation. University of Michigan Press, 1959.

Bergonzi, Bernard. *A Study in Greene: Graham Greene and the Art of the Novel*. Oxford: Oxford University Press, 2006.

Blake, William. *The Complete Poetry and Prose of William Blake*. Ed. David V. Erdman. Anchor, 1988.

Blanchot, Maurice. *The Unavowable Community*. Barrytown, NY: Station Hill Press, 1988 [1983].

Blanchot, Maurice. *The Book to Come*. Stanford, CA: Stanford University Press, 2003 [1959)].

Boehmer, Elleke. *Colonial and Postcolonial Literatures. Migrant Metaphors*. Oxford: Oxford University Press, 2005.

Bosco, Mark. *Graham Greene's Catholic Imagination*. Oxford: Oxford University Press, 2005.

Brennan, Michael G. *Graham Greene: Fictions, Faith and Authorship*. London: Continuum, 2010.

Brock, D. Heyward, and James M. Welsh. "Graham Greene and the Structure of Salvation." *Renascence* 27.1 (1974): 31–39.

Brown, Gillian. *The Consent of the Governed: The Lockean Legacy in Early American Culture*. Cambridge, MA: Harvard University Press, 2001.

Burgess, Anthony. "Politics in the Novels of Graham Greene." *Journal of Contemporary History* 2.2 (1967): 93–99.

Butler, Judith. *Giving an Account of Oneself*. New York: Fordham University Press, 2005.

Butler, Judith. *Precarious Life*. London: Verso, 2004.

Camus, Albert. *The Rebel: An Essay on Man in Revolt*. Trans. Anthony Bower. Vintage, 1991 [1951].

Chapman, Raymond. "The Vision of Graham Greene." In *Forms of Extremity in the Modern Novel*. Ed. Nathan A. Scott. Louisville, KY: John Knox Press, 1965. 75–96.

Chatman, Seymour. *Story and Discourse: Narrative Structure in Fiction and Film*. Ithaca, NY: Cornell University Press, 1980.

Christopher, Renny. *The Viet Nam War/the American War: Images and Representations in Euro-American and Vietnamese Exile Narratives*. Amherst: University of Massachusetts Press, 1995.

Conrad, Joseph. *Heart of Darkness*. Ed. Ross C. Murfin. Boston and New York: Bedford/St. Martin's, 1996 [1899].

Conrad, Joseph. *Lord Jim*. London: Penguin, 1994 [1900].

Conrad, Joseph. *Nostromo*. London: Penguin, 1994 [1904].

Conrad, Joseph. *The Secret Agent*. Oxford: Oxford University Press, 1983 [1907].

Conrad, Joseph. *Victory*. London: Penguin, 1979 [1914].

Couto, Maria. *Graham Greene: On the Frontier: Politics and Religion in the Novels*. Basingstoke: Macmillan, 1990.

Darian-Smith, Kate, Elizabeth Gunner, and Sarah Nuttall, eds. *Text, Theory, Space: Land, Literature and History in South Africa and Australia*. London: Routledge, 1996.

De Vitis, A. A. *Graham Greene*. Boston: Twayne, 1986 [1964].

De Vitis, A. A. "Greene's *The Comedians*: Hollower Men." *Renascence* 18.3 (1966): 129–46.

De Vitis, A. A. "The Catholic as Novelist: Graham Greene and François Mauriac." In Evans, ed. 112–26.

Derrida, Jacques *Aporias: Dying – Awaiting (One Another at) the "Limits of Truth."* Trans. Thomas Dutoit. Stanford, CA: Stanford University Press, 1993.

Derrida, Jacques. "Before the Law." *Acts of Literature*. Ed. Derek Attridge. London: Routledge, 1992. 181–220.

Derrida, Jacques. *Dissemination*. Trans. Barbara Johnson. London: Continuum, 2004 [1972].

Derrida, Jacques. *The Gift of Death*. Trans. D. Wills. Chicago: University of Chicago Press, 2008 [1999].

Dobozy, Tamas. "Africa and Catholic Crisis: Graham Greene's *The Heart of the Matter* and *A Burnt-Out Case*." In Hill, ed. *Perceptions* 427–57.

Donaghy, Henry J., ed. *Conversations with Graham Greene*. University Press of Mississippi, 1992.

Donaghy, Henry J. *Graham Greene, an Introduction to His Writings*. Amsterdam: Rodopi, 1983.

Douglas, Mary. *Purity and Danger: An Analysis of Concept of Pollution and Taboo*. London: Routledge, 2005 [1966].

Douglas, Tom. *Scapegoats. Tranferring Blame*. London: Routledge, 1995.

Dundes, Alan. "*Introduction to the Second Edition*." In Propp, xi–xvii.

Eagleton, Terry. "Reluctant Heroes: The Novels of Graham Greene". In *Graham Greene. Modern Critical Views*. Ed. Harold Bloom. New York: Chelsea House, 1987. 97–118.

Edmonton, Rod. *Leprosy and Empire: a Medical and Cultural History*. Cambridge: Cambridge University Press, 2006.

Eliot, George. *Adam Bede*. Ed. Margaret Reynolds. London: Penguin, 2008 [1859].

Eliot, T. S. "Baudelaire." *Selected Essays*. New York: Harcourt Brace, 1950. 371–81.

Emerson, Gloria. "Our Man in Antibes. Graham Greene." *Rolling Stone* 260 (1978): 45–49. Rpt. in Donaghy, ed. *Conversations* 123–38.

Erlebach, Peter and Thomas Michael Stein, eds. *Graham Greene in Perspective: A Critical Symposium*.Berlin: Peter Lang, 1991.

Erdinast-Vulcan, Daphna. *Graham Greene's Childless Fathers*. London: Macmillan, 1988.

Esposito, Roberto. *Bìos: Biopolitics and Philosophy*, Trans. Timothy Campbell. Minneapolis: Minnesota University Press, 2008.

Esposito, Roberto. *Communitas: The Origin and Destiny of Community*. Stanford, CA: Stanford University Press, 2010.

Esposito, Roberto. "Community, Immunity, Biopolitics." *Angelaki. Journal of the Theoretical Humanities* 18.3 (2013): 83–90.

Evans, Robert O. "Existentialism in *The Quiet American*." *Modern Fiction Studies* 3.3 (1957): 241–48.

Evans, Robert O, ed. *Graham Greene: Some Critical Considerations*. Lexington: University Press of Kentucky, 1967.

Falk, Quentin. *Travels in Greeneland: The Cinema of Graham Greene*. 2nd ed. Dahlonega, GA: University Press of North Georgia, 2014.

Fanon, Frantz. *The Wretched of the Earth*. Trans. Richard Philcox. New York: Grove Press, 2004 [1961].

Fichte, Johann Gottlieb. *Addresses to the German Nation*. Trans. R F. Jones and G. H. Turnbull. Chicago and London: The Open Court Publishing Company, 1922 [1808].

Ford, Ford Maddox. *The Good Soldier*. London: Penguin, 1977 [1915].

Foucault, Michel. *The Order of Things*. New York: Random House, 1970.

Freiburg, Rudolf and Susanne Gruss, eds. *But Vindicate the Ways of God to Man: Literature and Theodicy*. Tübingen: Stauffenburg, 2004.

Friedman, Alan Warren. "'The Dangerous Edge': Beginning with Death." In Meyers, ed. 131–55.

Friedman, Alan Warren. *Fictional Death and the Modernist Enterprise*. Cambridge: Cambridge University Press, 1995.

Gamer, Michael Crews. *Breaking the Carpet's Pattern: The Border Novels of Graham Greene*. Berkeley, CA: California University Press, 1987.

Gilvary, Dermot and Darren Middleton, eds. *Dangerous Edges of Graham Greene: Journeys with Saints and Sinners*. New York: Continuum, 2011.

Girard, René. *The Scapegoat*. Baltimore: Johns Hopkins University Press, 1989 [1982].

Girard, René. *Violence and the Sacred*. Baltimore: Johns Hopkins University Press, 1977 [1972].

Godwin, William. *Caleb Williams*. Oxford: Oxford University Press, 2009 [1794].

Gordon, Hayim. *Fighting Evil: Unsung Heroes in the Novels of Graham Greene*. Westport, CT: Greenwood Press, 1997.

Gorra, Michael. "On *The End of the Affair*." *Southwest Review* 89.1 (2004): 109–25.

Greene, Graham. *The Man Within*. London: Vintage, 2001 [1929].

Greene, Graham. *Rumour at Nightfall*. New York: Doubleday, 1932 [1931].

Greene, Graham. *Stamboul Train*. London: Vintage, 2005 [1932].

Greene, Graham. "Henry James: The Religious Aspect." *Collected Essays*. New York: Viking, 1969 [1933]. 33–44.

Greene, Graham. "Henry James: The Private Universe." *Collected Essays*. New York: Viking, 1969 [1936]. 21–34.

Greene, Graham. *England Made Me*. London: Vintage, 2006 [1935].

Greene, Graham. *The Fallen Idol. The Third Man* and *The Fallen Idol*. London: Vintage, 2005 [1935]. 99–130.

Greene, Graham. *A Gun for Sale*. London: Penguin, 2005 [1936].

Greene, Graham. *Journey without Maps*. London: Penguin, 2006 [1936].

Greene, Graham. *Brighton Rock*. London: Penguin, 2004 [1938].

Greene, Graham. *The Confidential Agent*. London: Vintage, 2006 [1939].

Greene, Graham. *The Lawless Roads*. London: Vintage, 2002 [1939].

Greene, Graham. *The Power and the Glory*. London: Vintage, 2004 [1940].

Greene, Graham. *The Ministry of Fear*. London: Penguin, 2005 [1943].

Greene, Graham. "The Portrait of a Lady." *Collected Essays*. New York: Viking, 1969 [1947]. 44–50.

Greene, Graham. *The Heart of the Matter*. London: Penguin, 2004 [1948].

Greene, Graham. *The Third Man. The Third Man* and *The Fallen Idol*. London: Vintage, 2005 [1950]. 1–98.

Greene, Graham. *The End of the Affair*. London: Vintage, 2004 [1951].

Greene, Graham. *The Living Room*. New York: Viking, 1954 [1953].

Greene, Graham. *The Quiet American*. London: Penguin, 1977 [1955].

Greene, Graham. *The Potting Shed*. New York: Viking, 1957 [1956].

Greene, Graham. *Our Man in Havana*. London: Penguin, 2007 [1958].

Greene, Graham. *A Burnt-Out Case*. London: Penguin, 1975 [1960].

Greene, Graham. *In Search of a Character. Two African Journals*. London: Penguin, 1980 [1961].

Greene, Graham. *The Comedians*. London: Vintage, 2009 [1966].

Greene, Graham *Travels with my Aunt*. London: Vintage, 1999 [1969].

Greene, Graham. *The Honorary Consul*. London: Vintage, 2004 [1973].

Greene, Graham. *The Human Factor*. London: Vintage, 1999 [1978].

Greene, Graham. *Dr Fischer of Geneva, or the Bomb Party*. London: Penguin, 1981 [1980].

Greene, Graham. *Ways of Escape*. London: Vintage, 1999 [1980].

Greene, Graham. *Monsignor Quixote*. London: Vintage, 2010 [1982].

Greene, Graham. *The Tenth Man*. London: Vintage, 2010 [1985].

Greene, Graham. *The Captain and the Enemy*. London: Penguin, 1999 [1988].

Gregor, Ian. "*The End of the Affair*." In Hynes, ed. 110–25.

Greimas, Algirdas Julien. *Structural Semantics: An Attempt at a Method*. University of Nebraska Press, 1984.

Guevara, Ernesto. *Guerrilla Warfare*. Ed. Brian Loveman and Thomas M. Davies Jr. Lanham, MD: Rowman & Littlefield, 2002 [1985].

Guevara, Ernesto. *The Motorcycle Diaries: Notes on a Latin American Journey*. Minneapolis: Ocean Press, 2013 [1993].

Hemingway, Ernest. *A Farewell to Arms*. London: Arrow, 1994 [1929].

Hill, William Thomas. *Graham Greene's Wanderers: The Search for Dwelling: Journeying and Wandering in the Novels of Graham Greene*. San Francisco, CA: International Scholars Publications, 1999.

Hill, William Thomas, ed. *Perceptions of Religious Faith in the Work of Graham Greene*. Frankfurt: Peter Lang, 2002.

Hitchcock, Alfred, dir. *I Confess*. Warner Bros, 1953.

Hitchcock, Alfred, dir. *North By Northwest*. MGM, 1959.

Hitchcock, Alfred, dir. *Spellbound*. United Artists, 1945.

Hobbes, Thomas. *Leviathan*. Ed. Richard Tuck. Revised student edition. Cambridge Texts in the History of Political Thought. Cambridge: Cambridge University Press, 1996.

Hoskins, Robert. *Graham Greene: An Approach to the Novels*. New York: Garland Publishing, 1998.

Hume, David. *A Treatise of Human Nature*. Ed. David Fate Norton and Mary J. Norton. Oxford: Clarendon Press, 2007 [1738].

Hynes, Samuel, ed. *Graham Greene. A Collection of Critical Essays*. Englewood Cliffs, NJ: Prentice Hall, 1973.

James, Henry. *The Figure in the Carpet and Other Stories*. Ed. Frank Kermode. London: Penguin, 2007 [1896].

Jameson, Fredric. *The Political Unconscious: Narrative as a Socially Symbolic Act*. Ithaca, NY: Cornell University Press, 1981.

Jameson, Fredric. *Postmodernism, Or, the Cultural Logic of Late Capitalism*. Durham, NC: Duke University Press, 1991.

Kant, Immanuel. *Critique of Practical Reason*. In *Practical Philosophy*. Ed. Mary J. Gregor. Cambridge: Cambridge University Press, 1996 [1788]. 133–271.

Kant, Immanuel. *Critique of Pure Reason*. Ed. Paul Guyer and Allen W. Wood. Cambridge: Cambridge University Press, 1998 [1781].

Kant, Immanuel. *Lectures on Ethics*. Ed. Peter Heath and J.B. Schneewind. Cambridge: Cambridge University Press, 1997.

Kant, Immanuel. *The Metaphysics of Morals*. In *Practical Philosophy*. Ed. Mary J. Gregor. Cambridge: Cambridge University Press, 1996 [1797]. 353–603.

Kelly, Richard M. *Graham Greene*. New York: Frederick Ungar, 1984.

Ker, Ian. *The Catholic Revival in English Literature, 1845–1961*. Notre Dame, IN: University of Notre Dame Press, 2003.

Kettle, Arnold. *An Introduction to the English Novel*. Vol. 2. London: Hutchinson, 1953.

Kierkegaard, Søren. *Sickness unto Death: A Christian Psychological Exposition for Upbuilding and Awakening. Kierkegaard's Writings, vol. XIX*. Ed. Howard V. Hong and Edna H. Hong. Princeton, NJ: Princeton University Press, 2013 [1849].

Kohn, Lynette. *Graham Greene: The Major Novels*. Stanford, CA: Stanford University Press, 1961.

Konstan, David. *Pity Transformed*. London: Duckworth, 2001.

Kramer, Beth. "'Postcolonial Triangles': An Analysis of Masculinity and Homosocial Desire in Achebe's *A Man of the People* and Greene's *The Quiet American*." *Gender Forum. An Internet Journal for Gender Studies* 14 (1996). Web.

Kulshrestha, J. P. *Graham Greene: The Novelist*. Delhi: Macmillan, 1983.

Kunkel, Francis Leo. *The Labyrinthine Ways of Graham Greene*. New York: Sheed & Ward, 1959.

Kunkel, Francis Leo. "The Priest as Scapegoat in the Modern Catholic Novel": *Ramparts* 1 (1963): 72–79.

Land, Stephen K. *The Human Imperative: A Study of the Novels of Graham Greene*. New York: AMS Press, 2008.

Lawrence, D. H. *Lady Chatterley's Lover*. London: Penguin, 1960 [1928].

Leigh, David J. "The Structures of *The Honorary Consul*." *Renascence* 38.1 (1985): 13–25.

Leighton, Stephen. "On Pity and Its Appropriateness." *Mitleid: Konkretionen eines strittigen Konzepts*. Ed. Ingolf Ulrich Dalferth, Andreas Hunziker, and Andreas HunzikerDalfert. Mohr Siebeck. 2007. 99–118.

Lejeune, Philippe. *On Diary*. Ed. Jeremy D. Popkin and Julie Rak. Manoa: University of Hawaii Press, 2009.

Lévinas, Emmanuel. *Totality and Infinity: An Essay on Exteriority*. Pittsburgh, PA: Duquesne University Press, 1969.

Lewis, R. B. W. "The 'Trilogy' of Graham Greene." *Modern Fiction Studies* 3:3 (1957): 195–215. Rpt. In Hynes, ed. 49–74.

Lingis, Alphonso. *The Community of Those Who Have Nothing in Common*. Bloomington, IN: Indiana University Press, 1994.

Lodge, David. "*Foreword*." In Gilvary and Middleton, eds. xi–xiv.

Lodge, David. *Graham Greene*. New York: Columbia University Press, 1966.

MacIntyre, Alasdair. *After Virtue. A Study in Moral Theory*. 3rd edition. Notre Dame, Indiana: U of Notre Dame P, 2007 (1981).

Malamet, Elliott. "The Uses of Delay in *The Power and the Glory*." *Renascence* 46.4 (1994): 211–23.

Malik, Meena. *Graham Greene: A Feminist Reading*. New Delhi: Atlantic Publishing, 2009.

Marcel, Gabriel. *The Philosophy of Existentialism*. Trans. Manya Harari. New York: Carol Publishing, 1995.

Martín Salván, Paula. "'Being involved': Community and Commitment in Graham Greene's *The Quiet American*." In *Community in Twentieth Century Fiction*. Ed. Paula Martín Salván, Gerardo Rodríguez Salas, and Julian Jimenez Heffernan. London: Palgrave, 2013. 105–22.

Martín Salván, Paula. "Community, Enquiry and Auto-Immunity in Graham Greene's *A Burnt-Out Case.*" *Lit: Literature Interpretation Theory* 22:4 (2011): 301–22.

Mauriac, François. "Graham Greene." In *Men I Hold Great.* New York: Philosophical Library, 1951. 124–28. Rpt. in Hynes, ed. 75–78.

McCarey, Leo, dir. *An Affair to Remember.* 20th Century Fox, 1957.

McCarey, Leo, dir. *Love Affair.* RKO, 1939.

McCormack, Frances. "The Later Greene: From Modernist to Moralist." In Gilvary and Middleton, eds. 263–75.

McGrath, Alistair E. *Historical Theology: An Introduction to the History of Christian Thought.* London: Wiley Blackwell, 1998.

Meyers, Jeffrey, ed. *Graham Greene: A Revaluation: New Essays.* New York: St. Martin's Press, 1990.

Miller, J. Hillis. *Ariadne's Thread.* New Haven, CT: Yale University Press, 1992.

Miller, J. Hillis "The Grounds of Love: Anthony Trollope's *Ayala's Angel.*" In J. Hillis Miller and Manuel Asensi, *Boustrophedonic Reading/ Black Holes.* Stanford, CA: Stanford University Press, 1999.

Miller, J. Hillis. "How to be 'In tune with the right' in *The Golden Bowl.*" In *Mapping the Ethical Turn: A Reader in Ethics, Culture, and Literary Theory.* Ed. Todd F. Davis and Kenneth Womack. Charlottesville: University of Virginia Press, 2001. 271–85.

Miller, J. Hillis. *Others.* Princeton, NJ: Princeton University Press, 2001.

Miller, J. Hillis. *The Ethics of Reading.* New York: Columbia University Press, 1987.

Miller, J. Hillis. *Versions of Pygmalion.* Cambridge, MA: Harvard University Press, 1990.

Miller, J. Hillis and Manuel Asensi. *Boustrophedonic Reading/ Black Holes.* Stanford, CA: Stanford University Press, 1999.

Miller, J. Hillis and Julian Wolfreys. "Why Literature? A Profession: An Interview with J. Hillis Miller." In *The J. Hillis Miller Reader.* Ed. Julian Wolfreys. Stanford, CA: Stanford University Press, 2005. 405–22.

Miller, R. H. "The Saddest Story." *Renascence: Essays on Values in Literature* 51 (1999): 132–43.

Murdoch, Iris. *Existentialists and Mystics.* London: Penguin, 1997.

Murdoch, Iris. *The Sovereignty of Good.* London: Routledge, 2001 [1970].

Nancy, Jean-Luc. *Noli Me Tangere: On the Raising of the Body.* Trans. Sarah Clift, Pascale-Anne Brault, and Michael Naas. Fordham, NY: Fordham University Press, 2008.

Nancy, Jean-Luc. *The Inoperative Community.* Ed. Peter Connor. Minneapolis: University of Minnesota Press, 1991.

Nashel, Jonathan. *Edward Lansdale's Cold War.* Amherst: University of Massachusetts Press, 2005.

Nietzsche, Friedrich. *The Twilight of the Idols and The Anti-Christ.* Ed. Michael Tanner. London: Penguin, 1990 [1889; 1895].

Nordlof, John. "Faith and Disloyalty in Greene's African Fiction." In Hill, ed. 459–78.

Oele, Marjolein. "Suffering, Pity and Friendship: An Aristotelian Reading of Book 24 of Homer's *Iliad.*" *Electronic Antiquity: Communicating the Classics* 14.1 (2010): 51–65. Web.

Olson, Lester C. *Emblems of American Community in the Revolutionary Era: A Study in Rhetorical Iconology.* Washington, DC: Smithsonian Institute Press, 1991.

Orwell, George. "The Sanctified Sinner. Review of *The Heart of the Matter*, by Graham Greene." *The New Yorker*. July 17, 1948. 61–63. Rpt. in Hynes, ed. 105–9.

Parkinson, David and Graham Greene. *The Graham Greene Film Reader. Essays, Interviews & Film Stories*. New York: Applause Theatre Book Publishers, 1994.

Parry, Benita. *Postcolonial Studies: A Materialist Critique*. New York: Routledge, 2004.

Pathak, Z., S. Sengupta, and S. Purkayastha. "The Prisonhouse of Orientalism." *Textual Practice* 5.2 (1991): 195–218.

Pendleton, Robert. *Graham Greene's Conradian Masterplot: The Arabesques of Influence*. Basingstoke: Macmillan, 1996.

Pierloot, Roland A. *Psychoanalytic Patterns in the Work of Graham Greene*. Amsterdam: Rodopi, 1994.

Prasad, Keshava. *Graham Greene: The Novelist*. Classical Publishing, 1982.

Propp, Vladimir. *Morphology of the Folk Tale*. Ed. Louis A. Wagner. University of Texas Press, 1968 [1928].

Rai, Gangeshwar. *Graham Greene: An Existential Approach*. Atlantic Highlands, NJ: Humanities Press, 1983.

Rimmon-Kenan, Shlomith. *Narrative Fiction: Contemporary Poetics*. London: Routledge, 2002 [1983].

Rorty, Richard. *Contingency, Irony, Solidarity*. Cambridge: Cambridge University Press, 1989.

Roston, Murray. *Graham Greene's Narrative Strategies: A Study of the Major Novels*. Basingstoke: Palgrave Macmillan, 2006.

Sartre, Jean-Paul. "A More Precise Characterization of Existentialism." In *Selected Prose. The Writings of Jean-Paul Sartre*. Ed. Michel Rybalka and Michel Contat. Northwestern University Press, 1985. 155–60.

Sartre, Jean-Paul. *Bariona or the Son of Thunder*. In *Selected Prose. The Writings of Jean-Paul Sartre*. Ed. Michel Rybalka and Michel Contat. Northwestern University Press, 1985. 72–136.

Sartre, Jean-Paul. "Existentialism Is a Humanism." In *Jean-Paul Sartre: Basic Writings*. Ed. Stephen Priest. London: Routledge, 2001 [1946]. 25–46.

Sartre, Jean-Paul. *Notebooks for an Ethics*. Chicago: University of Chicago Press, 1992 [1983].

Sedgwick, Eve. *Between Men: English Literature and Male Homosocial Desire*. New York: Columbia University Press, 1985.

Shaftesbury, Anthony Ashley Cooper, Third Earl of. *Characteristics of Men, Manners, Opinions, Times*. Ed. Lawrence E. Klein. Cambridge: Cambridge University Press, 1999.

Sharma, S. K. *Graham Greene, the Search for Belief*. New Delhi: Harman Publishing House, 1990.

Sharrock, Roger. *Saints, Sinners and Comedians: The Novels of Graham Greene*. Tunbridge Wells: Burns & Oates, 1984.

Sharrock, Roger. "Unhappy Families: The Plays of Graham Greene." In Meyers, ed. 68–92.

Shelden, Michael. *Graham Greene: The Man Within*. London: Heinemann, 1994.

Sherry, Norman. *The Life of Graham Greene: Volume 1: 1904–1939*. New York: Viking, 1989.

Sherry, Norman. *The Life of Graham Greene: Volume 2: 1939–1955*. New York: Viking, 1995.

Sherry, Norman. *The Life of Graham Greene: Volume 3: 1955–1991*. New York: Viking, 2004.

Shuttleworth, Martin and Simon Raven. In "The Art of Fiction" series. *The Paris Review*'s series (1953): 25–41.

Sinha, Sunita. *Graham Greene. A Study of his Major Novels*. New Delhi: Atlantic Publishers, 2007.

Smith, Grahame. *The Achievement of Graham Greene*. Brighton, UK: Harvester Press, 1986.

Smith, Rowland. "A People's War in Greeneland: Heroic Virtue and Communal Effort in the Wartime Tales." In Meyers, ed. 104–30.

Snyder, R. L. "'What or who is King Kong?': Graham Greene's *The Captain and The Enemy*." *Renascence* 65.2 (2013): 12–540.

Sweetman, Brendan. *The Vision of Gabriel Marcel: Epistemology, Human Person, the Transcendent*. Amsterdam: Rodopi, 2008.

Thomson, Brian L. *Graham Greene and the Politics of Popular Fiction and Film*. Basingstoke: Palgrave Macmillan, 2009.

Tönnies, Ferdinand. *Community and Civil Society*. Ed. José Harris. Cambridge Texts in the History of Political Thought. Cambridge: Cambridge University Press, 2001 [1887].

Unamuno, Miguel de. *The Tragic Sense of Life in Men and Nations*. Trans. Anthony Kerrigan. Princeton, NJ: Princeton University Press, 1972 [1913].

Watt, Ian. *Conrad in the Nineteenth Century*. Berkeley, CA: University of California Press, 1981.

Watts, Cedric. *A Preface to Greene*. London: Longman, 1997.

Waugh, Evelyn. "Felix culpa?" Review of *The Heart of the Matter*, by Graham Greene. *Commonweal* (July 16, 1948): 322–27. Rpt. in Hynes, ed. 95–102.

Weil, Simone. *Gravity and Grace*. Lincoln, NE: University of Nebraska Press, 1997 [1947].

Weil, Simone. *Lectures on Philosophy*. Cambridge: Cambridge University Press, 1978 [1959].

Weil, Simone. *The Need for Roots*. London: Routledge, 2002 [1949].

Whitehouse, J. C. *Vertical Man: The Human Being in the Catholic Novels of Graham Greene, Sigrid Undset, and George Bernanos*. New York: Garland, 1990.

Williams, Raymond. *Keywords. A Vocabulary of Culture and Society*. New York: Routledge, 2011 [1976].

Wise, Jon and Mike Hill. *The Works of Graham Greene: A Reader's Bibliography and Guide*. London: Continuum, 2012.

Wood, Allen W. "General Introduction." In I. Kant, *Practical Philosophy*. Cambridge: Cambridge University Press, 1996. xiii–xxxiii.

Ziolkowski, Eric. *The Sanctification of Don Quixote: From Hidalgo to Priest*. University Park, PA: Penn State Press, 2000.

Žižek, Slavoj. *The Sublime Object of Ideology*. London: Verso, 1989.

Index

Note: "n." after a page reference denotes a note number on that page.

Printed and bound by CPI Group (UK) Ltd, Croydon, CR0 4YY